Praise for: **BORN TO BE MILD**

'A feast of 60s and 70s nostalgia. Wonderfully vulgar and
irresistibly funny. Read it and wince.'

Kate Saunders, *The Times*

'Brilliant... I howled with laughter. You'll be hooked.'

Bill Leckie, *The Sun*

'A laugh-out-loud trip through teenage angst played against a
soundtrack from the 70s. Sweet!'

Ian Macfarlane, *Sunday Express*

'This is The Rotters' Club with scuffed knees... as
multi-layered as the Faces' feather-cuts. Evokes perfectly
the era between The Beatles and Bowie, space travel
and spacehoppers.'

Phil Shaw, *The Independent*

'Bloody funny... it has all the elements necessary to make
a great novel - sex, Stingray and the 70s. And what a relief
to discover I was not the only one who thought a certain
Gerry Anderson puppet was gorgeous!

Alan McKinlay, *Daily Mirror*

'From the moment I picked it up, I started laughing and that
went on until the last page. Very funny.'

Nick Szczepanik, *The Times*

A CIP catalogue record for this book is available from
the British Library.

ISBN 0-9552466-0-1
978-0-9552466-0-9

Published by

Hot Air Publishers,
10 Marigold Court,
Red Lake, Telford,
Shropshire TF1 5ZN

Reproduced, printed and bound in Great Britain by Cox and
Wyman, Reading, Berkshire

born to be mild

Dave Armitage

ABOUT THE AUTHOR

Dave Armitage was born in 1958 and is a journalist with the Daily Star newspaper. This is his first novel though plans for a second are well under way. He lives in Shropshire with his partner Jo.

ACKNOWLEDGEMENTS:

Thanks to the countless people who were good enough to cast a critical eye over early drafts and offered advice or encouragement. Special thanks to Nick, who got his big red pen to it. I am also grateful to those who went out of their way to help like Mervyn Jones of Raleigh in Nottingham and John Wheeler and Simon Martin at Cadbury Schweppes plc. Thanks to Palitoy for Action Man. Special mention must also go to Keith Cox and his boys who managed to rescue an entire manuscript locked in an ancient Mac and not only get it out intact but drag it into the 21st Century. Thanks to Jeremy Novick and Mick Middles for Wham Bam Thank You Glam (© JMP) a superb book which gave me a quick shot of the 70s any time I needed one!

The input of my friend Carl and Daren Sykes (www.onestopchoppershop.co.uk) should not go unmentioned either. Thank God for them and the likes of Robert Opie who take pleasure in hanging on to bits of the past. Without Robert, the cover would not be what it is. Thanks and it's worth visiting www.museumofbrands.com. Also a big thankyou to Andy Serle and Dave Instone for all their valuable tips. Special thanks to Tricia Freeman for her hard work and flair on the book. And finally to Jo for putting up with me when this whole project became all-consuming.

To Mom and Dad.

1

THE FINAL COUNTDOWN

Friday, November 11, 2005

It had all the ingredients for being a thoroughly miserable day and the funeral was hours away. The eleventh of the eleventh - a sombre enough date in itself. Outside it was grey and damp and as I glanced at the front of my morning newspaper, there seemed little chance of it offering any light relief. There was a picture of Carol Vorderman outside York Minster attending a memorial service for her Countdown mate Richard Whiteley. York Minster? I had read it right. York Fucking Minster. And to compound things, around two thousand people had attended the service. There was me thinking he was just a quiz show host. How wrong can you be? Come on, I'm sure old Twice Nightly Whiteley was a thoroughly decent bloke, but York Minster? Two thousand. It was insane. I was starting to feel slightly disturbed by it all when a mischievous thought cheered me. I pictured the minister saying something like 'and, in accordance with Richard's wishes we will now sing hymn number . . . I'll take two from the bottom . . . and one from the top please!'
Carol slots the cards into the order of service board with that precise click of hers and he says 'hymn number three . . . six . . . four.' Now that would be a fitting end. The thought warmed me. If I was Twice Nightly that's the way I'd have wanted to be remembered - not the man who died of irritable vowel syndrome. I'd really want to lay it on thick. And when the mourners trudged outside, I'd want them to look at the headstone and splutter with laughter at the inscription:

R.I.P

IN LOVING MEMORY OF

CHDRIRA TWELIEYH

Now that would be class. Go out with a conundrum. I'd like the public to remember me for having a really memorable funeral rather than being some guy who wore garish jackets and first came to prominence because a ferret bit him. It was one of the very first famous out-takes. A sort of It'll be Alright on the Twice Nightly. God bless that fucking ferret. At least I'd give Whiteley some credit - he'd served his time. These days it doesn't take much to be a celebrity. The tribute i nside the paper left you in no doubt he was something of a fanny merchant. I came from an age when the only Fanny on the box was Craddock. She was just about the only cook on the box as well. Heaven. It was all so much more civilised then.

Nowadays it seems you only have to be able to make an omelette and rant at a few people and you are a millionaire overnight. I flicked through the pages and there was little to cheer me. Jamie Oliver had been lamb basted for cutting a sheep's throat on TV. That had gone down like a lead balloon. I'll write in and suggest he should cull some of his colleagues - that would be reality TV with a real difference. Watching Aynsley or Anthony Waffle-Thompson being slowly roasted over a spit certainly had its appeal. I stopped briefly at page 17 to see a picture of Donny Osmond holding his first grandchild. What the hell was going on? And then there was Gary Glitter in the brown stuff way up past his six inch platforms and facing the possibility of death by firing squad. Jesus had the Thai authorities only just heard Another Rock and Roll Christmas?

And so the day had promised to be one with little cheer before I'd even walked through the church gates. And then it happened. I'd never been slapped at a funeral before. I couldn't imagine I was the only person it had ever happened to but that was no comfort. Thwack . . . just like that. And then she embraced me . . . and half apologised . . . and cried . . . and it was over . . . we hugged . . . and we went inside. This had all the hallmarks of being an appalling day.

2

QUADRIPLIGIA

I'd always thought Quadriplegia was a Who album until Jimmy Hunt chose to educate me for the one and only time in his miserable life. Call me cruel, but there was something almost heart-warming about the two lines of frozen snot under his nose. Jimmy Hunt . . . kung fu fighter ... boxing prospect . . . self-proclaimed best footballer . . . self-proclaimed best bird puller... fag thief . . . sweets thief . . . money thief . . . school bully extraordinaire . . . total wanker. And now as he sat here in his wheelchair just in front of me, a flicker of recognition crawling across his face, I presumed I was supposed to have some sympathy. I couldn't muster any. I hadn't set eyes on any of the Hunt family for a few years and not seen Jimmy for, a long time. He was straining in his chair and there was an unpleasant odour just briefly, as if he really was that excited to see me. I nodded and smiled indifferently. I acknowledged his older brother Ged who was guiding him down the tarmac path which weaved between the gravestones. It was bitterly cold with a lung-bursting, fierce wind, dictating little time for small talk. What was I supposed to say anyway? How sorry I was? How you wouldn't wish something like that on your worst enemy? Thirty-odd years had merely served to make me totally indifferent to the hand fate had served Jimmy. I didn't wish anything on him anymore. I'd done okay for myself. I had a couple of carpet shops. I wasn't a rich man, but I was doing all right. I lived four or five miles away these days and that, plus business, dictated I only bumped into most of them very occasionally. The things he'd done in the past - the torn blazer, the long walk home

4

because he'd pinched my bus money, the Chinese burns - were behind me. I'd moved on - and at a much brisker pace than he'd ever have managed if he'd been able-bodied. And what had he become? Quadriplegic. It's probably Latin for totally bolloxed. Thirty years on and I can recall the buzz around the village that a young lad had been seriously injured in a fall on holiday in Spain. It wasn't long before it was confirmed that it was Jimmy and that he was lucky to even be alive. The story went that in early hours horseplay he'd jumped from a first floor balcony into a swimming pool which had been emptied. Good move. One minute he'd been an over-robust picture of health, the next a virtual cabbage unable to eat a Rich Tea unless someone made it soggy for him. He'd been very lucky, they said. How fucking lucky was that? But today wasn't about Jimmy. We were here paying respects to another of us who had passed on. I nodded to Ged and made my way towards Hadley's Holy Trinity Church. Big Joe and my dad were standing under the yew near the entrance. They had been lifelong pals - well certainly for the past 40 years or so when the huge guy with the laugh that could crack open Party Sevens, moved near us. Big Joe White from Antigua. Who would have thought it? My dad was livid when he first heard Jamaicans were moving in by us. Yet in seemingly no time he and Joe had become massive mates. Inseparable almost. They drank together, holidayed together and trusted each other with their lives. Dad used to say they looked like a couple of negatives. If anyone wanted an abject lesson in racial integration - those two were it. I liked Joe too and his wife Marie. Big Joe was a bear of man, a gentle Uncle Remus kind of guy who just wanted to get on with his life and not do anyone any harm. I shook Joe's hand and hugged my dad. Mom had gone inside because it was so cold. Pele embraced me and I hugged him too and made a crack about the quality of his cashmere coat. Pele was a millionaire - several times over, some said. You couldn't tell - apart from the coat that is. He hadn't changed. Wouldn't. Probably couldn't. When I think about the state of his family's garden across the road from us, I should have got an inkling he'd make a fortune in scrap. Clearly he had a sharpness and business sense we hadn't given him credit for. Good luck to him.

'Still shit at football?' I whispered in his ear. He laughed. All these years later and everyone still knew him as Pele. Some didn't even know his real name. And all because he was terrible at football. It just sort of stuck and somehow it suited him.

Suddenly I was almost knocked over by a large woman's over-enthusiastic greeting.

'Jesus Christ.' It seemed a hardly appropriate greeting, given the location.

'Dunny,' she squealed excitedly.

"Well, bugger me,' I said with a relieved gasp, a quick double-take confirming exactly who it was. Belinda Smart . . . my God, I barely recognised her. I'd had sex with Belinda on numerous occasions - she'd just never been there at the time.

I felt like saying 'What happened?' but it's not a particularly good line to put on someone you haven't seen for quite some time. It kind of alerts them to the fact that something drastic has happened in the intervening years. It certainly had. Belinda was almost two years older than me and had widely been regarded as the prettiest girl in the village. Two good reasons why she would never have looked at a scrote like me.

'Good to see you Dunny. Hey, you've hardly changed! Are you going over to the pub later with the rest of 'em?'

'I was going to catch up with a few old faces, yeah.'

'Great, I'll see you there then. We can catch up on old times. Bet you hardly recognised me. Mind you, I have changed a bit since you last saw me eh?'

'We've all changed love,' I said with a smile.

I felt uncomfortable and slightly sad that I felt like pitying Belinda. She would have hated that. But I couldn't help reflecting that she had become a shabby and rather bulky shadow of how I'd chosen to remember her. Perhaps it was me - perhaps I'd changed more than I cared to realise from the wide-eyed, somewhat awkward young lad, who had adored her from a distance.

One of the last times I'd seen her properly was when she was heavily pregnant for the first time in that hot summer of '76 and I couldn't help wondering if she had never truly recovered from that. She had been such a slip of a girl. I can recall dad commenting on how the sun glistened in her chestnut hair. She could have been no more than 10 then. The cutest kid in the street had blossomed from then on . . . by the time she was 17 it was as if not having a nice car prohibited you from having any place in her affections. And so they came, a procession of lads from the area in a seemingly never-ending parade of cracking motors.

I was 15 and probably pretty annoying. She wouldn't have looked at me twice and who could blame her? We'd all changed, that was true enough. I still had a full head of hair, but it was losing the fight with the grey.

I wondered if she looked at me and wondered whatever happened to the gangly youth in the patchwork shirt who used to give her lip. We'd all changed . . . and we were all going to more funerals with each passing year.

3

CONSPIWACY THEOWY

Funny things funerals . . . Jimmy obviously hadn't been capable of bullying anyone into giving him a miracle cure in the 30 years since the accident; Belinda was a granny twice over and had the dimensions of an average sized barn and now we were discussing Donny Osmond. By now only a few of the funeral party remained in the narrow front bar at The Compasses and the room was thick with smoke and nostalgia. The service had been followed by a buffet in the lounge of The Lord Hill at Ketley Bank and the few of us now intent on making a night of it had walked down the bank to The Rose and Crown before finishing up in The Compasses down in Beveley. The conversation had turned to Donny and though I certainly hadn't started it, my last remark had caused something of a stir. It was Belinda's sister Joy, who was my age, who had said Donny had just brought out his autobiography and how she'd seen him on Richard and Judy recently and he was still as lovely as ever.

Okay, hands up, but I do feel it was a very fair point. If Donny was such a thoroughly decent bloke and all-round good egg, then why did he let his sister sing Paper Woses? It was obvious to anyone that Marie clearly didn't know her 'R's' from her elbow and for that reason - and not that reason alone, I might add - I've always treated Donny with some suspicion.

I'm not one to bear a grudge - the last 30 years have just flipped by - but when I was 13 Donny managed to get himself on the walls of seemingly every love-struck teenage girl in the universe. So yeah, I have got a problem with him and the fact that three decades on, Belinda now reveals she and a friend had been to see him in concert in Birmingham just two weeks ago, hasn't helped. Scars may fade, but they never completely disappear. Neither does Donny, it seems. Suddenly I'm a spotty teenager in a tanktop and a patchwork shirt again. When Donny fucked off in the mid-70s I'd been presumptuous enough to assume it would be forever. I imagined he'd be a preacher or living on some vast estate in Utah by now. But no, he was spotted on TV recently and apparently says that even after all these years he doesn't have a problem with people still asking him to sing Puppy Love. Well, he might not have . . . but I DO.

'He still looks fantastic' said Belinda breathily. 'David Cassidy was on the other night and, well, he still looked good even if he was a bit gaunt. But Donny. Well he looked . . . just brilliant.'

Brilliant. David Cassidy's gaunt appearance was of little consolation. Boyzone, Westlife, Boys 'R' Us, I can cope with because they are not of my time. Donny, David and the pre-magnolia Michael Jackson were the bees-knees, long before dog's bollocks mysteriously became a phrase describing excellence. Seems petty, but even now, I struggle with it. And so I launched my verbal smart-missile with devastating impact, having the temerity to even suggest that Donny and his brothers might just have actively encouraged their little sister to go with Paper Woses if only because she was a lisper of Olympic proportions.

Judging by the dropped jaws you'd have thought I'd just suggested that Mother Theresa had died of syphilis. How could I have the gall to believe there could be a darker side to Donny? Pint in one hand, cigarette in the other, I sensed a definable hush among the women of the group, as Belinda urged me to justify such a preposterous statement.

'That's a dreadful thing to say Dunny.'

'Why?' as even Donny himself asked, I recall.

'She couldn't help having a lisp.' Belinda continued.

'I'm not saying she could. That's not the point. The point I'm making is that when some dimwit suggested she should try Paper Woses, are you seriously telling me one of her brothers wasn't

9

smart enough to point out that just perhaps it wasn't really her song?'

'Well it went to number one.'

'So did Grandad . . . and Ernie . . . oh, and Mouldy Old Dough, but that's hardly the point either is it?'

'So?'

'So, what I'm saying is, how come one of them didn't say that on account of Marie's lisp, she might be better off trying a different number. But no, they all sat back and let her get on with it didn't they? That's the point. I'm surprised Donny didn't suggest she do Wockin' Wobbin and really take the piss?'

'Jeezus Dunny, you're a twat. Well, I thought he looked fantastic the other night.'

'I saw it. He DID look fantastic,' I agreed somewhat grudgingly. 'I didn't want him to look fantastic. I wanted him to be fat, losing his hair and possibly discover that he'd ditched his missus and set up home with a 14-year-old Mormon choirgirl - or choirboy for that matter.'

'You really should see a psychiatrist Dunny,' Belinda grumbled.

How many reasons did I need to hate Donny Fucking Osmond? I wasn't about to forgive him for invading my teenage years that easily. That squeaky-clean image still didn't wash with me. No amount of Clearasil or Phisohex would scrub my theory clean. Off the top of my head I could think of countless reasons to despise him . . .

• He was a multi-millionaire by the time he was 15.
• He'd met Pan's People.
• He didn't go to school.
• He'd kept Virginia Plain off the No1 spot.
• He didn't smoke or drink.
• My mom liked him and hummed his songs.
• He gave tons of money to The Morons.
• His favourite colour was purple (How the hell did I remember that?)
• He held his microphone in a particularly stupid way.

I could go on. I had a problem with the lot of them. Donny, Jay, Alan, Beaky, Mick, Titch and Qwackers. As for Little Jimmy spraying spit all over the Top of the Pops camera . . . well, I ask you. And, on reflection, to make matters even worse, you just got the feeling that one spiteful, improper thought about Marie and you'd end up with a visit from the Mormon Mafia and wake up with a horse's head on your pillow - a crazy one at that.

Marie looked like butter wouldn't melt in her mouth. You got the feeling nothing would melt in Marie's mouth. The only thing likely to get past her perfect teeth was dental floss.

And now here I was debating the merits of the original teenyboppers, glam rock, kola kubes, Aztec bars, and all because Donny is back on our screens and still looking a million dollars. For any lad in 1973, Donny and Co were, quite frankly, a nightmare. We had no chance of ever aspiring to such heights. Us lads were very much on the morning side of the mountain, while Donny was basking on the limelight side of the hill. I couldn't help but admire his survival qualities when so many of his like had disappeared from the planet, never mind the charts.

Marc Bolan had gone into a tree; Elvis had gone into the bathroom; Freddie Mercury had gone God-knows where and Gary Glitter had merely gone into PC World. It bought a somewhat sinister slant to 'Do You Wanna Touch?'

Sweet's lead singer took the Hellraiser thing just a little too far; Keith Moon had brought a new meaning to Who's Next and even the Bay City Rollers were all fat and drawing benefits while one of them was in the nick for sex offences, I'd been told. I even found adulthood making me feel sorry that Les and his Rollers hadn't made a penny from their chart-topping days and were all stone broke. Cliff was last seen singing at Wimbledon and Tom Jones was going stronger than ever. Okay, so the knickers being thrown at him were now several sizes bigger and damp through incontinence rather than frenzied excitement, but fair play to him. There were only two Beatles left - one best known by a whole new generation as the voice of Thomas the Tank Engine and the other for marrying a bird with one leg. I liked Macca - always did. How fucking annoying it must be when some 16-year-old says: 'Oh yeah, are you the guy who married the bird with one leg?' I mean, how can you say: 'Well, yeah, but I wrote Yesterday and Hey Jude . . . oh yeah man(Macca would say man) I helped change the face of a generation as well.'

Clean-living Donny's longevity as a human being was never really in question. But now he stood there in rather bizarre company with Keith Richard,Charlie Watts, Ozzy Osbourne and Alice Cooper, corpses all those years ago, as the men who had stood the test of time.

The trip down memory lane had been inevitable and not just because Katie, the 17-year-old new barmaid was wearing flares and platform shoes. She had almost split her pierced belly button with laughter when I had casually observed that I'd worn flares 30-odd years ago. I sounded so like my dad it was scary. We were not that long into a brand new century, and you knew a merry Christmas was just around the corner because Noddy Holder was telling us so on the juke box just like he did every year

So here it is . . .

4

NOT SO SMART

Belinda had just popped outside to make a phone call and left me reflecting. God, if she had an inkling of the grappling and grunting we had participated in over the years she would either have presented me with an Olympic gold or, more probably, slapped my face. She had been on the 'A' list and had remained there for years. Time was that the very mention of Belinda Smart's name was enough to send anyone's pulse racing. She was a teenage sensation - a guaranteed hard on from 100 yards or 100 metres as our entry into the Common Market would later try to dictate. She was the most desirable girl in our street . . . and now this. As she rested herself on the bar stool just a couple of feet from me, I couldn't help noticing her straining midriff had taken on the proportions of a VW Beetle bonnet. Time, four children by three different fathers, hadn't been kind. Once, the difference in our ages had been collosal - now it wasn't even a consideration. She wasn't far off 50 but, then again, much as I hated it, I was closing in on that milestone too.

   Belinda had most definitely been a title contender. There was no doubt about that and I began to mentally juggle who else had held such a distinction. There would have been the likes of: my mom's friend Jenny, Sally James, Blondie, several women in the underwear section of the Freeman's catalogue, Babs from Pan's People, Cherry from Pan's People, any of Pan's People come to think of it, Susan Dey from the Partridge Family, Paula Wilcox, Anne Aston from the Golden Shot, Lulu, the blonde in Abba, the brunette in Abba, Kate Bush, Suzi Quatro and the aptly named Mrs Robinson, the lab assistant at grammar school who happened to be my best mate's mom. As my tastes widened, virtually by the week, you could throw in the girl in the Nimble balloon; the lead singer with Middle of the Road; Julie Andrews; Lynsey de Paul; the woman in the Hai Karate adverts; the dirty looking Oriental bird on the Mastermind game box and Sally Thomsett.

Looking at Belinda now, the thought crossed my mind of calling an extra-ordinary general meeting of the list committee to consider a motion to have her stripped of her place. A sort of impeachment no less. Yet even considering the fact I was the chairman, secretary, treasurer and had absolute final attorney on my personal Who's Who, it just would have seemed unfair. I couldn't pretend otherwise. And so, to my eternal credit, I was forced to concede, that her place in my own personal history was hers of right. Any kind of mental Tippexing would have been out of order. I comforted myself with the recollection of just how beautiful she had been and the posse of blokes in smart motors who had clearly agreed with me at the time. Some quick mental arithmetic told me that it must have been about the early Summer of '72 when everyone, including my dad, noticed something quite incredible had happened to the girl at No1.

It's only now I realise exactly what my dad meant when he innocuously observed something to the effect of 'Belinda's growing up these days.' I would have been 14 in the August and she was 16 just over a month later. Something quite spectacular had happened during the previous winter. Santa had dropped all sorts of things down Belinda Smart's chimney. She just changed overnight. Her walk had become more of a slink and a pair of magnificent breasts had suddenly appeared from nowhere. The carnival queen judges were suitably impressed. Belinda's knockers had been unleashed, metaphorically speaking, on an unsuspecting world, along with Donny, David and Michael.

Belinda returned, thanked me for the half of Strongbow and couldn't have realised that with every passing moment she was having to mentally drag me back from that summer of 1972 - Seaside Shuffle, Rockin' Robin, Silver Machine, Wig Wam Bam, Sylvia's Mother, School's Out, Rock and Roll(Part 2) and all that

14

. . . Do Ya Wanna Touch? YEAH!

5

CLD IT B 4EVER?

As Belinda returned, I couldn't help marvelling at how I, a man who often struggles to remember what he did the previous day, had now suddenly acquired recollection powers of quite astonishing proportions.

'You sent a Love Heart to David Cassidy.'

'Christ, Dunny, can't believe you remember that? That's donkey's years. Ah, bless . . .'

It was hard to forget really, because it had made front page news in the local paper. Things stick out as milestones at that age. You know the kid who gets a firework in the face; the first one to get knocked over by a car . . . that kind of thing. Belinda had sent him a single Love Heart. Not only that, but the soppy cow had simply posted it to 'David Cassidy, America' and - this gets better - didn't even put a stamp on it! Venomous and sustained ridicule doubtless followed, when she received the ultimate putdown to all her tormentors. Weeks later, Belinda received a signed picture from Darling David with a personal message on it and consequently ended up with her picture on the front page of the Shropshire Star. I can still see it! Remember it? How could I ever forget?

'You were in the paper.'

'You're right. I was.'

'I know I am. I couldn't stand David bloody Cassidy anyway and then that happens. I mean to say, not only is the guy a great looking pop star adored by millions of girls but he turns out to be a really top bloke as well.'

'Oh he was gorgeous.'

'Well yeah, but I was a 13-year-old with acne at the time and

. . . well, you just don't fucking need it.'

'Oh Dunny, you are a funny one.'

Funny, well that's as maybe, but around the time my hormones had started to kick in, having David, Donny and Michael around, well, it just wasn't really that humorous at all. It's absolutely no consolation to me that Michael's face has fallen off all these years later - I wanted it to happen then - and preferably live on Top of the Pops.

'So what did it say then?'

'You're cute, I think.'

'Sick making.'

Fair play to him, he replied as well. Advancement in years had given me enough certain good grace to acknowledge that as being a wonderful gesture any of his teenage fans would take to their grave. It looked like it was going to stick with me too. Could It Be Forever? I started to fear it just might. The general school of thought was that Darling David and the rest of the Partridge Family would disappear off the face of the earth no later than 1975 and here I was in a bar 30 years later with vivid memories of that pearly grin and his breathy vocals, involved in deep discussion about him.

'You must have been dead chuffed when that dropped through the door,' I added graciously.

'Oh it was just fantastic. Imagine that when you are a kid. I remember my mom coming into my bedroom and saying I'd got a letter and that it was from America. It was a big letter as well, you know, so I was just so excited.

'I bet.'

'I opened it and there was this picture of him in a denim jacket and he'd written on it. I cried . . .'

'Well, you would, wouldn't you?'

'I was jumping around the bedroom, screaming. I couldn't believe I'd got something that he'd actually touched let alone written on. It was one of the most wonderful things that had ever happened to me. It still is. I can't remember ever being so excited before - or since, for that matter,' she said, a twinge of bitterness seeping to the surface. As she said it, it was if she realised, it just never gets better than that. It was her Torvill and Dean moment. Straight sixes for Cassidy. The boy done good. Follow that you fuckers.

'Oh it was lovely. He was the most gorgeous guy on the planet and the thing was, I just knew that he'd written on it - that's what was so good about it.'

'For definite?'

'Oh yeah, he'd put 'To Belinda, Thanks for the gift. Hope you like this - and, hey(in an American kinda way) I remembered to put a stamp on! Love - David X'

'Tight arse,' I just couldn't help exclaiming.

'Oh it was lovely,' she cooed.

'I kissed that picture last thing at night and first thing in the morning.'

'Hope he doesn't get strapped for cash or you'll get a letter asking for the postage back.'

'Only jealous.'

'Too bloody right.'

It was an unfair remark. What a great thing to do. What a super guy. Tosser. Beneath it all, I was kind of touched by the innocence of it all. Things had changed so much. I mean posting something for a start. That would be considered an extravagance these days. Mobile phones and E-mailing, somehow made posting something seem positively prehistoric. But I mean, if you wanted to send someone a Love Heart then there was only one way to do it - by post. And back then, you'd have to wait at least a month for a reply. If you'd been daft enough to send it to somewhere as vast as the United States without so much as a street number, name, town, or even a state to give the US Mail a clue then you really did have no right to expect any kind of reply. Elvis had clearly got it wrong when he said you'd better not mess around with the US Mail. Obviously you could and they loved nothing more than a massive challenge. Or perhaps, as I suspected, was David Cassidy just THAT famous?

Love Hearts . . . now there's another thing. Do they still make them? I guess so but I'm sure they've had to update them to cater for more enlightened times. Would kids today still get the same pleasure from twee little expressions of fondness such as 'Be Mine', 'I'm Shy' or 'You're Cute'? Had Love Hearts, unbeknown to us fortysomethings, been forced to go the way of everything else and smash through the sweets watershed? I grimaced at the thought of expressions of devotion such as 'Txt me', 'Donkey Dick', 'Great Tits' and 'I Swallow'. Suddenly the days of Cherish, Puppy Love and How Can I Be Sure? seemed somehow endearing.

'You're so funny,' Belinda said with a grin.

'Why?'

'Fancy remembering that.'

'It obviously made a bigger impression on me than I realised.'

'Ah bless.'

I felt like pleading with Belinda to stop blessing me. The last thing I needed right now was blessing. The Belinda Smart seal of approval had long since ceased to be of any importance, infact it had long since ceased to be.

I'd heard somewhere along the way that she had got married and had kids but whether it had been to the guy with the orange Bond Bug, the twat with the black Capri who thought he was the lead singer in The Rubettes or any other of her considerable list of suitors had been of little or no consequence. The summer after Belinda's trip to the tit factory when she went to work in the hairdresser's had seen not so much a spark of interest in her newly acquired charms but a raging forest fire. The two years age difference between us lurched into a chasm virtually overnight. As I rode the streets on my beloved Raleigh Chopper, the parade of visitors to the Smarts at No1 had to be seen to be believed. And now, more frighteningly than before, as I enquired about them, Belinda had to dig deep into the far reaches of her mind to come up with so much as a name for some of them. Guys who had more likely than not, at the very least, kissed her, would have been astonished to know they had cruelly been

19

dragged into the wastepaper basket of Belinda Smart's hard drive. The guy on the scooter with the crombie overcoat; the spotty one with loafers which clicked all the way up the road, that fella with the multi-buttoned Karmens with patch pockets and, more surprisingly, the David Essex lookalike with the Harrington jacket.

'You sure?'

'Positive,' I countered.

'David Essex? I'm sure I'd remember . . . oh I know, yeah, you mean Sam Johnson.'

'I never knew his name,' I said dismissively.

'Yeah, Sam, bless him. He lost his leg on a motorbike.' Now Sam was being blessed.

'Careless of him.'

'Dunny!!!'

Well, honestly. You were the top girl in our street. Everyone fancied you.'

'You are sweet . . . you always were a little cutie,' she smiled, playfully slapping the back of my hand.

'God you were gorgeous,' I added, the past tense disturbingly coming to the fore of its own volition.

'You didn't did you, Dunny?'

'Loads of times.'

'Dunny! I meant did you have a soft spot for me?'

'That's one way of describing it. Not that accurate, but . . .'

'You're terrible.'

That I could risk such forwardness reasonably safe in the knowledge that Belinda might know I wasn't trying to get her into bed was perhaps the most painful part of all. The passage of time had certainly been harsher to her than most and this seemed an opportune moment to explore more mundane matters.

'Did you say it was your daughter's birthday? Eighteen . . . scary isn't it?'

'Tell me about it. Just get her off my hands and they've all gone. Don't mean that really - she's a great girl.'

'All?'

20

'Yeah I've got four - Katie's the youngest,' she said motioning in the direction of the pretty girl behind the bar.

'Bloody hell. No'

"Yeah, Katie behind the bar. She's my youngest. Didn't you know she was mine Dunny? That's shocked you annit?'

'None of us are getting any younger you know. My eldest lad is 27; John's 25 and Lindy's 22.'

'Jeeeezus.'

'Oh, I'm a granny - twice over.'

Belinda might just as easily have branded 'Fuck me' on my forehead with a red hot iron. Her being a size 20 or whatever was bad enough for starters; four kids from 27 downwards, wasn't great; but a granny? It was like a nightmare unfolding before me. Now I realised I'd had improper thoughts about her daughter. Could this possibly get any worse?

'What does your husband do?' I said trying to somehow divert myself from the enormity of it all.

'Bugger all, that's why I kicked him into touch.'

'Oh right.'

'Lazy sod. You'd have thought I might get it right after the first two, but show me a deadbeat and you can guarantee I'll end up with him. There's no decent blokes left. What happened to all the nice ones?'

'It happens,' I said somewhat unsympathetically.

'Happened to me that's for sure. Never said anything about this on the Love Hearts eh Dunny?'

'Wouldn't have been right somehow. Imagine being 14 and being given a sweet saying *Life's bollocks* or *Let's divorce*. Just not the same . . .'

Belinda made a move to leave, confirming she'd make the final party arrangements with Terry the landlord in a few days.

"Lovely seeing you again Dunny. See you in another few years eh? Been smashing talking to you.'

'And you. Take care.'

Belinda stood alongside me and pecked me lightly on the cheek. 'Don't leave it so long next time. Hey, Katie, if he gives

21

you any lip, just tell me. I'll sort him'

'Yeah.'

'I've really enjoyed the chat. Look . . .' she said fumbling in her bag.

'Here's my mobile. If you fancy giving me a ring sometime and we'll catch up on old times again. It's been a right laugh. see you folks . . .'

I took the piece of card, noticing Terry's knowing look as Belinda made her way out of the lounge door. The door swinging shut was Terry's cue to pounce.

'Your chopper obviously made a big impression then Dunny,' he smirked.

'Hey, that's my mom, you're on about,' Katie intervened.

Strolls down memory lane were one thing - being dragged down an alley liberally daubed with dog shit was something else. Belinda, it seemed, had gone to seed after being impregnated by half the universe and was making it fairly obvious that she was up for a date; my Raleigh Chopper was a rusting wreck long since discarded. My heroes were either dead, gay or child molesters . . . and it seemed like even Love Hearts had led us up the garden path.

At long last Belinda was beckoning me in the direction of her bedroom door and I wanted to be dragged, screaming and kicking in the opposite direction. She was wondering where all the good blokes had gone . . . they just got fed up waiting.

6

NO STRINGS

So there you have it. You love commitment; we want it strictly no strings - a touch surprising really when you consider the first girl we fell in love with was a puppet. You search endlessly for Mr Right while the majority of us had changed our names to Wrong by deed poll. The first girl we fell in love with was half-woman, half-fish and couldn't speak a fucking word. Yes, Marina off Stingray captured the hearts of a generation of young boys and from that point on you should have known that maybe none of you would ever quite match up.

Was it Rudyard Kipling or Mr Kipling who said 'Give me the boy 'till he's seven and I will give you the man?' Well, whoever it was he does make an exceedingly good case and therein lies your problem. None of us have white chargers - a five-year-old Ford Mondeo, maybe. The dice were loaded against us from the start and basically we've been completely bolloxed from birth.

Until Pan's People came along our only heroes were puppets or men who wore dodgy outfits and make-up. Our first influences weren't so much role models as ... models. We were never going to aspire to be Troy Tempest or Scott Tracy and we didn't have a cat in hell's chance of being Batman. We were pre-colour TV; pre slo mo and action replays; pre mobiles - basically prehistoric.

What chance did we have of even turning out just okay? Ours were the days of Spanish Gold sweet tobacco, kali and Opal Mints before some half-wit without a proper job decided to re-name them Pacers. We had Pink Panther candy, Super Mousse chocolate bars, Aztec, Icebreaker, Parma Violets, Cherry Lips, Five Boys, Bazooka Joe and Anglo bubbly, Skippy the bush kangaroo, Cat in the Hat books, TUF Wayfinders, Subbuteo, Magic Robot, Wacky Races, Raleigh Choppers, Brut, Hai Karate and Spangles. Vesta Chow Mein, powdery lumps 'n' all was just about as exotic as it got.

Man hadn't even gone to the moon never mind made one massive leap for mankind on it. We were the kids who were made to eat prunes and congealed custard and semolina for school dinners, when the only good thing was the multi-coloured sponge pudding which must have had more 'E's' in it than a screech of brakes. We were even positively encouraged to think we were crap. We were made of slugs and snails and puppy dogs' tails while you lot were somehow magically assembled with sugar 'n' spice and all things nice. We had no self esteem before the phrase was even thought of. We invented not having it. The only exotic spice we encountered wasn't Posh or Scary, it was Old. We grew up in the days when you weren't supposed to get too dirty on Sundays and everything was closed. So you whiled away the day until tea time when you had a bath and ate salmon sandwiches and celery while Harry Fucking Secombe warbled away in front of a river. Dad said he was really funny in The Goons. Well what happened? No wonder Spike Milligan was glad you died before him so you couldn't sing at his funeral. We were the kids who had golliwogs on jamjars and at junior school Miss Chappel taught us how to sing Puff the Magic Dragon. Imagine the uproar that would cause now - Mrs Chappel would have had the Honalee Gay Rights Movement picketing the school gates for encouraging kids to sing about anything called Puff, even if he was magic. All that frolicking in the autumn mist - I think not. It's not as if Puff was gobbling anyone up, as dragons do, but then perhaps that would have been their objection.

This was pre-CD, more LP and EP and light years before anything as revolutionary as Now That's What I Call Music One. We had to settle for Top of the Pops Volume Six and Hot Hits Volume Four. The only decent compilation albums around were Motown Chartbusters but they had the distinct

24

disadvantage of actually being sung by the original artists and so cost quite a bit more. So if you couldn't really afford Diana Ross from Detroit you got Stella Jones from Stockport and your mom still assured you that it sounded exactly like the original while deep in our hearts of impressionable hearts we just kind of knew it didn't.

We were weaned on The Woodentops; Andy Pandy; Rag, Tag and Bobtail and Tingah and Tucker and our first toys were freakish Potato Head men and a sort of Identikit picture thing where you moved iron filings around with a magnet to make faces which all ended up looking like The Hood or the lead singer with Mungo Jerry. Yeah, that's us, girls, just blokes who wanted to be in International Rescue or wear tights inside our pants just like Batman. He got Robin - it might just as easily have been thrush.

Digital watches hadn't even been thought of and when they burst onto the scene they cost an extortionate amount of money. These were times when Daleks were the scariest thing on TV and when we eventually got to the stage where we got spots and a bad attitude, God gave girls Donny, David and Michael to wet their pants over. Just when we thought they'd pissed off into a dollar-laden early retirement we discovered it wasn't so much a case of bye, bye but Bye, Bye Baby. Along came those Rollers from wherever Bay City was in fucking Scotland. Cheers! What did we get? Gary Glitter, an overweight paedophile who wore a dodgy wig and somehow managed to cram eighteen stone into a Bacofoil suit. Sweet hadn't got a clue what to do and neither did my dad who just walked away from the telly shaking his head when he saw them in all that make-up. My favourite was Marc Bolan, a corkscrew-haired dwarf who wore women's shoes and was acclaimed as the poet of our generation for his meaningful lyrics like 'Dubber-ehda-dubereehda, de da; da de da de da de da da, dubereehda , de da , de da, de da, Oh Deborah, always looks like a Zeborah . . .'

Dad said he was crap and was convinced there was something funny going on between him and the bongo player, but though I can see flaws now, I thought Marc spelt with a 'c' was a genius. Jesus Christ! It's only now that I can pick the stitches of some of Bolan's more meaningful lines like 'Metal Guru is it you, yeah, yeah, yeah' or 'Purple Pie Pete, Purple Pie Pete, his lips are like lightening girls melt in the heat' He was my very first pop idol and then even he went and got killed in a Mini. He deserved a more glamorous death - any dumbo can do that.

And then when we were Kung Fu Fightin', my old man warned me that if I didn't master the basic steps of a waltz and a foxtrot I might as well forget any chance of ever pulling a decent bird. Just as he was beginning to despair of me, along comes The Hustle and then John Travolta completely blew dad's theory out of the water. Jesus, it's like us telling our kids that if they don't learn to do The Hustle, The Bump, The Footsie or The Pogo, they are condemning themselves to a life alone.

So stick all that in the Melting Pot(Blue Mink, 1968, sung by a bird with a set of gnashers which suggested she could give you a blow job and carry out a neat circumcision at the same time) and throw in decimalisation and metrication just as you'd learned the old stuff and it's no wonder we're walking around in a daze. PC? We didn't have Political Correctness or a Personal Computer. The only PC we had was Dixon of Dock Green. We had the calculator thrust upon us only to be told we couldn't use them at school . . . I rest my pencil case.

So is it any wonder all of us men a bit over 40 have had our brains scrambled? God I've become my dad again. It's just what happens. In exactly the same way as my grandad revelled recounting how he could buy five Woodbine, four pints of beer, a box of matches and still get change out of sixpence; then my father would tell me about the orange and a brand new penny because there was a war on. Now I've been struck by the same affliction - I didn't want to be. I tried desperately to avoid it but the virus has indisputably infected another generation.

Listen, I wasn't deprived, hard done by, or anything of the sort, but give me a break . . . kids today, well, they just don't know they're born!

My dad wondered if I was homosexual because I wanted a 'doll' - Action Man - and when I hit my teens I thought two dabs of Brut would have girls falling at my feet. Man had landed on the moon by then and taken about half as long to do it as it took me to reach puberty. These were pre-Girl Power days. The only proper female pin-ups we had were Pans People until 1976 when Charlie's Angels came along and I was 17 going on 18 then. Ah, Pans People . . . Big Babs, darling Cherry, Louise, Ruth and Dee Dee. They gave us teenage boys plenty to think about. When I eventually lost my virginity, I was too blissfully carried away to realise I'd actually committed a criminal offence(hang on, don't even go there - SHE was 15) and just thinking about my best mate's mom was enough to give me a hard-on for weeks. Hey and it wasn't just us with a puppet fetish - 15 million people tuned in to watch the Basil Brush show!

And so now divorced and separated women the nation over down their pints, compare tattoos and tongue studs and wonder where all the decent blokes went. Girls, we were never there - we have been spiralling off course since we were about eight.

It must be galling to find you've come a way distant second to a girl whose entire wardrobe comprises of a few bikini tops and a couple of scallop shells. The seeds were sown at a criminally early age. The die was cast . . . and from that point on we were beyond redemption. Marina had just about everything and at the time we naively didn't even realise her inability to speak would eventually be looked upon as something of a wonderful bonus. No 'does my bum look big in this?' No 'what are you watching this rubbish for?' or 'you don't want another one'. Nothing like that, just the occasional splash of her flipper and a wistful, contented grin and we were captivated.

Tin Tin, that sultry brunette with the cute accent off Thunderbirds, was from the same mould, no pun intended. Our boyhood fancies wouldn't continually demand hugs - just a quick squirt of WD40 or a lick of Ronseal and they'd be happy for years. It really could bring a whole new meaning to 'It does exactly what it says on the Tin Tin'.

Not that surprising then, come to think of it, that Daryl Hannah got us all going again in Splash. A lost generation seeking new direction and Daryl beckons us to jump off that quayside never to be seen again. To disillusioned, fed-up males the land over it was escapism of epic proportions - Reggie Perrin with scales.

Pledging your life to Marina would have had untold advantages beyond the comprehension of a seven-year-old. If she was quiet, you wouldn't be thinking 'She's got the hump with me' and if you suspected she had you could always just piss off upstairs knowing it would take her an absolute age to slither up to have it out with you. Marina wouldn't need 15 pairs of shoes, infact she wouldn't even need the odd pair of flip flops. She wouldn't ask you if you'd noticed anything different about her appearance because it never fucking changed and if you took her away for the weekend she could cram her entire wardrobe into a toilet bag and be ready in two minutes flat. Marina wouldn't delay things by complaining her hair was still wet - it was permanently wet and she wouldn't sue for half of your cash if ever it ended in divorce. She hadn't got any pockets for a start and she'd probably just piss off and find another cave rather than take half of your home. Your kids would come home with a sackful of swimming medals and you wouldn't have to spend half your life telling them not to go on frozen ponds and worrying if the police would knock on the door to tell you they were missing feared drowned. Marvellous.

Marina wouldn't have been expensive to take out either. You can almost imagine it - a few beers, chippie on the way home: 'Pie and chips please and a nice chunk of raw cod for the missus!' Fantastic. She wouldn't turn up at a party worrying if someone would have the same outfit on and she could piss in the sea without looking sheepish about it. And so lads, from early childhood, we were totally fucking ruined. Women just somehow never shaped up after that. How could we have known that our male role models, the men who helped mould our characters from an early age, had set impossible standards?

28

We would never be aquanauts, pilots or astronauts - not even John the sad bastard Space Monitor in Thunderbird 5. No matter how good a job we had we would never call around at your front door on one of those hover scooters. We were earmarked to under-achieve from those formative years on and yet you still wonder why we are like we are . . .

For three weeks in The Seychelles, read two weeks in Minehead. How about a holiday on Tracy Island? Wow, now there's something to set the mind racing. In the mid-60s anyone who took a summer break in Spain really had something to crow about. British holidays were the norm be it in a caravan, boarding house, hotel or the Butlins and Pontins packages which had become so popular. No matter where I went my mind would often wander to what it would be like sunning myself on Tracy Island. Only trouble was it was a secret location so how the fuck would you find it? But then again, how the hell could it be secret with all that activity going on? Just supposing Thomas Cook, never mind Captain Cook, couldn't find it, someone outside the Tracy family must know where it was.

It would throw up its own problems though. I mean to say, you'd be scared shitless if you were admiring the pictures and suddenly those eyes lit up and someone started talking to you. And just imagine having a leisurely dip when the swimming pool started moving about and Thunderbird Fucking One blasted into the air.

Your lilo would disintegrate in seconds if you hadn't drowned already. They wouldn't be able to hang around would they? You couldn't have International Rescue being held up for a few minutes while the pool was cleared.

You could be taking a leisurely walk around the edge of the island when suddenly the palm trees flopped flat to the floor and Thunderbird Two came up on its ramp ready to roar off. I guess that's why they never opened it up to tourists and Jeff Tracy didn't seem the type who needed the cash anyway. Was he giving Lady Penelope one the minute the boys were off putting their lives on the line? Those dodgy beads of sweat were a bit of a giveaway come to think of it. And the girls all wonder why men over 40 are fucked in the head?

7

EASY RIDER

Neil Armstrong might have made one small step for man and one mighty leap for mankind in July of 1969 but it was bugger all compared to what landed in the garage of 78 Sandpiper Road just a few short months later. December 25, 1969 - a date which will forever be etched in my memory. Reminiscing with Belinda had merely brought it home to me that there are milestone points in your life when it's probably as well a greater being doesn't peep out of a cloud and say 'Enjoy it, because it just doesn't get any better than this.' It's your very own Torvill and Dean straight sixes moment.

Every indication had been that I'd more than likely be getting a sensible bike for Christmas. My dad's 'well, we'll see' was usually an indicator that I'd be getting something I would grow into. I was eleven and we weren't rich - a deadly combination. Don't get me wrong, this is not some tale of a poor boy's battle against adversity and my parents were brilliant, but if money was growing on trees then I couldn't see any orchard and it seemed like almost everything I really wanted was either deemed impracticable or something I'd grow out of in no time. Last year's present had been just what I wanted - a pair of George Best Stylo Matchmaker boots with the sidelace and the autograph - but it had taken 12 months to discard the two pairs of thick socks I'd had to wear to stop them slipping off every time I kicked the ball. And so to the bike. I might have been an only one, but I certainly couldn't just have anything and everything I wanted and so while a racer would have been my No1 choice when dad took me around the shops to have a look,

31

I'd made the mistake of showing an interest in a normal bike. Dad thought racers were dangerous; dad thought everything was dangerous. I lived in constant dread of getting caught swallowing bubbly gum because he was always warning me that if you swallowed it, it wrapped around your heart and killed you. Even Spangles were dangerous to dad. If he'd have had his way he'd have smashed them with a toffee hammer first and allowed me to eat shards of blackcurrant flavoured glass rather than risk me swallowing one whole. And taking that kind of mentality into account, there was no way I could see me waking up to a racer. The very word 'racer' conjured up images of me hurtling down the road at 60mph and into the path of an oncoming articulated lorry. If you're going to have a bike have one that someone else would at least consider pinching. When you're an 11-year-old lad there are standard things to be met - like not being standard. A bike had to have a crossbar and it definitely doesn't require a basket or anything which looks like it would accommodate one – front or back.

I guess I must have woken with a mix of excitement and trepidation that Christmas morning, thrown some clothes on and gone through the usual pleasantries of opening pressies from aunties and uncles before being ushered into the garage to go and see my new bike. What happened next still makes me go weak at the knees. I'd been led to believe that I was going to be rewarded for passing my eleven plus, but Jesus wept. It was completely covered in all that stiff brown paper you get from hardware shops. You could see it wasn't a racer because of the handlebars. I tore the paper frantically and glanced up at my mom and dad, I felt like I'd got an honours degree in . . . in . . . I don't know . . . being a son. I just stared at it and then stared at it again. It was bright yellow. The shape, the sheer chunkiness of it. It was phenomenal. It was a thing of beauty. A Chopper . . . a Raleigh bloody Chopper, no less.

'Like it?' dad asked, though he knew he didn't need to.

'Oh man . . . It's fantastic.'

'They're the latest thing,' said mom.

'I know.'

'Thought you'd like it,' said mom. I swear she had a tear in her eye.

'Like it? I love it. Oh man alive just look at it - thanks.'

I hugged my mom and dad and sighed(just slightly) on being told that I'd have to come in for just a bit because it was still very early. I wanted to hug the bike - a Raleigh Chopper, with a real gearstick, hi-rise handlebars, a fuck-off back wheel and a seat with a huge reflector on the back that looked like it had come off one of the motorbikes I'd seen on tele on a Saturday afternoon. I was Arthur Lampkin. I couldn't wait, so I went indoors to sling on some playclothes so I could go in the garage and just sit on it. It had a stand. A stand! This bike had everything. I would be the envy of the street. Racer? Who wanted one of those. This was the kiddie. Even the sound of it stirred me - Chopper. It looked tough and it even sounded tough. It was quite possibly the best damned bike in the world and it was mine - as of 15 minutes ago. It was the best.

'Now just go steady,' dad said opening the garage doors. Steady? This beast didn't do steady. It didn't know careful. I'd seen the adverts proclaiming The Wild Bunch are coming with three kids on these bikes from another planet.

'Brrmmmm . . . born to be wild,' I shrieked gleefully.

'Mild more like,' said Dad. 'Just be careful.'

* * *

I'd been relaying every last ounce of that feeling to Terry the landlord, when our conversation was interrupted by a slightly flustered Belinda making her way back to where I was sitting at the bar. Terry glanced at me knowingly, as she apologised for bringing me back to the 21st century with a jolt.

'My car won't start. You couldn't give me a push could you Dunny?'

'No problem.'

'You're a darling. I told that fella of mine that it was on the

33

blink but does he take any bloody notice? No. Fucking useless. Men eh . . . hopeless.'

It seemed a shade inappropriate to include the whole of mankind in that sweeping generalisation particularly as one of thcm was about to givc hcr a bump start. Belinda pointed me in the direction of a Ford Mondeo which had seen better days and I motioned her to get in and stick it in gear. I couldn't help noticing the Baby on Board sticker dangling from the back window, like some exclamation to a world that couldn't care less. Not having kids myself, I admit to being totally perplexed by Baby on Board stickers. What purpose do they serve? Does it mean 'Forgive me for driving like a twat, but there's a delicate human being in here?' As a driver, I don't want to run into someone else's car in the first place and the fact that there's a sticker informing me there may be other human life in there, matters fuck all to me. I suppose some would argue if the car is found on it's roof then it's a way of telling rescuers they might find a tot in the back, but don't ask me. What do I know about it?

I shoved and I pushed and Belinda waved at me and yelled her appreciation through the window as the car spluttered to life. I stood there catching my breath for a few minutes. I wasn't sure whether it was my knackered lungs or the exasperation of seeing the 1971 carnival queen, the belle of the ball, hurtling off in the distance in an eight-year-old Ford Mondeo. What happened to the orange Bond Bug; the yellow Ford Escort Mexico, the black Capri or the Cortina that had been painted to look like Starsky and Hutch's? Three husbands, four kids, not forgetting two grandkids, a huge arse and one major hang-up about men. I'd probably once dreamed of emerging from a car park panting breathlessly after a rendezvous with Belinda, but how times had changed. There were a lot of things I'd felt about her over a period of years. Even in my most jealous moment I'd never wanted it to be sympathy. There was a sad, almost pathetic desperation about her. She was still looking for Mr Right. The girl who had the world at her feet had somehow managed to stumble across a part of it that had collapsed beneath her. A life

34

of unfulfilled dreams and sporadic maintenance payments. I gulped the sharp night air and made my way back into the pub.

8

LOVE THY NEIGHBOURS

I'm guessing that broken homes and divorce came to Britain as part of the Common Market because they were noticeable by their absence in 1965. It would have been around the Spring of '65 that my parents John and Jean Dunn, and me moved into No78 Sandpiper Road - one of the smart new semis on a then half-completed estate. Strange, from that point on everything in my life is vivid, but up to the age of six I'm left clutching an abstract collection of smells, sights and sounds. My parents lived with my gran and grandad in Wolverhampton for a year or so while the house was being completed. I'm not quite sure how that came about, probably to do with them saving up money or something, but it doesn't really matter. A psychologist would probably have a field day with such a hotch-potch of recollections, but I would imagine everyone's the same. I vividly remember my mom or gran, maybe both, cooking in the kitchen with World Wide Family Favourites on the radio. Loads of requests I didn't understand from people called Simon and Charles who were in BFPO whatever and saying they missed home so much and couldn't wait to be back for Christmas. Cutting shapes out of pastry seemed much more interesting, so the sentiment was lost on me.

I recall big slabs of green soap shaped like bullion bars; my grandad coming home for his dinner smelling of engine oil and putting his cap on the mantelpiece; Wagon Wheels the size of dartboards; the Tufty Club; gran on her hands and knees polishing the red front door step; the mangle just outside the back door; and grandad diligently checking his pools coupon and saying 'ah, well, work on Monday.'

I remember the butcher's boy delivering a joint of meat with a little piece of flimsy paper on the top attached by a little metal skewer which looked like a ski pole; grandad having steel splinters in his fingers and the Betterware man. And that's about it really and I take comfort from it rather than worry about my seemingly sparse and faint recollections because I'm sure if I'd been beaten or locked away in a dark room for hours on end, I'd remember it. It was unspectacularly good and safe and warm. More Johnson's powder than itching powder.

Within 18 months of moving into the home which would prove to be my solid base for around 13 years, our house had virtually all the trappings indicating a family doing okay at that time. We didn't have a car because mom didn't drive and my dad found his Honda 50 - NRE 77B - a more than suitable mode of transport to work despite the fact that he was 6ft 3in. I can't believe I can still remember that registration, particularly bearing in mind that if you were to ask me what I had for lunch yesterday it might well take me a good 20 minutes to come up with the answer and even then only with the proviso that I could come back to you and make amendments. But for some strange reason I can - NRE 77B - an unspectacular machine particularly if it was teeming with rain, but one etched inexplicably on my memory.

No78 was up at the very top of the main artery road of the estate where all the cul-de-sacs which sprouted off it were named after birds. The estate was basically built in the shape of a big upside down thermometer with Sandpiper stretching all the way to the top culminating in a circle around a grassed area affectionately known as the Top Patch. You could sense a feeling of having 'arrived' a little as the houses gradually filled up with those fortunate enough to have a deposit and the means to arrange payments on the £2,875 to purchase one. If money was no object, the builders had offered to put some new-fangled central heating in for an extra £100, but on the advice of my gran, my parents had been told not to overstretch themselves and so we had a gas fire in the main room with living flame coal effect and precious little else. That wasn't a problem for most of the year, except my bedroom was directly above the garage and had it not been for my electric blanket, I might easily have woken one night and gone out declaring I might be some time. But impoverished it certainly wasn't.

There were ten houses around the Top Patch, two sets of semis from the nape to the crown of the circle with two detached bungalows sitting at the very top. No78 was the furthest up on the left, next to an alleyway which led to the playing fields, railway line and the mounds where we spent endless hours playing. The alleyway comprised of six-foot fence panels either side and must have been about five feet wide and thirty feet long. It bi-sected our garden from the first bungalow which is where the Smarts lived. The Smart's house originally started the sequence of odd numbers which ran down the other side of the road, though they had become the first to name their house - Roma - taking the first two letters of Ron and Maureen. Next to it was No3, empty when we moved in, but quickly filled by a retired couple - Mr and Mrs Watson. The Watsons probably had grown up children, maybe not, I can't remember ever finding out. They had two sausage dogs, which they treated like kids.

Mr Watson spent most of his time tending his greenhouse and cutting crescent shapes in his front lawn to put bedding plants in. He was the king of the slug pellet, which says it all really. I can't imagine a more painful death than eating something which blows you up and my dad's slug remedy of sinking a half-filled glass of beer into the soil and letting them drown in it, did have its merits. If he wasn't tending his tomatoes or cutting crescents, old Mr Watson was spraying. In the winter months he made wine; along with sloe gin and marrow rum. To the uninitiated, Mr Watson would go to great lengths to explain how easy it was to make marrow rum. All you needed was a pair of tights or stockings and insert a marrow with the seeds scooped out, he'd explain. The mind boggles. Then you pack the marrow with brown sugar, hang it up and leave it to ferment, whereby the juice seeps out, is strained in the tights and leaves a lethal potion dripping into any

38

available receptacle. Something like that anyway.

Mrs Watson would have been lucky to have anything resembling a marrow near her tights. She was something of an oddity; an immaculately groomed woman with a purplish-pink bouffant beehive who talked to her dogs with a lot more affection and understanding than ever went in Mr Watson's direction. They really were the odd couple of the street and I'm not on about the dogs. Whatever happened to sausage dogs, incidentally? Did some strange virus wipe out certain breeds of dogs in the mid-70's or did Princess Anne's Staffie just eat the lot of them? Suddenly, canine standards you had grown up alongside seemed to mysteriously disappear. Where did the Lassie dogs go? What happened to miniature poodles? Does The Queen own the last corgis on the planet? She won't if Anne has anything to do with it. Something went on there and we just weren't told about it. When I was a kid Alsations were as nasty as it got. Bull terriers, Rottweillers and their like just weren't heard off and mastiffs were things you got behind your ears and if you had them removed it meant you couldn't swim in the deep end.

The first of the semis was Pele's family - the Joneses. Pele quickly became a founder member of our gang although at that time he answered to his proper name of Richard or Rich. The actual moment when Rich became Pele and took on a nickname which would last him a lifetime, isn't precise. But I can remember roughly when and why it came about. It's bit of boy thing, but nicknames can be like that. There was a kid at school called Stephan Rogers who unwillingly became known as Einstein because he was a brainbox, but Rich's christening as Pele came about for totally opposite reasons. Quite simply he was shite at football; just one of those kids with no natural aptitude for a ball. Rich was virtually always the last one to be picked out from the line, marginally ahead of the fat kid you stuck in goal. There was always a Jumbo in goal - every playground or park had a Jumbo - and then next in line of succession for the crown of being totally fucking useless was . .

. Pele. And so the name stuck. Pele - a lasting tribute to be named after a more famous No10 than Downing Street and, quite simply because it was totally inappropriate.

Pele came from a large family, he was the middle one of three boys and had two younger sisters. His house was always chaotic and reeked of cats and babies. Even as a kid you'd have to be really desperate to have a drink of squash at Pele's. His mom always seemed to buy the really cheap squash, you know the sort, 15 litres for about 10p, which no matter how much you put in the glass, always ended up tasting like cat's piss and the plastic beakers were always so heavily scratched you couldn't see through them, almost as if to disguise the contents. God love him, he was a top lad, but he got some stick off us because his house was always a tip and the shambles of overgrown garden hid a collection of old gearboxes and panels off cars that Pele's dad always seemed to think would come in handy one day. Mr Jones was one of those blokes who'd never throw anything away in case it *came in handy*. You name it - a piece of tatty wood - Pele's dad would keep it. And when the shed that he'd thrown up himself was full, the handy objects spilled out all over the back garden until they rotted or rusted and outlived any chance they ever had of being useful.

That was a source of considerable annoyance not only to The Watsons in the bungalow next to the Joneses but to the aptly-named Gardners in No7, which was somewhat reluctantly joined to it. The two houses looked like one of those before and after cameos. Before the rendering on the front of the two houses had been given the chance to turn from magnolia to nicotine colour, Mr Gardner had painted their half a pale yellow with the demarcation line clearly defined right down the middle at the front. If it was a gesture meant to shame the Jones family in any way, it failed horribly. The rendering on the front of Pele's house was allowed to go through the various stages of off-white, quite naturally. The Gardners took pride in their house. Their only daughter Josie was at university and wasn't a frequent visitor. They spent hour upon hour tending their tidy borders and lawn and could occasionally be seen tossing any one of a number of offending items back over the Jones' side of the tiny picket fence.

* * *

My best mate Rob Robinson lived next door in No76, the house adjoining ours. Rob was six months older than me, a little on the chubby side with raven-black hair and was often plagued by his irritating younger sister Rosemary. She was two years younger and answered to Rosie on the infrequent occasions when she was being pleasant. Rob's Dad Geoff was a strange kind of guy to work out at times, though for the most part he seemed okay. Mom said he was a bit of a 'ladies' man' who fancied himself as Jason King. I guessed that he might just be the hairiest man in the world; absolutely covered from head to foot in a thick black mat. He had a bushy black Peter Wyngarde-type moustache and sideburns so thick, you wouldn't have been surprised to see a robin's nest in them. He had to shave the rest of his swarthy face twice a day, which is mightily impressive to a young lad of any age. He could whistle so loud with two fingers that it actually hurt your ears, which also won full marks from a seven-year-old. He was a steam train enthusiast and had a track in the garage and was also a local football referee who you'd often see setting off on a Sunday morning resplendent in his black, neatly pressed kit, which he did himself. He was a really smart man, though he always seemed to have really grubby hankies, which Mrs Robinson made no secret of her contempt for. It wasn't so much the bogeys, but the black stuff he seemed to get all over him from his work in the factory, I still have vivid memories of how horrible Mr Robinson's hankies were. It must have had a lasting effect because from that day to this I've never owned one. They must rank among the grossest things around and when I think of the days when one of the tasks expected of the woman of the house was to boil hankies to get them clean and darning socks, it's a good job divorce wasn't so easy in the olden days or else it's doubtful any of us would ever have been born. He could be deadly quiet at times, barely acknowledging your presence and even at an early age you could sense Rob's mom wasn't always entirely at ease in his company. Penny Robinson was lovely - the prettiest mom in the road by a running mile. She had a cute face and a really slim figure. She had closely cropped blonde spikey hair and a cheeky smile which showed off her lovely white teeth and she was great fun. She also had amazing, very large breasts. Quite simply, Mrs Robinson was a top mom and we all had a real soft spot for her. Mr and Mrs Robinson had always called me Dunny from an early age. I liked that. Rob's mom worked part-time as a lab assistant at the local boys' grammar school, which was in Wellington, about three miles from our village. I never quite knew exactly what she did, but it sounded quite important which didn't surprise me because she exuded intelligence.

Nos 74 and 72 were empty when we moved in and stayed that way for what seemed like quite a while. We'd go around and play in them until one day a big warning went around because someone had written something on the plaster upstairs and upset the builders so we were banned from going anywhere near them.

Dad said that he'd looked at No72 but it wasn't going to be finished in time or something like that and there was a problem with a drain and the mortgage on it or something and so we didn't have it. This mortgage thing that adults spent their entire life talking about sounded very, very confusing and not very interesting at all.

Dad said he was glad he didn't go for No72. Our house was better. Mom loved our house. I loved our house. We were all happy. It was near perfect and I only say 'near' because my dad had big plans for it but always added the proviso of 'when we're on our feet.'

The garden was quite big and would be really nice once we were on our feet and we were going to have a tarmac drive once we were up on our feet. It seemed No78 had cost us so much that we were going to be stretched for quite a while. That was fine, I just worried at times how long getting on our feet might take.

Was my family going to be like some desperately weak giraffe, never quite getting up and then collapsing in a heap in one last agonising push? I was scared that it could inexplicably crumble one day, but it didn't and in no time at all we would have most of the trappings of a young family going places - a deep freeze, a tropical fish tank and we were even going to have the phone put in. Good lord.

Dad said the only thing that might change things was if 'blacks' moved in on the estate. Hey, come on, this was late 60's Britain, and anyway he was sure most of them couldn't afford to live in nice houses like ours. Dad said he just didn't want the street smelling of curry. He'd got nothing against them, he said, he just didn't fancy having them in the street and certainly not in one of the houses up at the top end. Boy, was he in for a big shock . . .

9

UNJUST DESSERTS

Why the fuck Jimmy Hunt was made one of the meal monitors at junior school is still something which baffles me to this day. As you get older you get to learn that promotion quite often isn't merited - infact it's often bestowed on people who aren't up to the job. Brilliant - not very good at your job, so they give you a pay rise to watch over people who can do it better than you. Life is cruel and I should have picked up on one of life's great ironies a bit earlier than I did when Jimmy was made monitor of our table. There hadn't been any debate or informal discussion about it - it just happened. There were nine to a table at Hadley Junior School, four down each side with the designated monitor at the head of the operation. There was a great sense of injustice on Table Three in 1965 as it was casually announced that Jimmy would sit at the top of the table and oversee the distribution of the food from the metallic trays which were handed out. The rest of us took it in turns to be water monitors which was scant consolation. In fairness to Jimmy he was consistent. If the food was shite, he gave us all bigger portions than himself and when anything really tasty was offered, he virtually ate the lot. On the occasions when Mrs Peterson walked past as puddings were being served, he'd distribute things evenly with the sort of sadistic grin which you knew meant not to eat it too quickly because he would reclaim some of it the minute she had returned to the far end of the dining room. Jimmy's menace ensured he bulked himself up for his karate exertions on the odd occasion that we got chips or good puddings. But when it was prunes and congealed custard, semolina, lumpy potatoes or anything like that, the likes of Rob and me were left half-gagging to try and empty our plates.

As if that wasn't bad enough, we were encouraged to say 'Thanks Jimmy' for his personalised style of meal distribution or risk getting a Chinese burn the minute we got outside. The whole procedure was like a scene out of Oliver. It was positively Victorian at times. Just thinking back about it, makes me shiver. The metallic taste of the water from dented jugs; the scratched glasses marked 'Duralex, France'; the scramble to get out. Being left handed didn't help either. I ate 'the right way around' anyway, thank God, but was actually *forced* to hold my pudding spoon in my right hand. To this day I've never actually got the hang of it, but was made to feel awkward and dumb even though it was patently clear that I was one of the brightest kids in the whole bloody school. And so my reward for being bright, top of the class in almost all subjects and going to school smartly turned out was to emerge from meals with dribbles of pudding down my grey shirts because I was deemed to be somewhat backward in the eating department. I found it hard enough getting semolina anywhere near my mouth anyway, but to do it right handed as well was something which bordered on torture. My mom went ballistic and returned from a trip to see the headmistress with a right flea in her ear that she'd virtually been accused of mollycoddling me for not trying to correct the problem in the first place.

All that and to be served up my food by Jimmy fucking Hunt - even now it has to rank as one of life's great injustices. He wasn't just a psycho he was a bit like the school meals he dished up - half-baked. Jimmy Hunt wasn't even in our class for reading and writing because he had 'difficulties.' He didn't have difficulties, he was fucking dumb and disruptive. So where's the justice in that system? He has problems getting to grips with reading and writing and goes into a class for special tuition; my brain tells me instinctively to hold my spoon in my left hand and I'm treated like some kind of spastic. Incidentally, on the subject, whatever happened to spastics? Did they just disappear?

Did they cure it or did they become called something else? There were spastics around when I was a kid - and mongols. I'm pretty sure mongols became Down's Syndrome in a sort of PR move somewhere down the line but I'm still not sure what happened to spasticity. Terrific word though - sounds a bit like a Police album to me. Perhaps they banned it. They just might have done. They seemed to ban everything else when I was a kid.

When we were growing up , almost anything half-way decent ended up being banned. I could have thought up Banned Aid long before Sir Bob came along in a bid to launch a global attempt to get some of my favourite things off the strictly prohibited list. We used to have these fantastic balsa wood gliders which were self-assembly, though that description is perhaps stretching the point a bit. You'd buy them in a little flat-pack and basically there was a body section with a slit in it, through which you fed the wings. There was a tiny kind of metal clip which you attached to the nose and a tail fin. On the bottom was a little notch into which you inserted the enclosed elastic band and away you went. They were brilliant fun but because some twat in a spare moment when he'd nothing better to do decided they might easily take another child's eye out, they were wiped off the face of the earth at a stroke. That was the whole point for Christ's sake. The balsa blinders were just one of a number of things which the authorities stamped BANNED on. It was almost as if we were a guinea-pig generation - you know, find something that they really enjoy and stop them having it. We had gobstoppers the size of golf balls, note the past tense. BANNED. At my junior school they'd ban anything. If it was great fun - ban it. I remember buying an 007 Powerball, a new-fangled thing which were really tremendous. They were black as coal and hard as titanium and one good, meaty, thwack into the playground and they'd be over the school roof. Brilliant. BANNED. I don't know why they bothered banning them because they were so fucking powerful you were guaranteed to lose the darned things within an hour of having it anyway. There wasn't any need to ban them apart from the small consideration that thrown in an incorrect manner you would have no problem fracturing someone's skull with one. I ask you, what is the point of having toys, whatever, if you can't do damage with them? They just cease to be fun. My junior school banned conkers because they were dangerous. The fact that kids had been playing conkers for hundreds of years didn't seem to come into it. The only time I ever saw someone come within a whisker of his life over conkers was when Mo Singh had the audacity to smash Johnny Jones' 67er only for it to be discovered that his conker was wood and had been turned on a lathe by his father. Last time I saw Gurdial he was the millionaire head of a clothing empire which just shows it's never too early to start out with enterprising ideas. Potato Puffs even found their way onto the prohibited list just because it had been on the news that some kid in Halifax had choked to death on a packet. I ask you! One of the ice-cream companies came up with the brilliant idea of making a cone with a bubbly gum in the bottom - BANNED. War cards - BANNED. There was no let up, and the girls didn't escape Scot-free either. They only had a few months enjoying clackers and driving a whole generation of parents bonkers with the noise, because it turned out that they could fracture your wrist. BANNED. Dr Scholls sandals, with the wooden bottoms - BANNED. Later on, platform shoes - BANNED. Even when they brought in something educational and useful - the pocket calculator - they ended up banning it. We were the generation which saw in the fantastic new dawn of the calculator and what happens - BANNED. Fuck me, there's kids today with computers that can tap into the secrets of The Pentagon or wipe-off the debt of a Third World country at a stroke and no one bats an eyelid, yet we weren't allowed to take calculators to school. No wonder we're bitter.

There was no stopping 'em and even the pop charts weren't safe from interference. Personally the decision to ban Jane Birkin and Serge Gainsbourg's Je T'Aime . . . Non Plus, made little or no difference to me. They were just moaning and getting hot under the collar about her moaning and getting hot under the collar. They thought it was far too sexual and there was me just assuming she'd been hit by a Powerball. How wrong can you be? Non plussed? You bet.

And I think it's for that reason as much as anything that I have a problem with the decision makers of this world. What do they know about anything? The whole fabric of our society is fatally flawed by the people in power, be it at school, the lawmakers, the religious leaders or politicians and whatsmore I can prove it. It's only later in life that you discover, often at your own personal cost, that a frighteningly high percentage of the people promoted at work get moved up to get them out of the way. They end up telling other people who are ten times better at doing the job, what they should be doing.

Look at councillors, particularly those who go on to be fully-fledged politicians; the bulk of them are absolute tossers. When I saw a 15-year-old William Hague addressing the Tory Party Conference from the podium, I didn't think 'Now there's a young man destined for greatness.' I just couldn't believe what a wanker he was. Anyone who spends hour-upon-hour reading Hansard at 12 should be banned from telling us what to do. But they don't prohibit the things they should, you see. And he's not alone is he? To be a politician at an early age means you have had to spend almost every evening of your life going to meetings, sub-committee meetings, rallies etc, etc. Now who honestly wants to do that when you could be out on the pull or playing darts? Show me someone who does and I certainly won't be voting for him.

The church? It's riddled with half-wits and social misfits. Explain to me how a man who has supposedly never experienced sex and never been married can sit in a confessional box and advise people on how to handle things and where they are going wrong. It's absolutely fucking nonsensical. What does he know about it? The square root of fuck all, that's what. What a job. I'd make a good priest, because I've done most of the things causing such angst among my flock and would know nearly all the implications of the particular fix any member of my parish was

48

in. That apart, it's an absolute criminal waste that the one man who can't do anything about it, gets all the best tips! Straying housewives; 15-year-old girls confessing all their secrets and what do they get? Three hail Mary's and an Our Father. I'd tell them not to worry about it and if they wanted any hands-on advice, they knew where to find me.

The minute you wake up to that crap, the nearer you are to cracking it. The police aren't the brightest people in the world - or the most honest. I'm generalising, I know, but it's a fact. A police superintendent I happened to go to school with was caned for breaking into the school tuck shop as a 12-year-old. I rest my case. I saw him over a pint years later and as the occasion became more relaxed I asked him how a man who had shown the flair of Ronnie Biggs and only got two 'O' levels ever managed to rise up the ranks of the police force with such remarkable speed. You know what he said? He said that it helped to have a criminal mentality to deal with the people he had to deal with. He kind of argued that you needed to know how to force open the door on the school tuck shop and plan a getaway to be on exactly the same wavelength as the cretins he had to deal with every day. I almost swallowed it. I just watched him pour his 12th pint down his throat, get into his car for the 15 minute drive home and couldn't help wondering about his mates in the murder squad.

10

MERCURY RISING

It's little wonder, when you consider all the contributory factors, that anyone whose junior school years started in or around the mid-60s grew up to be mentally suspect. Infact when I recall how one of my junior school teachers used to tip mercury onto the top of his desk as we all huddled around, to show us it's fascinating qualities, it's a wonder some of us grew up at all. I'm pretty sure Mr Richards, a coins-in-pocket-rattling military sort of man, who always had little spots of white spittle in the corner creases of his mouth, must have told us not to touch the stuff, but whatever . . . Honest to God, he'd get us all to assemble around his desk and tip out this quicksilver stuff onto the wooden desktop. We watched transfixed as the globules wobbled their way around the table. Jesus, this stuff was absolutely deadly. If you thought Freddie Mercury was dangerous, get a load of the real stuff. And there we were, just seven or eight years of age within touching distance of it. Imagine if they did that now - Mr Richards' heels wouldn't have touched the ground as he was booted out of school, his career in tatters, never to be seen again. And it's against that kind of backdrop that us 40-somethings need a little understanding. Mr Richards had one of those blackboards that at the time was quite possibly the most advanced of it's type. It was actually on a kind of roller system and his idea of punishment was to get anyone guilty of incurring his wrath to wipe the whole of the board clean with a blackboard duster. Jesus, never mind mercury poisoning, it's a wonder half of us didn't develop the blackboard equivalent of asbestosis in later life just through inhaling microscopic particles of chalk. We had inkwells in that classroom as well. I swear to God if I were to walk back into it now and witness it just as it was, you could be forgiven for thinking that you had entered the Dickensian era. You wouldn't have been too surprised if Martin Chuzzlewit or Smike were sitting behind grainy, wooden desks, held together by ear wax, hardened blotting paper and several generations of bogeys.

Then of course, there was glue-sniffing. Only trouble was we were high on glue and solvents before it was even known to be a danger and so that was okay. My dad actually introduced me to it when he bought home my first Airfix model plane kit - a Spitfire or Hurricane, or at least one of the easy ones, just to introduce me to what became a national pastime. We all loved making them and in our innocence not one of the nation's sniffers ever realised we were doing anything wrong, because the dangers weren't common knowledge. That's the thing you see, tell someone something is prohibited and they hurtle headlong towards it. Give them a modelling kit with extraordinary smelling tubes of glue - I think it was called plastic cement - and throw in a tiny tin of equally mind-bending paint to decorate it and we were happy for hours - absolutely off our fucking faces without even realising it.

Junior school teachers encouraged it and, the nation over, kids could be seen with their heads rammed into massive tins of Bostik and Copydex while the more vulgar among us would roll up dollops of it and suspend them from our noses like huge strings of snot. I even recall making kites in the fourth year of juniors where, when we had eventually assembled the balsa dowling rods and paper, we were required to coat them with a waterproof varnish called, believe it or not, DOPE. Honest to God - dope - and the stuff smelled fucking great and if it happened these days teachers would be instantly dismissed. High as kites on dope, fuck me I can see the headlines already.

Kids today, with their mobile phones and i-pods just wouldn't believe it. I paint an impoverished picture and I heartily apologise for that but thirty years of progress makes it all seem more like one hundred and thirty. I-Pod? When we got a break from close encounters with deadly chemicals, we'd pass the time playing milk bottle tops. Yeah, smelly flattened foil milkbottle tops. They were virtually a currency in our playground. Various pupils would set up stalls in the corners of the yard and shout out the prices on offer if you managed to skim one which landed on theirs. 'Four and your own one back' was an often heard call and occasionally there'd be mayhem as someone who had quite clearly inhaled some mercury earlier sprinted through the yard shouting 'scrambles!' Now what this particular cry indicated was that the aforesaid mercury victim was bounding his way across the playground and as the cry 'scrambles!' reached a deafening pitch, he would hurl all his milkbottle tops into the air, sparking a mass frenzy among the rest of us to catch them as they came down. Now come on, knowing that, is it any wonder that we are all stark raving bonkers? I mean tell me about it eh, grazing knees, scuffing shoes and risking life and limb to get your hands on the odd couple of stinky milkbottle tops. On summer's days we'd even go around burning each other with magnifying glasses. It was tremendous fun. And the girls, what fantastic pastimes they had too. They would do handstands against the playground walls and show off their navy knickers. Marvellous that, because we weren't very interested then. Years later, you'd virtually have to do handstands to get anywhere near their knickers. Oh yeah, and they used to French knit. That has to be one of the most bizarre things you could even contemplate doing. The equipment was astonishingly complex - a cotton reel with four tiny pins nailed in to the top. Then as if by magic, if you wound wool around the pins in a certain way, a knitted tube would start to snake it's way out of the bottom of the cotton reel and I think the general theory was to try and see who could knit the longest tube or something. It was the sort of thing that Blue Peter latched onto. Val, Peter and John would urge young girls the length and breadth of Great Britain to send in their tubes of wool so they could be made up into blankets for the poor people of Biafra or Ethiopa or some other impoverished, drought-hit land. What the fuck did they want blankets for? Can you just imagine, you haven't eaten for fucking weeks, it hasn't rained for years and it's 140 degrees in the shade and when you've crawled 15 miles to where you heard the plane land, some twat comes out and gives you a multi-coloured knitted woollen blanket which is about half-an-inch thick? Well when that happens you really should wake up to the fact that your luck has well and truly fucking deserted you.

And so some of those girls got together with some of those boys and had families and now their kids are taking drugs and mugging old people. Is it any real wonder? Imagine trying to show a perplexed kid today the finer points of playing bottletops. They would just look at you in the same way that I looked at my parents when they were trying to explain that they played with hula hoops - not the things you eat - and spinning tops. 'You're bloody ruined you are!' Well, sorry mom, but you did it. And now we're doing it and doubtless in twenty years time, the kids of today will be exclaiming in disbelief 'You don't know you are born - when we were kids our mobiles were as big as fucking Mars Bars and if you had more than four parts of your body pierced your parent (singular), would go barmy!' And they'd ground you so you couldn't get drugs for a week, but the dealers now had a neat way to send them via your laptop anyway.

It's incredible. I actually used to love those selection boxes comprising of chocolate replica smoking stuff. Yeah, a chocolate pipe with chocolate matches and some chocolate cigarettes and a cigar. Can you imagine that now? There'd be marches on parliament. There was an abundance of stuff like that. Liquorice pipes with little red hundreds and thousands on the end representing the glowing tobacco; candy cigarettes, the lot. And we could get Spanish Gold tobacco, a kind of sweet tooth-rotting brown candy stuff which came in a plastic replica of the pouch adults got the real stuff in. It was the 1965 equivalent of a drug-taking selection box you'd get these days. You know the sort of thing, a chocolate syringe, a liquorice lace ligature so you could get the vein up. Wow, that could really take off . . . MPs couldn't help but encourage that.

These were the good old days, we never thought we'd refer to like that. The days when bonfire night actually just lasted one fucking day, sometimes two if November 5 fell awkwardly. The days when cats and dogs didn't need counselling for nervous breakdowns because Guy Fawkes celebrations didn't span three fucking weeks. The days when hedgehogs seeking shelter in bonfires just had a 1-in-365 chance of being cremated alive and there were only an eighth of the cars on the road. Progress hasn't been kind to hedgehogs all told. Yeah, the good old days when being a two-car family was a sign that you'd arrived - not that you just hadn't got any kids.

Designer gear? Forget it. Dunlop Green Flash was about as cool as it got. Remember plimsoll bags? Nike they were not. Huge material bags made by your mom with your name stitched on and a draw tight cord. They made fantastic weapons easily capable of knocking a classmate right off his feet with one carefully aimed swing. When you finished with a girlfriend at junior school in those days, you actually had to pluck up the guts to tell her or at least let her get the message by letting it be known that you were now going out with her best, soon to be worst, mate, or merely swiping her with your plimsoll bag. No texting. No easy way out for us. There just HAS to be someone who was the very first person to be dumped by text. There's no way of ever knowing really. Unless it was Mr Motorola's daughter perhaps who just happened to be going out with a Nokia heir. And because of their dads, they were among the first to have mobiles. There's someone out there. Perhaps they aren't even aware they were the first to be dumped by text message. One, curt cruel 'We're through' or should that be WR THRU and history was made.

Doubtless in the future, people will get engaged by text. Perfectly plausible - maybe even marry by text across some staggering distance. Just tap in 'I do' and then when the pastor says 'you may now kiss the bride' just send a little X across the airwaves. Ah, technology. Where would we be without it? Well, we were cutting edge once, you know . . .

11

RADIOGRAM GA GA

There were occasions when the yellow formica table in our kitchen resembled The Somme after dad had taken delivery of half a hundredweight of meat. There were only three of us but we had recently had a new fangled freezer - a Kelvinator - and my parents, on the premise of saving fortunes, now only dealt in pork, lamb and beef by the ton. Dad would proudly work out how much it had cost him for half a pig which included 96 sackfuls of pork chops, before proclaiming what a difference the freezer had made. Mom was anything but a snob but seemed happy enough that the family seemed to be keeping apace with the numerous technological wonders changing everyone's lives right now. We had a serving hatch, a curly cord light and it wouldn't be long before we had the phone put in. Dad seemed to spend an eternity ramming it home to me that he didn't really want me to give the number to anyone in case they rang. Okay, got that . . .

Our house didn't have a name and I don't feel deprived for that. There's something distinctly sad about people who give their houses names, particularly those who compile it from the first couple or so letters of their own rather ordinary names. So as the Romas, Micas, Ronmars and their like emerged like some frightening form of cell division, our humble 78 stayed just that. Perhaps even scarier than the Dunroamins were those taken from some far-flung foreign place the occupants had quite probably never even been to. Quite likely they had just taken the name from some travel book or feature thinking it was a sun-kissed bay in Mauritius when actually it meant something rather mundane like public library, slow down, turn right or horse shit tipping point. If you're going to give your house a name then why not just call it Albert or something and be done with it.

Dad, for some reason, resisted the temptation, though I suspect that was in no small part down to the fact that the Johnsons at No70 had wasted no time in proudly displaying Hillview on their house, barely a week after my father claimed he'd mentioned that as one he'd considered to Reg Johnson over a game of darts. He pretended he wasn't bothered but you could just tell he harboured a lasting suspicion of the Johnsons from that day on though steadfastly insisting they were welcome to it because he thought the very notion stupid.

Hey, but we were the first in the street to have a serving hatch and seeing as that was in absolutely no doubt, dad possibly got some bizarre satisfaction from the proliferation of serving hatches which were dutifully knocked into the separating walls of kitchens and dining rooms in the neighbourhood. Serving hatches were definitely cutting edge, but quite what purpose they actually served was hard to fathom. I mean it wasn't as if any of us had staff or anything - a little something to make the butler's job a touch easier. But, there you go, meals were prepared and placed onto the wooden top of the serving hatch, completely by-passing any thoughts of just walking the three or four yards through the door at the other side. Marvellous. How did we ever cope without them? All that time they saved.

The Johnsons soon had a serving hatch, but they would have, wouldn't they? The Joneses, Powells, Woods, Williams' and all the rest followed suit in no particular order and grateful mothers on Birdsong Estate would extol the virtues of this most fantastic concept in home decor since Vymura while occasionally quietly grumbling that the only real drawback was that it made the dining room a bit draughtier. Big fucking surprise - knock a three-foot-by-two-foot hole smack in the middle of the wall and fill it with two ill-fitting doors or those multi-coloured plastic ribbon-type things you see on kitchen doors in cheap takeaways and wonder why half the family are walking around with stiff necks. Still, what a boon in summer. The serving hatch era was well and truly upon us.

Now add to the trusty hatch a tropical fish tank and it was little wonder my dad thought he was in the running to be president of Coolville. He never tired of telling us how he marvelled at its relaxing, therapeutic qualities, yet to this day I can't see why. He was forever out of his comfy armchair tinkering with the bloody thing and just checking that the guppies, neon tetras or whatever weren't in a distressed state, though quite what they had to be manic about escaped me. When one of the black Mollies had the good grace to give birth, you could have been forgiven for thinking that my dad was going to start getting sympathy pains. Ironic really, since they just kind of spit them out without the slightest fuss and then wait for nature to take its course. Then the Angel Fish had the audacity to eat all of dad's new family. Old Angel Eyes never recovered from that indiscretion and had not one fluid ounce of a chance of getting back in my old man's good books. The poor creature which had been admired so lovingly for the previous few months was suddenly isolated in the fish tank's very own Chamber of Horrors along with the other fishy equivalents of Harold Shipman and Myra Hindley. He or she was immediately slammed into solitary confinement in a separate kind of tank which floated within the the main aquarium until it was farmed off to one of dad's friends from work who obviously didn't have a problem with accepting a psychotic killer into his home. Dad even threw in his copy of 'How to Keep Angel Fish' just for good measure - not so much a gesture of good will, more an indication that he was washing his hands of this particularly vulgar species. The shit-chomping Catfish must have been delighted with its elevated status, just going to prove that every dog, or cat in this particular instance, has its day. The minute dad handed over the Angel Fish guide book you could just tell there was to be no last minute reprieve.

But the crowning glory was the piece of furniture which might so easily have not so much been delivered to our house, but carried in military style to a fanfare of trumpets. Now the radiogram is something of a sore point with me and I dare say countless thousand others of my age at the time because the idea of getting one was introduced under the guise of it being a family present. I can recall having a kind of Dunn team meeting when the notion was first put forward, the perfectly reasonable explanation being that if the massive decision was made to go ahead and get one, I needn't expect too many big presents that particular Christmas because the radiogram was an expensive piece of equipment. Fair enough, the logic was sound and I was old enough to take on board a new-found maturity that would welcome being consulted over this momentous decision. The theory, as explained to me, was that I would be free to play my records(in stereophonic sound) whenever I wanted to, but the whole family would be able to use it. Fine in principle, except that the only real times I managed to get at it was whenever mom and dad had gone to bingo or the Saturday night dance at the Hadley United Services Club, because that apart, dad was either hogging it with music he felt deserved a wider audience or I was told that I couldn't put on my 'rubbish' because mom wanted to watch TV. Dad explained that the stylus had a diamond in it and God forbid if you tried to lift the playing arm without the requisite care - dad's glare could knock a rhino off its feet at a hundred paces. And with it came the most life-changing horrendously shit collection of LP's that some sadistic bastard at Reader's Digest could spawn. You name it, if it was in a bargain 12-record box set, my dad would get it, to such an extent that after barely a few months you would have thought the darned radiogram was propped up on the bloody things. Readers Digest must have hit on the idea that it didn't matter who the artists were, so long as it was a brand of music which brought out the full extent of this new concept stereophonic sound there would be millions of people gullible enough, including my old man, to buy the wretched things. And so it ensued that my life would never be the same again as dad let the sounds of Manuel and The Music of Mountains, countless brass bands and Roger Fucking Whittaker, not so much flow over him, but consume his, and everybody else's, whole being. Just who the fuck was Manuel? Where were the mountains he came from? Why didn't he have a fucking surname? It didn't occur to me at the time, because it just doesn't, to tell my dad that Manuel, far from being a Latin rhythm master, was quite possibly a session musician who lived in Islington and just spent 23 hours a day in a studio banging the bloody things out. He wouldn't have gone for that anyway. Dad must have really believed that Manuel was a guy lucky enough to be discovered by a fortunate and eternally grateful record executive holidaying with his family in some Alpine village.

Roger Whittaker - I ask you. My dad actually had a record of his which was totally whistling. Honest to God! Now don't get me wrong, when it comes to whistling I can't think of anyone on this planet more accomplished, but do me a favour eh? And dad would sit there pursing his lips as if accompanying Roger in some sort of whistlealong, assuring me that one day I'd grow up to realise T Rex were a pile of shit. No proper words, no meaning to any of the songs, he'd insist. No dad, not like Roger Whittaker's Greatest Whistling Hits. I'd got a slight problem with whistling anyway because I never managed to master it. I'm not talking to the standard of making a best-selling LP, just to make any sort of noise that didn't sound like you were blowing your nose. I couldn't whistle with grass; I couldn't wolf-whistle and I couldn't whistle in that happy-builder kind of way which brickies and postmen used to do around that time. And so quite possibly with that shortcoming in mind, I've always found people who whistle grossly irritating. Thankfully it's not a common pursuit anymore, but had I been an adult in the 50s when it was obviously considered a particularly trendy and manly thing to do, I might well have ended up getting 25 years for administering the mass slaughter of a bunch of workmen as they gleefully went down the pit or into their steel furnace whistling their fucking heads off.

The box-set syndrome encompassed many musical concepts, not least the string of well-known classics played on a variety of somewhat obscure instruments like steel guitars, Hawaiian guitars, French horns, steel drums, whatever - and surely it wasn't just my dad who seemed intent on owning the fucking lot. Around that time a succession of naff artists wafted through our living room among them Bert Kaempfert, Andy Williams, Mantovani, Perry Como and Nana Mouskouri - The White Rose of Athens. Her shoulder length raven hair with the flick and black glasses made her look like some starchy school secretary but it certainly made an impression with my old fella. Dad thought she was sexy; mom thought he just had a thing about women with glasses and I just couldn't help thinking maybe he needed fucking specs. Let us not forget The Spinners, a particularly irritating band who seemed to be on nearly every telly show of the time - Parkinson, Morecambe and Wise, you name it they couldn't go through a series without having The Spinners on at least twice. I can't remember a single song they sung which considering the amount of times I must have heard them suggests my brain had somehow magically managed to delete them. Funny thing is I can picture the one with the funny face, the smug silver-haired small guy and one huge coloured guy with a voice which sounded like it was being dredged up from a gravel pit. The rest of the line-up I wouldn't recognise if they walked into my local and bought me free beer all night - which, if they had any sense of wrong-doing, they would.

But outstripping the lot by a mile was the man who must have come criminally close to mentally scarring me - James Last, a German band leader who thought he was Joe Fucking Cool and churned out LP's at a phenomenal rate of knots. It was just absolutely incredible how many albums that guy managed to get out and just to cap it all some idiot had struck on the idea that each one's title should start 'James Last Goes . . .' So not only was the goatee-bearded Kraut mind-numbingly irritating to listen to but you'd be ready to climb onto the pelmets just at the thought of James Last Goes . . . wherever. Mom and Dad went on bus trips all over the place to see The James Last Orchestra and pretty quickly built up a frighteningly large collection of vinyl with titles such as James Last Goes Pop, James Last Goes

Samba, James Last Goes For a Walk in The Black Forest and James Last Goes South Pacific. Why the fuck couldn't James Last just go? And so it was with a mixture of boyish mischief, musical brainwashing and frustration that I embarked on one of my first attempts at adult humour - an exercise which went spectacularly wrong. One Christmas on from getting the radiogram, I decided to pen a fictitious letter to Santa supposedly from my dad. To me it seemed a good way of getting over one or two points in a humourous kind of way; to dad it reeked of taking the piss in a manner unbecoming my years. To say he wasn't amused would be putting it mildly. I received a big lecture on how ungrateful I was; was told in no uncertain terms that only when I was old enough to appreciate good music could I have an opinion on such things. I was informed that if that's the way I felt about it then the only solution was to get myself a record player for my bedroom and sit up there on my own and listen to my rubbish. Yeeeees!! Out of darkness cometh light. The pen clearly was mightier than the sword and my few, well chosen words, had engineered an extremely productive outcome even if it had come on the back of a major bollocking.

Although I didn't keep the letter, because that didn't seem such a good idea at the time, I can remember the rough outline of how it went. I thought it was amusing; I think mom detected some early promise and more than the odd telling observation in it, but dad, well . . . he just didn't quite ever see the funny side of it. It went something like:

"Dear Santa,

I am a particularly sad man who lives at 78 Sandpiper Road and last year you kindly bought my family a radiogram for Christmas. We have all had so much pleasure from it. So this year rather than socks or an Old Spice box set, I wonder if you would be kind enough to bring me some more James Last LP's. The family do enjoy them so much and we understand that he is bringing out another dozen to coincide with this festive season. I have been very good all year except for not allowing my son to play any of his records on the radiogram when he wants. So with that in mind I wonder if you would mind bringing us some nice LP's that the whole family can have hours of pleasure from. Any of the following would be lovely: James Last Goes Off His Head, James Last Goes Off With his Best Friend's Missus, James Last Goes for a Walk in a Black Forest Gateau, James Last Goes into Broadmoor. Yours Sincerely, John Dunn.

PS: my ungrateful son doesn't seem to like any records that come in boxes so don't bother with him this year but his mom would like any of the following: Ken Dodd, Acker Bilk, Andy Stewart, Des O'Connor or The Seekers.

It went down like a lead fucking balloon.

12

G.I. JOANNE

Politically incorrect? Me? You're kidding. Listen, my generation found their feminine side very early on and I can remember it being a particularly enlightening experience. Without wishing to sound sad or dismissive, there are few real highlights from those extremely formative years between six and eleven. For the sake of brevity we'll call them the junior school years, which considering that's exactly what they were, is a perfectly reasonable all-embracing tag. We didn't have Farrah Fawcett, Jaclyn Smith, Cheryl Ladd or even The Bionic Woman - we had Valerie Singleton, who was more of a mother figure until you reached that age when you suddenly realised she'd got a cracking pair of tits and wasn't that bad looking after all. By the time you'd come to terms with the fact that you wouldn't mind a dabble with Val, you were at the stage where you would have shagged anything even it was made out of sticky backed plastic. It was a male orientated world. Enter Action Man . . .

Now Action Man was something completely different when it appeared on the scene, so different that G.I. Joe singlehandedly so nearly caused a riot in our house. He might just as well have stormed in through the roof with all guns blazing because my dad would have been ready for him, make no mistake, when he heard the shattering news that his son was desperate for a doll for Christmas. Fuck me, he was not happy about it one bit. He tried his hardest to disguise his disappointment when my mother, who I'd sensibly broached the subject with first, broke the distressing news.

'Well, Muldoon, Pele and Rob are all getting one,' I argued.

'Why do I have to be so different?'

Anyway, Action Man showed just what strong stuff he's made of when he stormed his way into my toy collection despite my dad's protestations.

'What do you want a doll for?'

'It's not a doll!'

'Well what is it then?'

'It's a sort of action toy for boys . . .'

'It sounds like a doll to me'

'Well it's NOT'

'What's it called again?

'G.I. Joe'

'Sure it's not G.I. Joanne?' dad guffawed in that mortified daddish way.

'So, can I have one then or not?'

'Well, I'll see what your mom says. Do you want me to get you Ken as well? A friend for him kind of thing?'

'Ha, ha.'

Dad knew Ken was Barbie's hairdresser-type boyfriend and believe you me, G.I Joe was nothing like bloody Ken. G.I. Joe wouldn't so much just beat Ken up no problem, he'd doubtless slash his chest open with one lightning strike of his bayonet which would have Ken's innards dribbling all over his bri-nylon polo-neck. Ken? Nice one dad, only you could come out with that one. Had Ken got a helicopter? Could Ken survive in minus 40 degrees in his slacks? I don't think so somehow.

I should have known it was a mistake to mention that the first outfit I wanted to get for my soon-to-be new pal was the Arctic survival kit, surprisingly a kind of white affair with fur trim around the hood with goggles and skis etc. Talk about leading with your jaw. Dad was ready and perfectly poised to deliver the knockout blow.

'Well, I don't see why not. Tell you what, we'll get you some nice white high heels and a handbag to go with it if you like. *She'll* like that. Go nicely with that mink hat.'

'It's a hood, dad. It's what you'd wear if you were in the

Arctic fighting.'

'Fighting what? Penguins?'

'Oh I don't know . . . just fighting. Fighting anything.'

"Fighting the cold probably. Well he must have been look, his willy has fallen off.'

I realised then it was pointless arguing. There was little use explaining to my dad that we wanted to attach our Action Men to clothes lines and pelt them with stones - last one clinging the winner. It was pointless trying to argue that we'd push our GI Joe's out in ponds in empty biscuit tins and bombard them with the large chippings to be found under the railway sleepers by the banks where we played. G.I. Joe was a culture shock to my old man and one he accepted only grudgingly.

I hadn't got my dad down for being old fashioned, but maybe hindsight will allow me to correct that observation. It was just like with most dads, he wasn't always happy with things which made us highly delighted. His bubbly gum theory was pretty scary stuff when you are seven. A little girl died in our village one year - just collapsed in the street and died. It was years later before I discovered that she had suffered from pleurisy or something similar because my dad had told me she'd swallowed her bubbly.

And it was at the start of the Junior School Years that my parents moved to Sandpiper Road, a place which would only evoke images of wading birds paddling contentedly in an estuary to those who didn't know it. Sir Peter Scott or Bill Oddie, unlike Kilroy, had not been where the houses were. David Attenborough had almost certainly never been anywhere near the place and, if he had, his binoculars wouldn't have picked out much more than the odd starling, house sparrow or occasional pair of breeding house martins that for reasons known only to themselves flew thousands of miles back from South Africa to nest in the eaves of a few of the houses. The theory that they came back year after year was scientifically and ornithologically sound. But one deranged bird with a sense of direction matching its ambition, must have started the trend which posed the question why? Sandpiper Road, circa 1964, was the main artery of a largely semi-detached housing development in Hadley, one of a number of small villages destined to be swallowed into a faceless new town sprawl which would eventually become known as Telford. Councillors in their wisdom had agreed to the proposal to designate the road names after birds. The fact that a Sandpiper hadn't been within 100 miles of the place was quite obviously immaterial. It sounded suitably exotic. They wouldn't have got away with a Hummingbird, but Sandpiper? Yeah, it was British. It was close enough. Bereft of wildlife, no - but neither was it, or ever had it been, a salt marsh or estuary. If The Gorbals sat rooted at the bottom of the scale at one with Britain's Best Kept Village at 100, then Hadley would quite possibly be proud if someone in their wisdom ranked it anywhere around the 35-40 mark.

Birds being the criteria, the cul-de-sacs which sprang off Sandpiper Road were accordingly named Curlew Close, Kingfisher Way, Oystercatcher Drive, Nightingale Court etc. It gave the place an air of respectability which alternatives such as Thrush Drive or Shag Avenue would have most definitely struggled to carry off.

We moved in sometime in the late summer of 1964. We weren't the first in and we weren't the last but by the time I'd got my bearings, new school, new mates, new everything, the whole of the estate was finished and fully occupied. It sounds vaguely dismissive to say my formative years between six and 13 amounted to little more than memories of Bazooka Joe bubblegum, England winning the World Cup and Tuf Wayfinders when in the same period Martin Luther King and Robert Kennedy had both been assassinated and Christian Barnard had performed the world's first heart transplant operation. But that's the way it is when you're a kid. I still struggle with the fact that he ended up pegging it through heart failure. How can that come about? It just doesn't seem right somehow. But what the fuck difference did that make to your life when you were eight or nine? None at all. Jesus, there were far more important things to busy yourself with. Did anyone get those X-ray specs for which you had to send off six zillion Bazooka Joe comic strips along with a dollar to some fucking obscure place in America? What did a dollar look like for a start? I unashamedly don't know of anyone who sent off for them, although we all wanted to, and if they did they are probably still waiting for them to this day. Didn't see through that then did you? No, those years to me were about my dad taking me to see Goal - the official film of the 1966 World Cup and Kes; fishing for newts, big grandad ones, in the pool by the first banks; Wacky Races, Spirograph, The Magic Robot and Tuf Wayfinders.

Getting a pair of Wayfinders was a monumental day in my life and the fact that I can remember being the proud owner of a pair perhaps explains a lot about how some of my generation lost their way. Tuf Wayfinders were a sturdy new kind of shoe which mums and grans the country over approved of. And while that would normally be a good enough reason to give them as wide a steer as possible, these were different. They had a compass in the heel and on the bottom of the moulded plastic soles were pawprints - yes PAWPRINTS. It was a particularly fine example of TV advertising at its very finest - kids splashing into huge puddles and keeping their precious tootsies dry and then having an instantly accessible guide to any wild animal tracks you might find in and around a West Midlands street. If my memory serves me correctly there was a lion, a cheetah, a rhino and a couple of others which I obviously never had the need to identify as I stumbled around on safari in the deepest, darkest outposts of our village. Imagine the worst case scenario when as an unwitting nine-year-old you happened to stumble upon a suspicious track outside school that you felt warranted further investigation. No problem, off with the shoe, let's have a look - oh fuck it's a cheetah! Just my luck to get mauled to death by a big cat because I was standing there with just one shoe on - not that having both of my TUF Wayfinders laced up and ready-to-go would have done me much good in a one-on-one race with a beast capable of nigh-on 60 miles per fucking hour. Ridiculous but true and I fell for it along with tens of thousands of other schoolchildren and made Mr Tuf - only years later I realised that was FUT backwards - a multi millionaire into the bargain. I'd love to meet him, providing he wasn't eaten by a lion at the height of his earning powers, and tell him that I have finally realised he was taking the piss.

13

BLAZER GLORY

And so in September, 1969, my life was thrown into turmoil as I trudged my way to a new school wearing a barathea blazer which might easily have been made for Desperate Dan. My mom had the biggest, that being the operative word, say on the size of it, arguing that as I was shooting up at such a startling rate of knots, I didn't want one I would quickly grow out of. Although, no doubt, my hormones were contemplating coursing through my veins, I'd have needed to have been on steroids to fill this particular acquisition. My gran, beside herself with pride and the gloating-value of my eleven-plus success, had paid for it and insisted I had the best quality available, a particularly shrewd move considering it was about to be gobbed on by some of the 500-odd pupils of Wellington Grammar School who had all served their time as first years and now, to largely varying degrees, constituted membership of what could loosely be termed the big boys' club. The most relieved members of this particular faction were the new second years; the ones who had been the pond life of the pecking order for a whole academic year but now had their own fresh supply of krill to gorge on, gob on, or just merely use as objects of physical and verbal abuse. To add insult to injury it was a school rule that kids in the first three years must wear a cap at all times to and from school and while the older boys had experienced 12 months of dodges to get around this particular burden the new lads were, understandably scared to death of dreaded new things like prefects 'juggers' and detention. We were also petrified of a completely new set of masters we knew nothing about. The mere fact we now answered to masters rather than teachers had a certain air of menace about it and all of us quickly woke up to the fact that certainly the first few weeks were perhaps going to be even more difficult than first imagined.

And so when you are swimming in the bottom pool among the lowest forms of life, it's a modest but not unreasonable target to doggy-paddle until some smaller fry come along.

It's not just your trousers that get longer when you start at the big school. Suddenly, everything gets longer, not least the school day. Just when your parents are stressing how much you need your sleep, you are rattled out of bed earlier, get home later and work harder. As if that's not taxing enough, you are very quickly made to realise that from the minute you walked out of the junior school gates for the very last time, everything would now be geared to choices. You would take French in the first year and if you didn't take to it you could ditch it for German at the start of the second year; you would have Latin once a week and then you could drop it after a year. There would be woodwork and music for the new boys with all these mysterious new subjects being put onto nine 'lines' at the end of the third year where you had to then make the decision of your life by picking one off each line to make up the subjects you would take for your 'O' levels. The masters had explained to us how the subject choices would be presented to us come the time and the first thing that was made perfectly clear was that when it came to picking off the first few subjects the choice was . . . well, there wasn't one. Line 1 English Language (compulsory); Line 2 Mathematics (compulsory), Line 3 English Literature (compulsory), Line 4 Geography (comp), Line 5 History (comp) then the choice system kicked in, but even then only with conditions. Along with having to take one science you then had to wade your way through a minefield of subjects for tossers like woodwork, art metalwork, art, music, religious studies, general studies, technical drawing and the like. Whoopee shit! I think even then with two years ahead before I had to make the choices, William Hills would have given extremely short odds on me going for the classic arts-sided line; ie fucking off physics, chemistry, art metalwork, music and technical drawing, slide rule 'n' all. General Studies was a new one to me but it sounded okay - general nothingness. Marvellous. Just the job - so middle-of-the-road I might easily have invented it myself. I couldn't play an instrument, not even the recorder or the fucking triangle. I couldn't draw breath let alone still life and seeing as there didn't seem a sliver of a chance that Mrs Robinson would one day breeze into the art class, peel off her lab coat and present herself naked as a subject to draw, art didn't come into the equation either.

Up to secondary school what choices did you have to make for yourself? Hardly any as a matter of fact. Swimming or playing football? Bird nesting or fishing? Magpie or Blue Peter? What did you want for tea? It was all so simple. Now you had timetables for this and that, not just the one classroom but loads and the days of having one teacher for the whole year seemed light years ago. Now there were slide rules and protractors and woodwork aprons and homework fucking timetables - for a new thing called homework!

God, this had been a life-changing summer and only now was I largely unsuccessfully trying to grasp the inscription in the book Miss Orrick had given me when she had pulled me to one side on the last day of junior school.

When Miss Orrick had announced half way through the fourth year that the last hour on Friday would be spent by her treating us by reading a book, the suggestion was hardly met with wholesale approval. Some of Class 4 couldn't read Whizzer and Chips, and as one of the brighter ones I can't say I was pissing my pants in delight at the prospect.

'So' she announced. 'Every Friday for half an hour before you go home I'm going to read a wonderful book to you. It's called The Adventures of Tom Sawyer by an American author called Mark Twain and I think you will love it.'

That's what she said, virtually word for word, but I wasn't convinced and you could tell most of the rest certainly weren't, yet by the time we'd had the third or fourth reading, Friday afternoons couldn't come quickly enough and not just because we were going home for the weekend straight after. Miss Orrick read it with such enthusiasm that she single-handedly took us to the Deep South and we might easily have been sitting right there on the banks of the Mississippi, wonderstruck as we watched Tom, Huck Finn and Injun Joe acting out their adventures. It was marvellous and to the man, or boy, we were totally absorbed in her wonderful oratory. It's only now that I realise what a life-changing moment that was and how Miss Orrick had introduced me to books, proper books, albeit with off-putting titles. And on the last day, as the other lads all bounded out for ever, she asked me to stay behind for a minute.

'Did you enjoy the book Paul?'

'Yes Miss. Very much Miss.'

'Good. I'd like you to have it.'

'Thanks Miss.'

'Listen Paul. You can go a long way. I wish you well and I'm sorry that our paths must now go separate ways. You've been a pleasure to teach. Keep this and make sure to read it again one day,' she said as she hastily scribbled in the front.

'Thanks Miss. Thank you very much. I'd better go . . .'

'Take care.'

'Thanks Miss.'

Mom thought it was wonderful that Miss Orrick had given me the book and said she would write a letter thanking her for such a kind gesture. She didn't quite understand what the inscription meant but was sure that I would one day.

"To Paul. Keep the story of Tom and the fence close at hand and you won't go far wrong. Do well. With sincere best wishes MJO."

To be honest I didn't take on the full meaning of what she wrote that day and, to my shame, for some years totally forgot about it. And it was so much later that in telling the tale of how Tom Sawyer's Saturday morning in the summer looked certain to be ruined by his Aunt Polly's order to whitewash 30 yards of fence, nine feet high and how cunningly he got out of it, I realised Twain was pointing out that work consists only of what the body is obliged to do and play consists of what a body is not obliged to do.

Tom turns a nightmare situation to his advantage and when his playmates file past he persuades them that there's nothing in the world he'd rather be doing than whitewashing a fence. And as his pals plead with him to let them have a go, he not only gets them to do some but makes them pay him for the privilege. And as they worked and worked away, he sat and watched and counted the items his pals had traded to have a go at slapping on whitewash. The fence gets done by mid-afternoon and Tom has accumulated 12 marbles, a kite, a Jews harp, a piece of blue bottle glass, a key, some chalk, a glass stopper off a decanter, a tin soldier, a couple of tadpoles, a kitten with only one eye, a dog collar but no dog, four pieces of orange peel, a window sash and had a good idle time. If he hadn't run out of whitewash he'd have bankrupted every kid in the village.

Miss Orrick was clearly making a point but it was hard for me to comprehend when I might be old enough or clever enough to pull off such manipulation. Most of the boys at this school were older than me, bigger than me and the masters were brighter than all of us. How was it to be? Maybe she just meant for me to try it out when I was older. Yeah, maybe that was it. I'd get it when I was older and in the meantime I'd have to just muddle my way through like everyone else.

Getting a job, having a car, earning your own money and great things like that were bloody years away. Inbetween times, there were more pressing things in hand and hopefully really important things like puberty wouldn't be in the too distant future.

14

CURTAIN CALL

Reflecting on my teen years, well, let's start at the very beginning; a very good place to start, according to Julie Andrews. It's my 13th birthday -August 7, 1971 - a significant milestone in anyone's life. Julie Andrews had played a not insignificant part in my life up to that point. Hey, come on, she had featured in the first proper film you'd seen at the pictures(after Bambi) and we'd all loved her to death. Wasn't she just the best? She was nice looking in a favourite-auntie kind of way. She had a lovely face; nice teeth; was certainly never stuck for keeping you occupied and was always so inspiringly optimistic. Sure, she had her bad points. She yodelled, which like men who whistle, is a suspect characteristic and she was prone to ripping down the curtains to make dodgy play clothes, but all in all she was a top bird. A suspect nun, maybe, but a top bird. I swear to God, it's that puppet thing again, but I digress. Then she shocks the world by getting her kit off in SOB and suddenly we're all looking at her in a different light. Jesus, my mom wasn't happy about that; my dad feigned disinterest, while I found it particularly galling that having been actively encouraged, nay dragged to see Sound of Music, the pleasure of seeing Maria de-frocked as it were, was to be denied me. Suddenly the delights of Julie's curtains took on a whole new dimension. SOB? I could have fucking wept as the hills were somehow magically alive with the sound of hormones exploding. Julie getting her kit off got me thinking that she really should have been paid mega-bucks to do a re-make of that classic, a kind of alternative Sound of Music. It would have been marvellous and a box-office smash without doubt.

Come on . . . just imagine the eldest Von Trapp daughter could have said what we all knew she really meant as she danced around that bandstand singing 'I am 16' to the telegram boy. Greta(it was Greta wasn't it?) was definitely up for it.

'People I meet may say that I'm sweet, and willingly I agree' and all that bollocks. 'I need someone older and wiser telling me what to do,' Yeah, okay, it's probably best left there and it's not an unreasonable assumption that Greta giving head or getting her tits out in the bandstand, didn't really fit in with the general mood of the original film. It's a marvellous thought nonetheless and if Julie could ever have been persuaded to do a spoof of it, the permutations would be endless. 'I am 17 going on 18 . . . IIII'lllll take care of you.' Shag would fit without messing the music around too much.

Anyway, back to my birthday. As I flipped unspectacularly into my teenage years, Julie was no more than a passing fancy. By the day I turned 13 the female influences in my life were changing by the minute, though that was more down to me than them. Your mom starts to get really embarrassing; grans are just,well, grans; and there's usually an assortment of aunties and a number of cousins dependant on the size of your family. Nothing out of the ordinary in that. Then there was Belinda and Mrs Robinson. Rob's mom was sort of like an auntie but better because I saw her nearly all the time. Everyone seemed to love Mrs Robinson, except Mr Robinson, strangely enough. Our assumption that all the dads of the street must fancy her, were proved to be far from groundless as we were to advance through adolescence. By the time the testosterone had kicked in we all owned up to really fancying Rob's mom. Then there was Rob's sister Rosie, a horrid, soppy creature 12 months younger than me who tried her damndest to tag along on all our boy things. Occasionally, if Mrs Robinson had to go out we had to take Rosie along which invariably proved a pain even if it was prompted with the promise of some kind of treat on her return.

Rob and me did everything together and the only thing we

occasionally argued about was who fancied Laurence's sister the most. Belinda was two years older, had a movement like a Swiss watch and, though we didn't even enter her thinking, she would have had to have been blind not to have known we were fascinated with her. We weren't alone, everyone in the darned street thought she was gorgeous. She had a sister Joy, who was in our class at juniors.

Belinda Smart didn't so much grow into her surname but slipped into it with such a beautiful, effortless force no one heard the chains snapping behind her as she hurtled down the slipway to womanhood.

It would have been fitting if someone had smashed a champagne bottle down the side of her to celebrate the occasion. By the time she reached 16-17 they could have sold tickets for the event. Men and boys alike would have cheered and applauded excitedly at such a magnificent launch.

'I name this new woman Belinda Smart - may God bless her and all those lucky enough to ever get to have a go in her.'

Belinda was, quite simply, stunning. She was pretty in a Sally James and Jan Francis kind of way, rather than glam and unapproachable. She had a neat, chestnut page boy cut and wondrous pert breasts which, someone definitely told me, she put down to having a small back. I can't recall how that particular shred of information came in my direction because she was almost two years older than Rob and me. She was at an age where she was approachable to some lucky sods, but not us, though I'm sure I detected a certain affection when she called me 'Mong.' I could have been mistaken.

Funny thing names - some people's suit them and others never quite sit right, or if they do, for all the wrong reasons. She was Smart by name and smart by nature and by the time she was leaving school and for quite some time before she was onomatopoeically unchallenged. What a fucking bizarre word. I mean, it just doesn't do the very thing it's supposed to. The Oxford English Dictionary describes it as *'the formation of a word from an associated sound - eg sizzle, cuckoo'*. Fine, so

77

why the fuck isn't the collective term for words like that something more reasonable like 'soundslike?' While we're on the subject - why is abbreviation such a long word? I digress - back to names that either suit you for all of your life, part of it or plain never at all. Albert is definitely one you would have to grow into. It's sort of crap in a take-the-piss kind of way for about 45 years and then when you get past 50 it becomes a name which mysteriously sits more comfortably. In reverse, you could have the coolest name on the planet in your early years - something like Troy or Tyrone - and then discover later that it fits you like a pair of trousers you've had since you were 12. You grew out of it, but the name didn't alter. There are no universal rules to this phenomenon. Personal prejudices without doubt come into play. I have a problem with James despite the fact that most of the ones I've met after Jimmy Hunt seem to be okay kind of blokes. The nastiest bully at infants school, the wiry-haired, nutty bastard who quite probably invented being a total twat - well, he did to me anyway - was Jimmy Hunt and I fucking hated him. And that's why by virtue of him tipping one of those small bottles of stinky school milk all over my Clark's sandals when I was six, he forfeited the right to have any of my children named after him. I don't have any - not because of him - but if I did, and providing it was a boy of course, it would never be called James. I'm equally sure that there are loads of tough, good looking, sportingly adept Tims around, but somehow it just doesn't do it and Adrians really have a tough task convincing me they didn't spend most of their PE lessons time playing chess. The one guaranteed to make my heckles rise is Jonathan, not least because there must be about half a dozen different spellings and none of them seem right *Johnathan, Jonathon* - you get the picture.

Belinda's two girlie mates had names which suited them too, though that would be an unwelcome observation. Petra Garfield was the ugly one and somehow her name stank of mediocrity. She was another one who had a lazy eye and, to be honest, I think if I'd have been an eye in that face I'd have been lazy too;

bone idle would have been forgivable. In fairness, her parents weren't to know what Blue Peter would decide to name their dog but followed by the dull sound of a surname like Garfield, she really was struggling.

The middle one of the three was Sally Tonge, far more difficult to assess in the name game, when put under closer examination. There's little argument that Tonge is quite hilarious when you are a kid, but it conjures all sorts of more interesting pictures as the years unfold. She was attractive in a plainish way. Quite tall, taller than Belinda, she had a nice smile and wasn't nasty to us. Once tongues started taking on a whole new meaning, so did Sally.

What happened to lazy eyes? I wouldn't go as far as to say they were common but Petra and Joy Smart had them which meant they had a kind of eye patch underneath Milky Bar kid type glasses. It couldn't have been great. There were a lot of complaints around then that seem to have become nigh-on extinct. Do kids still get stys in their eyes? I haven't seen one for ages. What happened to Elephantitis? Women with tree-trunk legs , mottled as if they'd been in front of the fire for ages, seem somewhat scarcer these days. Warts don't seem half as common either. I knew kids who had fistfuls of the fucking things. I'm honestly not sure. Perhaps modern medicine has cut down a lot of it or even wiped it out in some instances. I hope so because if you were a kid afflicted by any one of them, it must have been hell. Not least because kids like me, needed no encouraging to take the piss.

15

THE DOWNWARD SLIDE

Finally becoming a teenager was something I, like most, couldn't wait for, but suddenly your birthday presents start to get a whole lot less exciting. While money is always most welcome, even though grandmas still seemed to think ten shillings could buy the earth, the pre-teen excitement disappears as rapidly as your spots decide they deserve a wider audience. It's marvellous that people see fit to give you the cash to get something you really want and at the time it seems really adult, but eventually you realise that it's just easier for them to do that than traipse around shops asking baffled shop assistants if they have got anything which might just drive a moody 13-year-old wild - yeah, Britt Ekland. I had some Brut after shave a good four years before a razor blade got near my face properly. Passing for grammar school hadn't helped really because inevitably there were really useful things that you would need which became presents. If I'd gone to the secondary modern maybe I'd have been given a flicknife, but now I was entering the world of Coles' Notes, Chaucer and associated bollocks. Jesus, we've all had those sort of things but on my 13th I got something which has to rank as the most useless fucking present of all time - a slide rule. Quite probably not useless to anyone with the slightest leaning towards technical drawing or mathematical equations, but for me, about as much use as metal fatigue in a zimmer frame. My dad thought it would be just the job, possibly thinking I was about to embark on a career as a space scientist or something similar, but I'm sure when he saw me using it as a slide trombone it didn't take him too long to work out that a letter of acceptance from NASA wouldn't be dropping through our letterbox. Aunt Mary had surprisingly bought me Get It On by T. Rex something I'd been listening to on Radio Luxembourg for a few weeks on a radio the size of the average suitcase. Mom had told my Auntie Eileen that I was showing an interest in poetry and so the Pam Ayres book had been really fucking well received. Mom also seemed to be under the impression that Rob and me liked Middle of the Road's Chirpy Chirpy Cheep Cheep. I mean, for fuck's sake, how do you tell your mom that the only good thing about Middle of the Road was the blonde lead singer in the hotpants? No, Rob and myself were where it was at man - Get It On was the hot single. I spent many a happy hour under the covers listening to Radio Luxembourg, waiting for that record to come on which seemed an eternity between the mind-numbingly numerous adverts for Peter Stuyvesant cigarettes and Stimarol chewing gum. I got a pair of Puma football boots and a Parker fountain pen which came in a set with a propelling pencil. Now, without sounding ungrateful, there's another thing which you soon get to realise has a usefulness factor of nil and ranks alongside the slide rule as great things not to bother wasting your time with. Have you ever seen anyone using a propelling pencil? No, neither have I. In a word they are shite and the inventor should have his balls cut off just for thinking they might catch on one day. To my mind, they are a bit like mosquitoes. Yeah, don't laugh. What useful purpose do mosquitoes serve? And do you know something? Mosquitoes are responsible for more deaths in the world every year than warfare. Isn't that scary? So fuck 'em off. You can't tell me that we don't have the technology to completely eradicate the darned things and I'm not talking with a personal interest here because I've only had the occasional nip on holiday. The do-gooders will argue that they are part of God's great plan, but so was fucking smallpox and we blitzed that off the face of the earth. You'll struggle to convince me mosquitoes serve any useful function whatsoever and I'm all for dumping them in the global equivalent of Room 101 along with propelling pencils.

Slide rules, I concede, serve a function though I still have not the slightest idea of how to use one and , strangely enough, as the years have rolled by have even less inclination to find out. Do people still use them? Do they still have any purpose in life or has the computer quite rightly relegated them to logarithm heaven or wherever it is baffling pieces of mathematical equipment go? It would be kind of nice to think that brainy kids are still having slide rules inflicted on them as presents but somehow I doubt it. Anyway, child geniuses probably think it's the best present they ever had. It almost leads me to say never trust a man who can use a slide-rule, but I honestly don't know of anyone. Having said that I haven't asked and whatsmore I genuinely don't care. I'm getting worked up just thinking about the fucking things.

Some years prior to all this I had always wanted an Etch-a-Sketch but for reasons best known to the powers-that-be I ended up getting a device which resembled a piece of trelliswork, which if I recall, was called something like Drawmaster . . . whatever. Etch-a-Sketch was 1967 state-of-the art technology though you quickly had to take on board the fact that unless what you were drawing was made up of rectangular shapes, say a house, you were basically knackered. If this sounds like the ingredients of a deprived childhood, forget it, they were a highly treasured childhood accessory of the time. My parents decided in their wisdom that the Drawmaster was far more educationally sound in that you could reproduce the outline of the coast of Australia or the Isle of Man if you wanted to - which you might until you quickly realise that a sheet of Izal from the school bogs does it far better and more quickly. The principle was that on the one end of this trellis-like plastic contraption was a pointer which dictated the movement of the pencil, felt pen, biro or whatever you had jammed into the hole at the corresponding end of the device. It was a fucking nightmare . . . the pencil needed something akin to a two-by-two paving slab on the other end to give it sufficient weight to make an impression and just as you had somehow managed to take the pointer round to the north coast of Tasmania, you quickly realised you'd picked the wrong starting point and the paper, exercise book, or whatever wasn't fucking big enough. I have this recurring nightmare that one day I'll bump into the inventor in some remote bar in a picturesque holiday destination and tell him how he darned near ruined my childhood. I can imagine the conversation.

'Another pint gaffer and one for . . .'

'Julian . . . cheers'

'Right, cheers Julian. So you live out here then?'

'Yeah, came out in the late 60's and never bothered going back, really. I've got a place in Surrey, but I rent it out. Just pop back twice a year to check things over. You know how it is!'

'Well, no I don't as it happens but nice one anyway. . .'

'Yeah, I've got a couple of holiday homes but my main residence is in the harbour over there,'

'Good stuff,' say I, glancing to a millionaire's playground nestling comfortably on the gentle slopes of a sun-kissed hill, sitting just behind the palm-lined coastal boulevard.

'The one at the back there . . . with the green tiled roof.'

'What that big fuck-off one?'

'Yeah,' the guy I now know to be Julian adds somewhat matter-of-factly.

'Jeez, nice place. Fair do's mate . . . you must have a good job.'

'No, actually I retired in 1971, I haven't worked since as such.'

So, I think just how seriously this guy is in danger of pissing me off. The fact that he hasn't worked for 30 years and he can be no more than late-50s is to be commended, but if he's made his bundle from arms-dealing or drug running, then I could quite happily sit back, comforted in the knowledge that though I might not have much, I've worked hard and diligently for every single last penny.

'What do you mean *as such?*'

'Well, when I was 25, I kind of invented this toy, educational aid, call it what you will - made a stack of quick money and got out. Just thought that there was a big wide, world out there to see and decided to call it a day.'

'As you do!'

Now, I'm impressed. Who wouldn't be? It's a story of epic proportions. I'll take my hat off to this guy. And I've just bought HIM a pint as well. What the fuck eh? . . . I'm about to discover just what he did, bestow upon him the praise he so richly deserves and maybe even have another beer with him as I while away another pleasant hour in paradise.

'Go on then hit me with it . . . what was it?'

'Dare say, you might even have had one . . . how old are you?'

'43'

'I bet you did . . .'

'Spacehopper!'

'Nope . . . but you're on the right lines. Remember I said educational. That's your best clue.'

"Educational . . . mmmm . . . Fucking hell, how many guesses do I get?'

'Many as you like'

'And a toy, yeah?'

'Yeah.'

'It wasn't that green thing that used to swing around and point a wand at the right answer and completely fucked my brains in for years . . . Magic Robot! Christ, you didn't invent the Magic Fucking Robot did you? I loved the Magic Robot . . .'

'No. Right lines though and the right era. But no . . .'

'Plastic . . . let me think.'

'I'll give you a clue. You could draw things with it.'

'No. Not Spirograph? Now that WAS my favourite. My absolute all-time favourite. I'm not having a beer with Mr Spirograph am I?'

'Hmm, no. But you're warm.'

'Well I was thinking of that Mastermind game with the Chinese bird on the box , but that would be later surely?'

'Yep. I mean, yeah , that was later. No, I didn't invent that either. Pity though - that did out sell mine.'

'Oh fuck it, I give in . . . honest you're doing my head in. Put me out of my misery Jules.'

'I'm sure you must have heard of it. I invented this ermm, device, I suppose you'd call it, called Drawmaster.'

'Not the trellis thing, with the . . .'

'Yep.'

'Fucking hell! It didn't work!'

'Worked for me - infact I've never worked since,' Julian grinned.

'Unbelievable. I must have spent three hours once trying to trace the outline of fucking Australia and . . . is it too late to sue?'

'Well, you know where I am.'

'So let me get this straight, right. You retired on the proceeds of that fucking contraption. It must have brought in an absolute fortune.'

'Well, the funny thing is, I actually only got pennies for every one they sold, so I didn't make as much as I should have done if the truth be told. That's multi-nationals for you.'

'Yeah, but how many of the fucking things did they sell?

'I'm not actually sure to be honest. I think at the last count it was about 26 million.'

'Life's a bitch . . . so you got 26 million lots of pennies in 1970-whatever?'

'Spread over three or four years, in fairness, but roughly speaking yeah.'

'And that was it. Never work again. Big killing. I take my hat off to you Julian. And so you just signed over the rights and that was the last thing you did eh?'

'Nearly. Then I wrote a book called 'How to use your Drawmaster' which sold about three million copies and I just called it a day after that.'

'How to use it! Hope you put the bit about the paving slab in early on. Hope you put in a chapter saying how a much easier way to trace the outline of Australia was to get a piece of Izal bog paper, and then just stick it on a clean page and hey fucking

presto!'
   'Do you wanna beer?'
   'Fucking right I do Julian . . .'

16

STICKS AND STONES

'Sticks and stones . . .' I assured my tormentor without total conviction. Names will never hurt you, so the saying goes, but they were making a darned good effort and whatsmore I knew that Pete Hunt wasn't averse to a bit of sticking and stoning if the verbals fell short of the mark.

'Val,' Pete repeated himself. Jimmy laughed approvingly at his brother's acidic wit.

'Fuck off,' I said in a really kind of soft, breathy way so as not to sound in any way threatening and putting myself in real danger of some form of physical torture.

The object of Pete's ridicule was my tanktop and there was no let up despite a couple of the girls insisting that it was 'alright'. Alright? I'd gone up to the rec thinking it was magnificent - now I wasn't so sure. The Hunt twins would have taken the piss regardless, but as Pete led the taunts, it struck me they might have a point. It was purple and white bands with a black slightly-scalloped trim. It was the latter feature which had been picked out by Pete for his cruel assumption that I was wearing a girl's tanktop. I insisted he was talking rubbish but my argument was hardly helped by the fact that the tanktops the twins were wearing had plain edges. Theirs were a matching pair, black with just two hoops in the middle of red and gold. They were cool and if I was forced to admit that mine might not quite match up, it surely didn't deserve this barrage of abuse.

'You fucking big Jessie,' Jimmy took up the attack.

'Val . . . Val, Val, Val,' Pete went on and it certainly wasn't the right time, if ever there would have been one, to tell him that he couldn't even say it properly.

'What d'ya mean Val?' I stupidly begged him to explain. I'd only done that so his warped thinking and stupidity could be exposed once more to a wider audience and hopefully turn the ridicule back on him but I should have known better. Pete's thought process had taken him from tanktop to pullover and there was only one logical association to be made, hence Val.

'Val Dooligan,' he chortled.

I felt like saying 'Doonigan you stupid, thick, twat' but it possibly wouldn't have been my best move. I decided to just let him get on with it, trying to get by with a shrug of the shoulders and a somewhat forced couldn't-care-less look. It might be lost on the Psycho Twins but maybe I'd get some sympathy from the girls once they'd decided to leave me alone.

'Dooligan, Dooligan, Val Fuckin' Dooligan,' Pete went on, almost singing it now. It was at times like this that you were left cursing cell division.

'Where's your funny chair, Dunny?'

God he couldn't even say rocker. Hardly surprising, when he was off his, but what was I supposed to do?

'Well I like it,' I said, which wasn't the greatest of answers to be honest.

'Well, you would Dunny wouldn't ya? And you know why? Cos yer a girl, that's why. And you wear girl's clothes. Spaz.'

'Nowt wrong with it,' I said, moving just inside the door of the gym towards the big open room where we played table tennis.

'Nowt fuckin' right with it.'

Pele was inside and I gratefully stepped forward to take the battered table-tennis bat he'd offered me. Pele was almost as embarrassed and annoyed as me, but was powerless to do anything. On account of the fact that I'd now got my back to the Psycho twins, I mouthed 'wankers' to my mate and was grateful for the understanding wink he gave me before serving the ball across the net. Pele understood. He'd been a victim of this pair before and inevitably would be again.

We were only a few points into the game and the barrage

seemed to have subsided when the look of horror on Pele's face alerted me to the fact that something was happening directly behind me.

'Dunny' he shouted instinctively, but it was too late as I felt a forceful, yet soft, damp thud right in the middle of my back and howls of laughter I instantly recognised.

'What the fuck?'

'That's better,' Pete screamed. 'That looks much better Dunny.'

The force of the blow had pushed me against the edge of the table and as I turned around to see just what had happened, I could hear Beryl the play leader, ordering Pete out and berating him for being so stupid.

'What's he done?' I asked as I felt my back was wringing wet. Pete had walloped me with a mop he'd pulled out of the metal bucket which was used to clean up the floor in the smaller kids play room. It had been used to mop up the aftermath of a poster painting session and I was now wringing wet with the dirty, purplish contents of the mopbucket.

'Aghh, Jesus,' I exclaimed.

'I'll get killed when I get home.'

'It should come out,' Beryl assured me. 'Get your mom to soak it straight away.'

I took it off, but the stuff was everywhere. It had now run all down my jeans and down my backside into my pants. I felt sodden, humiliated and extremely stupid and couldn't begin to think what my dad would say when I got home. It was little consolation that both Pete and Jimmy had been thrown out of the gym and told not to come back for a week. That wasn't going to help me when I got home. Pele suggested going outside for a while and trying to dry out on the grass at the back of the five-a-side pitch. It was ten minutes later when we went outside, made our way around the back of the gym and sat ourselves down by the big oak behind the goalposts. Pele glanced at me to see if I'd noticed the two figures about thirty yards away up by the alley leading back to our houses. I had and my guess that at least one of them would soon be over proved correct. As I noticed Pete slowly sidling over with Jimmy a couple of paces behind, I asked Pele for another update on the extent of the damage.

'Jeezus Dunny, it's fuckin' everywhere.'

'What about my shirt?' I asked. It was my best cheesecloth one, white before the intervention of the Cunt Twins.

'It's all over it mate. It's like a bloody tie 'n' dye.'

'You're kiddin'.'

'Nope. It's sort of . . . purply-blue.'

'What about my pants?' I enquired lifting the back out and inviting Pele to make a quick inspection as only close mates can.

'Same, Dunny. Fucking bastard.'

'Soz mate,' Pete muttered unconvincingly.

'Just a laugh, that's all.'

'Some fucking laugh.'

'Thought it was just water. Didn't know it had paint in.'

'Too late now,' I said more firmly than I normally would have dared.

'Gonna tell your dad?'

'Well I think he might just notice to be honest.'

'Don't drop me in it, Dunny.'

'Tough luck. What do you expect me to do?' I was getting braver by the minute as I witnessed the unusual spectacle of Pete fuckwit Hunt being very much on the back foot.

'Tell him you just fell over.'

'Oh right, sounds good. I'll tell my old man that I just accidentally fell into a mop bucket eh?'

'Say you slipped.'

'Look, my dad's going to fuckin' kill me. I only had this tanktop at the weekend, my shirt's ruined and, believe me, he's going to want to know how I've done it.'

I wasn't in the mood for making deals and we got up to make our way towards the alley, largely ignoring double-pronged appeals for immunity from the twins. As we got towards the bottom of the alley, they reverted to type and abandoned the 'be your best mate for ever' approach.

90

'Oi, Dunny. Before you go in. You fuckin' tell your dad and you'll get the biggest pasting of your life . . . oh, and that's a promise.'

I squelched towards our drive and considered my options - none of which carried much appeal. I seriously wished Jimmy and Pete were dead. They had the capacity to make my life a misery at times and it was so unfair. Everything else was pretty good and these two were just fucking things up. What made it worse was they seemed to get away with every single thing they did. The fear factor kicked in whenever their backs were against the wall and they always ended up getting off Scot free. It just didn't seem right. And it was about to happen again. In the time it had taken me from the bottom of our drive to the back door, I'd made up my mind not to grass-up Pete. Bear in mind that I didn't live at Windsor Palace. This was a short drive by anyone's standards, not one guarded by poplars that took you five minutes in your car before you approached the front of the house. This was short - it hadn't taken me any time at all to evaluate the merits of dropping Pete in the shit. As usual, I'd have to try and make up something half-way convincing and take the rap myself. Honesty pays was a favourite saying of my mom's - but like a lot of parental advice, it didn't seem to cross-over into my world a lot of the time. Mom took one horrified look at me and started stating the bleedin' obvious. She didn't think it would come out(guessed that); my dad was going to be furious(certainty) and that she wasn't convinced by my strenuous assertion that I wasn't quite sure who had actually done it(thought so). I'd explained the melee; it had all been very confusing; a mop had mysteriously come from nowhere as we were larking about; could have happened to anybody; was really sorry etc, etc. So what does she say?

'I hope those two didn't have anything to do with this?'

'Which two?'

'Don't 'which two?' me.'

'Na, they weren't even there,' I garbled, making out I'd just clicked who she could possibly be on about.

'Bad un's - the pair of 'em. I'll have words with them before too long.'

'No, no. Not this time. It wasn't them.'

Can you believe it? No. I couldn't fucking well believe it myself. Not only had I let them off the hook, but I'd handed them a cast-iron alibi just to really take the piss. Did I really say they weren't even there? Yep. Brilliant. It was hard to say whether I was more angry with myself than them now. I was a coward. Well, it wasn't that I was a coward, it was just that I was a bit scared of getting my brains bashed in. Same thing - coward. My dad hinted as much but added his own little twist to it in a vain bid to get me to sort out the problem.

'I can't fight your battles for you.'

'Don't want you to.'

'Listen, you're gonna have to stick up for yourself, sharpish.'

'It's just . . .'

'Hey look, I understand but let me give you a bit of good advice. Remember - a bully is always a coward. Mark my words.'

I tried to get the gist of it. Right. Jimmy Hunt, stockily built, karate three times a week and with an equally big twin brother in the highly unlikely event of me decking him . . . is a coward. And then an even bigger brother Ged. God knows what that made me then. He scared the shit out of me. Didn't sound like great advice to be honest, no matter how earnestly it had been delivered. These two had virtually got moustaches. They were bruisers and I was destined, on the odd occasion, to be the bruised. We might have been in the same year at school but they were only weeks off being a year older then me. The twins' birthday was September 2, just one day inside the school calendar year, whereas I was born on August 7 so though we were the same year academically, I was actually 49 weeks younger. I speculated whether if I was to catch them up by 49 weeks whether I too would have a sprouting of bum fluff on my top lip and perhaps I might be a good 49-weeks tougher. Nah, I doubted that very much. Dad's David and Goliath stuff was alright in theory but just like my pants and shirt - somehow it didn't wash with me. The summer of 1972 had hardly got off to an ideal start, but boy was it going to get better. It was just about to get so much better . . .

17

CRISPY NOODLES

I don't think it's taking things too far to say that Vesta should be brought before a European Court of Human Rights, charged with gross deception. Well, at least the lesser charge of totally making up exotic dishes. They made the fuckers up. What? Vesta the Vesta Chow Mein people? Yes! Someone at Vesta actually made the bleedin' things up and left an indelible imprint on an entire generation. Those crispy noodles that I learned to love, never really existed at all. I and millions of others, were brought up to believe that little explosions of beef flavoured powder was the taste of the Orient. When I first came across a pepper, both red and green, that didn't have the texture of Lego, my body rejected it. Someone at Vesta must be held responsible. It's enough to make weaker souls need counselling. I'd love to meet the executive who came up with that one and ask him what the hell it was all about. Vesta was as exotic as it got in the early 70s and though it barely registers on the Richter Scale now, my old man virtually accused me of eating rat.

But the smell, the exploding powdery bits in it, unchewable square bits of meat and the thought of Mrs Robinson serving it up dressed in her black slip still send shivers down my spine. Vesta Chow Fucking Mein; chop suey and paella too. How fucking classy is that? Three or four years later when Chinese takeaways really started to take off, the rogue Vesta exec was responsible for one of my most cringingly awful moments, only tempered by the fact that I was convinced the stupid Chink behind the counter had got it wrong and just couldn't understand me.

I'd popped into the brand new Chinese take-away in Portman Street to officially subscribe to the cultural revolution and on account of the fact that the only two dishes I knew were chow mein and chop suey, decided to play safe with the dish I knew best. Bring on the chow mein. I knew every single ingredient or so I thought and it was with some disappointment that I ended up trudging back to the Chinese with my carton to explain they just had not given me what I had ordered.

'Sowwy?' said the man I was to later be on first name terms with.

'I asked for chicken chow mein,' I insisted, pointing to the unrecognisable contents sitting in the carton.

'Yes.'

Yes what? Yes! What sort of an answer was that? How can you start to have a rational conversation with a man who clearly doesn't know what should be in one of his own national dishes. I needed better feedback.

I'd only taken the bloody thing back because my dad had seen me disgruntedly sifting through the pile on my plate with a fork. Now this. Dad had warned me.

'I told you - it's foreign muck. That's what that is. Bloody waste of money.'

'It's not, it's just that I wanted . . .'

'I told you before you went. You'd have been better off getting some fish and chips. At least you know where you stand with fish and chips. Foreign crap.'

I knew instinctively that I was in grave danger of getting dad's story about eating curry in Egypt only because it disguised bad meat for the 174th time. Sure enough.

'You won't listen will you? That's your trouble - never listen. When I was in Egypt doing my National Service, we used to get curry regularly and you know why?'

Go on, tell me. No, let me guess dad. Was it because the meat was all going off in the heat and they curried things to disguise the flavour? Bet it was.

'It isn't curry dad.'

'It's the same bloody difference. You know the Chinese eat rats don't you? Bloody rats. I ask you. And now they've come over here trying to sell us the bloody rubbish. Beats me. And now YOU want to pay good money to eat it as well, so if you're not happy with it take it back.'

'I'll eat it.'

'Don't bloody eat it if it's not what you asked for. Take it back.'

'Will you come with me dad?'

'Not likely lad. Wouldn't go within 100 yards of the place. They'll serve you anything them Chinese. Go on, take it back.'

I was running out of options. It might have been easier to just eat it, but it didn't look right. It was sort of wormy and . . . oh I don't know . . . it just wasn't right. I knew about these things. I poured it back into the container and made my way out of the door.

'Sowwy?'

'I asked for chicken chow mein and you gave me this.'

Mr Chung peered down into the container, looked back up at me, and looked somewhat surprised. 'Yes?'

'What is it?' I said nervously.

'Chicken chow mein.'

'Oh right.'

'What's that?' I pointed.

'Noodle.'

'Noodles'

'Yah. Soff noodle. Beansprout . . . and . . . chicken. Chicken chow mein.'

'Oh right," I said again. I wasn't very good at this complaining lark.

'So wos wrong?' Mr Chung went on.

'It's just not like I thought it would be.' Oh fuck it, I decided to tell him.

'Well for start off, you've forgotten the crispy noodles.'

'Crisp noodle?'

'No, crispy noodles. You put them on afterwards. Curly

96

yellow things . . . '

'No, no, no.' Mr Chung was having none of it.

'No crisp noodle. Saf noodle, beansprout, chicken. Chicken chow mein.'

I decided to play my trump card. There wasn't any soy sauce and that was indisputable.

'No soy sauce,' I said addressing him in a tone of voice that suggested he was either a good few years younger than me, profoundly deaf or insane. I was clearly a man conversant with this cuisine.

'Soy soss?'

'Yeah, no soy sauce.

'You want soy soss?'

'Yeah,' I said triumphantly, guessing he couldn't answer that particularly well made point.

'You won soy soss?'

'Yes, please,' I said firmly.

'Thirry-pence,' he said placing a weird- looking little bottle in front of me.

'Thirty pence. No. No. I don't want a bottle of it.'

'Soy soss. Thirry pence'

'Yeah . . . but not a whole bottle.'

'How you think soy soss come?'

'In a little sachet.'

'Sasha?'

'No. Sachet. A little silver plastic thing you . . . oh bollocks.'

'Thirry pence?'

He seemed to think I was joking. I wasn't. But having asked for the bloody stuff, I inexplicably started delving into my pockets to try and see how much money I could muster. Ten, twenty, twenty two, twenty-three, twenty-four . . . 24 pence and an Anglo bubbly.

Mr Chung magnanimously agreed to let me have it for 24p and he would stand the rest. Ah this hard-bargaining business wasn't so difficult after all. I walked home desperately trying to convince myself I'd won. I'd made my point. Perhaps he'd get it right next time. I'd got my soy sauce, albeit enough to fill 100 sachets and I'd swindled sly old Mr Chung of six pence. Not bad eh?

I ended up apologising. Clearly it was my mistake and so I trudged home with the re-sealed container to get a multi-tiered bollocking off my dad for even patronising the place, wanting to eat foreign crap and then failing to stand up for myself. I ate it in the end, if only to save some face, and you know what - it just wasn't up to Vesta's high standards. Perhaps they'd got it from a different part of China. It was a bloody big country after all. It was so big my dad reckoned one day they were all going to jump up and down at the same time and completely fuck the Americans and the Russians by shaking the entire planet. That's how big it was. It had turned out to be a big disappointment. I told myself that I must remember to ask Mrs Robinson about it when I saw her next. I vividly remembered the first time she had made it for us . . .

* * *

'I take it they meet with your approval!' Mrs Robinson exclaimed.

How did she do that? I quickly averted my gaze from her tanned legs and stepped alongside her to put the empty plate in the vicinity of the brown formica table.

Rob followed with his plate, a satisfied grin and an inquiry as to if there was any pudding.

'Angel Delight if you want some,' she smiled.

'Ahh brilliant, what flavour?'

'I'll have to make some, you can have what you want - I think there's strawberry, mint, butterscotch or banana. You decide boys.'

This was just about as erotic as it got. Mrs Robinson was standing at the sink in a black mid-thigh length slip having just introduced us to the delights of Vesta Chow Mein - crispy noodles 'n' all. She was feeding us up while getting ready to go out. Now we were going to have a huge dollop of Angel Delight. Wow. Mr and Mrs Robinson were going out to a dance that evening and though she was nearly ready, she was leaving putting her dress on to the very last minute for fear of spilling anything on it. That was fine by me, even if Rob thought she looked ridiculous.

I'd always liked Mrs Robinson. She was always kind to me and treated me and Rob just the same when it came to handing out sweets, biscuits or anything like that. She was really lovely. Just lately I'd been surprised just how lovely I thought she was. I couldn't tell Rob about it because it sounded a bit weird. I'd written a list out the other day of the best looking women I knew and she'd come fourth. That was quite unbelievable because she was miles older than all the rest. She was old . . . she was . . . well over 30.

18

PORN FREE

It's hard to know just when a teenage lad's mind turns to other things, but nature dictates that it will sooner or later. For any teenage boy in the 70s who hadn't castrated himself on the Sturmey Archer gearstick of his Chopper, the time would come soon enough. The very second some of the contents of your mate's mom's clothes horse are of more interest than what is in her biscuit barrel, you're bolloxed. It's one of those things that just happens. One minute you go round the house praying she will offer you a chocolate digestive, the next you're desperate for just a glimpse of her bra or anything which could help you colour by numbers.

It sounds laughable, almost unbelievable, but back then we were virtually starved of anything remotely resembling porn. Lynda Bellingham getting her tits out in Confessions of a Window Cleaner was about as hot as it got. She was prime meat back then but who ever would have thought she'd go on to become that institution that is the Oxo mom? God, it's that mom thing again. It used to trouble me, but alas, no longer. It's just a fact that teenage lads go bonkers for older women. Then you get older and go bonkers for teenage girls - that's life. The woman next door; the one across the road, your mom's friend; the woman who catches the bus; or one of those catalogue women. The change in perception is scarily rapid. Mrs Robinson went from a woman who made me orange squash and gave me a custard cream one minute, to a brazen harlot in black underwear tearing my clothes off in no time at all. It just happens and I stopped trying to justify it a long time ago.

No, teenagers of the 70s didn't have porn - the closest we got was mail order catalogues. The only vaguely see-through things in our house were Tupperware. So if you didn't have a catalogue mom or a big sister, you had to wait for one to be brought round to the house and an appropriate moment to start flicking through the pages of women in nighties and underwear, pretending to be looking at a shirt or jumper you might like for Christmas.

I'm sure there wasn't an actual definitive moment when I suddenly felt that riding other things would be infinitely more pleasurably than a Chopper. There was Belinda, Mrs Robinson or Babs from Pan's People. The days when a Chopper replaced puberty on my personal wish list were disappearing fast. And so wistfully I turned my attention to other things, not least Babs. It's all well and good Sir Cliff harping on about Why Should The Devil Have All The Good Music? but I've got to confess to being more than just a little pissed off when Jesus of Nazareth married Babs. Is nothing sacred? Our girls off Top of the Pops were virtually all we adolescents had to think about and some things should be religiously off-limits. So when Robert Powell got hitched to Busty Babs he must have known that he'd broken a lot of hearts. Our ration of Babs, Dee Dee, Ruth, Louise and Cherry was far too meagre as it was - three or four minutes every Thursday night. He tried to win us over later by starring in The Detectives with good old Jasper, but sorry Robert, still totally out of order. Flick Colby's girls were not only national treasures, they were the original exponents of Girl Power. There were five of them for a start, but they all had an individual identity and somehow they managed to convince you that little smile straight into the camera was for you and you only. In 1972, Charlie's Angels was still a good four years off and Blondie wasn't Hanging on the Telephone gasping Call Me breathlessly. We were kept astonishingly short of good fantasy material. Paula Wilcox, Sally Thomsett, Nerys Hughes and Anne Aston were the sex kittens of the time - but, do me a favour, this was soft porn you had to not only star in but, write, direct and edit yourself. Come on, Paula was lovely but her blushing coyly to Geoffrey

Bubbles Bon Bon at the very suggestion of Percy Filth, was about as raunchy as it got. Even the thought of Richard O'Sullivan stumbling across her or Sally in just their underwear at that flat they shared was kind of left hanging in the air - you never saw anything. When you were 14 you desperately wanted that kind of stuff and it just wasn't around. Man About The House was about as good as it got and while it was good, it wasn't that good. Chrissy(Paula) just didn't do it did she? Jo(Sally) gave the impression of being up for it but couldn't help leave you wondering if she was just as big a tease as her mate and so that left Yootha Fucking Joyce. Shocking as it may sound because she was pig-ugly, you were inevitably left wondering whether Mildred was perhaps the banker bet. She certainly wasn't getting it off George and if you seriously put your mind to it, the more attractive she got. It was just those teeth of hers . . . Lord knows, Jo had a fearsome set of gnashers, but Mrs Roper? She looked like she was breaking them in for Red Rum and the fact that you even fleetingly considered the prospect of riding Yootha, is a thought best dispatched to the farthest reaches of your memory bank. It's just that kind of school disco mentality - don't go for the really good looking one, her mate might be grateful.

Anne Aston was the gorgeous little thing who spent Sunday afternoons with sticky apple juice dripping down her fingers. She helped, or should that be hindered? Bob Monkhouse on the Golden Shot - compulsory family viewing before the salmon sandwiches came out. She wasn't as stupid as she made out - couldn't have been. This was hi-tech stuff in the late 60s/early 70s but a bit like showjumping when you pray they plough into a fence, or motor racing where you want them to burst into flames, the only good bit about The Golden Shot was when some tosser missed hopelessly or you got more than a fleeting glimpse of Anne's cleavage. There was something almost erotic about the way she fingered that half a Golden Delicious as the juice dripped all down it but just imagine bedding her! 'Left a bit, right, no left, left, right a bit, FIRE! Yeah, cheers Anne.

We wanted flesh and as much of it as was permissible - or not, as the case may be. Pan's People gave it us in bucketfuls and they became even more important than the artists who appeared on Top of the Pops. It seems strange looking back now but TOTP and the Sunday night chart show on Radio One was about it. The days of 24 hour music channels were way, way, into the distant future. This was pre-video, pre-interactive - the only choice you had was watch it or miss it. At least you knew where you stood. The announcement of the brand new Top 20 was broadcast on Radio One at 12.55 on a Tuesday afternoon! Now whose brainchild was that? All over the country, kids would nip off to the cloakrooms in the middle of lessons or take up a desk in the far corner of the classroom to slyly tune in to an announcement far more important than anything one of the masters might come out with. I can remember the music, like it was just five minutes ago as the DJ built up the tension and prepared to unleash the brand new Top Five onto the nation . . . de, de, de, de,de,de . . . dum,dum ,dum . . . DUM DUM . . . and this week's new No1 . . . no, it fucking can't be . . . it is . . . maybe last week's No2 has mysteriously slipped out of the Top 20, which just never happened . . . so it's got to be . . . it is you know . . . yes, confirms DLT with just twelve and a half seconds to the one o'clock news . . . this week's new No1 . . . you've guessed . . . too right I have . . . it's Lieutenant Pigeon - it's Mouldy Old Dough! NO! So you got 35 minutes of what's supposed to be OUR music on Thursday night, when you really should be doing your homework anyway and that's the last four or five minutes written off by seeing some stupid fat battleaxe plonking away on an old piano. It wouldn't happen these days - it just wouldn't happen. She'd be glassed or nutted by a teenage freedom fighter and quite rightly so. Why we allowed novelty acts to totally hi-jack our miserly 35 minutes of pleasure is lost on me. We should have lobbied parliament and got them to pass an act that what we wanted in the brief time allocated to us, was Sweet, Queen, T Rex, Slade, Bowie, Mud maybe and Pan's People definitely, preferably gyrating to a particularly suggestive song like Love to Love You Baby. Infact, never mind the artists, just give us 35 minutes of Babs and the girls grinding their groins.

It seemed like every single bloody week someone at the BBC decided it was compulsory to inflict at least one shite act on TOTP. It was almost like someone there was saying 'Hang on a sec, these kids will enjoy this too much.' So some bastard who did the scheduling must have insisted on throwing in a record either because he was a total killjoy or he just knew the act would fall over themselves to appear. The list is endless, but consider Benny Hill, Vince Hill, Ken Dodd, Neil Reid and you get the picture(yes, we see). I'll never forgive him, the leader of that particular pack.

We should have demanded our rights. I mean to say, I couldn't stand Middle of the Road, even though the lead singer was extremely shagable, but the memory of Pan's People dancing to Soley, Soley has never left me. Middle of the Road's lead singer was almost Soley responsible for the launch of hotpants. I can't remember her name, even though the lyrics to Chirpy Chirpy Cheep Cheep and Tweedledee and Tweedledum are inexplicably etched in my memory. But I can remember her legs and, more to the point, I can remember my initial disappointment that Pan's were doing their routine to Soley, Soley, evaporating the minute the cameraman zoomed in on the location. The girls were on a beautiful beach and were dancing at the water's edge in skimpy bikinis. Cherry looked fucking gorgeous and Babs, who just had this brassy edge to her, was busting out all over the place. Now if that's not a good enough reason to harbour a grudge against Robert Powell then you tell me what is.

Thank you Pan's - you were marvellous. You must know, some things go without saying, that every teenager in Great Britain cut their metaphorical teeth on you. Even our dads loved you to death, though they had to pretend they were reading the paper. You were, are, quite simply MARVELLOUS. Until you breezed into our lives, we had little or nothing. Lulu was nice enough and we would have forgiven her for being a Scottish midget if she had just got off the damned cover of that Freeman's catalogue and jumped into the underwear section, but man can not live on Lulu alone. Hang on a minute, come to think of it, she was on that bus with Cliff on Summer Holiday wasn't she? I told you - watch these fucking Christians.

We salute you Babs, Cherry and Co, you brightened our lives and though we got harder, the available porn didn't. Indiscreet I know, but how else can I ask such a question? Come on, which ones of you shagged which pop stars? I bet the groups of the time were always hitting on you. You were bigger than the lot of 'em and while I would reluctantly accept one of you had been between the sheets with, say, oh I don't know, David Cassidy, I just don't want to hear that the drummer from Wizzard or the unknown bass guitarist of Mungo Jerry managed to bed you. Let's face it, anyone who managed to do a sexy version of Gilbert O'Sullivan's Get Down - a song about a fucking St Bernard - gets my vote. That takes some doing, but you were all wearing sexy, short white nighties and wagging your fingers at the offending pooch. Get Down . . . what would the current version of that be? God, they'd have Babs' head in your groin area, no trouble. It still wouldn't beat what you did girls. You were sex personified and a grateful generation of British males quite literally stood in tribute to you.

19

PIPPA DEE

There was no big announcement that Pippa Dee was coming to our house. My mom obviously didn't think it was a big deal. How could I have possibly known it would change my life for ever? Pippa Dee took me unsuspectingly by the hand as I wandered aimlessly in the opposite direction to Action Man, Subbuteo, Chopper bikes and innocence. It had been a gentle slope up to now. Pippa Dee brazenly assumed the mantle of a bobsleigh, hurtling me down the Cresta Run of life without so much as a crash helmet or protective suit to stop me getting serious ice burns. If Pippa Dee sounds like some incongruously exotic girlfriend, then I'd happily leave that image hanging in the air and open to all manner of conjecture, but a little further explanation is perhaps necessary if only in the sure knowledge that the truth will come out. Pippa Dee was an occasional, and may I say, far too infrequent a visitor to our house. Pippa Dee introduced me to minor fraud, serious character building entrepreneuralism and voyeurism on a totally acceptable scale - not in any particular order. Pippa Dee was like Tupperware but with lace and straps and shiny, wonderfully coloured fabrics and I remain eternally grateful for the fact that as I careered towards adolescence, she brought a serious number of female neighbours of varying shapes, sizes and ages to our house with the sole intention of getting them to try on articles of lingerie on the landing. The reasons for the landing being the neighbourhood catwalk was frighteningly simple. We only had a three-bed semi - the kitchen was full of various snacks mom had to make as part of being a party host while the hall was unsuitable because it was tiny and was only separated from the outside world by a three-parts glass front door. Clearly changing rooms and serving hatches hadn't figured in the builders' plans. And so up the stairs they would all come, doubtless aware that I'd been banished to my bedroom with a number of bribes, but thankfully oblivious to the fact that there was a split in the panel of my bedroom door which provided a panoramic view of proceedings without the slightest chance of being caught. There might be a lot to be said for having a really handy dad who was forever fixing things, but it was at times like these that you got to really appreciate having an old man with a very relaxed attitude to DIY and a tool box which consisted of little more than a hammer, two screwdrivers(one dipped in paint) and an assortment of rawl plugs.

Pippa Dee, I was soon to discover, was the latest craze. My mom had got an honours degree in Tupperware. There was nothing my mom hadn't got a Tupperware container for. We already had a cupboard full of stuff we never used - cereal holders, unbreakable mugs with lids and re-sealable bowls - the lot. I swear to God I'd have been the not-so-proud owner of the world's first Tupperware satchel if mom had anything to do with it. Seemingly casting aside that stage of her life, she had agreed to be the first host in our street for a Pippa Dee party which, I confess, stirred not the slightest interest within me. Strange how major life-changing events can just pass you by at the time. All I knew about it was that I was sent to my bedroom with strict instructions not to even venture to the loo but was bribed for my co-operation with a generous supply of sweets and pop.

There was a battered dartboard with wire framed numbers perched precariously on the back of the door and that normally occupied me for what seemed like an eternity while neighbours arrived and they gassed and gassed for a fucking age until the first party-goer ventured up the stairs to try on one of the garments. It was made all the more intriguing because there were so many permutations. Right garment, wrong model; wrong garment, right model and just occasionally right model, right garment. It was like Top of the Pops - you never quite knew what would turn up. The thump, thump, thump of darts merely served to signal that the neighbour or friend of mom's currently occupying the landing, was either fat, old, distinctly unattractive or a combination of all three. Too often the sound of a different set of feet making their way upstairs led to bitter disappointment but occasionally you would get the dream ticket. And so it transpired that over a period of months and a couple of parties I had too fleeting glimpses of some of the nicest women in the street in next to nothing. It was usually just bras and slips but that was ample entertainment. Seeing Belinda's skirt fall to the floor as she tried a black slip on had been one of the highlights while the picture of mom's friend Jenny standing there with her back to me in a red lacy bra remains with me to this day. Turn around woman!

As my crash course in the delights of Pippa Dee developed it struck me that everyone was the winner. Mom was happy because she had girlie friends around and made a few quid into the bargain; dad and a couple of the other husbands were ecstatic because they were sent down the pub under the strict instructions not to return until 10ish and unbeknown to everybody I had the ringside seat that the husbands would probably have died for. Getting a supply of sweets and pop into the bargain was an additional bonus - it's that Tom Sawyer thing.

Hindsight is a wonderful thing, but I still chuckle at the thought of my old man walking down to the pub with a few of the husbands, rubbing their hands at the thought of a few pints away from the wives, getting back later than 10pm and not getting a bollocking with platefuls of sausage rolls, cheese and pineapple on sticks waiting for them when they got back because every fucking woman on the estate was on a diet.

I can imagine the conversation:

'Better take some crisps back for our Paul. Poor little sod's been stuck in his bedroom all night.'

This was pre-TVs in every kid's bedroom, any kid's bedroom for that matter. Play stations and computers were light years away. In those days you had to amuse yourself with the simple pleasures in life. Like darts in your bedroom and seeing all the women and girls in the street in various states of undress. Life was never meant to be easy . . .

Take for example the evening I got injured when mom made a random check, to see if I was okay just as Pat Kaye from down the road was trying on a black nightie. Crash! The dartboard embedded itself in my face. You try explaining to teachers and various classmates how you got '19' and '3' branded back-to-front on your forehead.

20

PUBIC LIABILITY

Whether it was Tom and the fence or being bribed with sweets to watch the Pippa Dee show, something definitely sowed the seed. I suddenly woke up to the fact that to gain financially or get a job done and have it put on a plate was the way to go about things. I decided to develop my first venture - taking bets on Wacky Races. I wondered if this was the way the top business minds started doing things. I opened a book on the outcome of the cartoon race and watched the cash start to flow in. I became known as the kid who would offer prices on the outcome and helped myself to the odd pennies and two pences that pupils of all ages ventured on the weekly cartoon spectacular. Occasionally I took a little hit, but not often and once word had spread around not only that I ran a book but that I could be relied upon to pay up - and promptly- I was bringing in as much as 15-20p clear profit most weeks. A fortune! I fancied doing it as a career but, typically, Wacky Races Turf Accountant wasn't on the list of options.

Be it Penelope Pitstop, Professor Pat Pending or the Anthill Mob, it was all about choices and pretty soon you get to find that picking and choosing becomes the essence of life. Choices, choices, choices . . . has it ever been anything thus? I can't recall exactly when we were first introduced to the idea of Careers Information advice but take it as read I would undoubtedly have been wearing a particularly long vest at the time. This, I must point out, had nothing to do with any particular career path I was considering but more that puberty was taking an agonisingly long time. Always quick to improvise, I'd discovered that if you wore a long vest the need to be publicly humiliated when changing for P.E. was avoided. Strategic positioning of towels, sports bags or whatever you could lay your hands on went a long way to hiding the fact that you were pubicly challenged. While the lads with developing appendages and bum fluff moustaches paraded around seemingly flaunting their recently discovered invitations to adulthood, I, not on my own I must add, found the long vest did the trick most of the time. The argument that the price they paid for pubic hair was spots and acne-scarred backs, was scant consolation as, at that point, I would have quite happily agreed to let someone stick Mount Etna or Vesuvius on my face in exchange for just a touch of body hair. Changing in front of your mates, or even worse those you weren't particularly pally with, was a relatively new thing. Of the gang back at home, the phenomena had only really crept in when we went to the baths. Muldoon was the most advanced among us by far, though Rob wasn't far behind. Pele and me might just as well have been immersed in Immac as we hadn't got a single hair between us that would have registered even the smallest ouch on the body wax scale. And so seemingly overnight balls dropping and Adam's apples appearing became targets that couldn't come quickly enough. And so with a neck which resembled Susan Dey more than Oliver Reed and balls like two tiny pickled walnuts, some higher authority decides in their wisdom that it's a great time for you to start taking a serious look at what sort of career path you would like to pursue.

I mean, do me a favour, how the hell are you supposed to seriously consider what you'd like to do for 40 years of your life when the first thing you do every morning is check your genital area in the vain hope that a hair has sprouted from somewhere? It's all arse about face somehow. You make decisions on subjects at 13 that determine what exams you do which in turn dictate or influence whether a future employer will consider giving you a job. A job that could very well determine how much money you bring in to look after your wife and family and dictate what sort of house you live in; where you go on holiday and when you might eventually be comfortable enough to finish work. Who the fuck decided that was such a great idea? I'd only just started masturbating when I had to decide on all that shit and somehow that doesn't seem right. God's teeth, give me just a little more time.

Self-discovery was the key-phrase in all this. Girls get told loads, all about periods and how not to worry and all that stuff. These days they get discussion groups at school with expert advice on how to cope with the dramatic transformation into womanhood. What do we get? Just a warning we'll go blind. It's a very important subject - a compulsory part of the secondary school curriculum, yet did we get a little instruction manual?

Did we hell. Like everyone else I guess, I just thought it was about time I joined the club after it became obvious that loads of the other lads were doing it. And then it goes out of shape and you think you have broken your dick before you've barely started. What a nightmare! Who are you supposed to ask about such a delicate matter? Are you supposed to tell your mates your penis has become a disfigured mess overnight? That would be guaranteed a sympathetic response. But, anyway, once I was up and running I was ready to make decisions on what job I'd like to do when I was about to leave school. It's only in later years that you get the bigger picture and realise that in an ideal world everyone should retire first and start work when they are about 35. Then you'd be much better equipped to make a decision on what you wanted to do for the remaining 30 years. It always seems such a gross injustice when some poor bastard slogs his guts out in a pit or foundry or even shoving forms from department to department in the Civil Service, only to drop down dead because he's totally knackered two months after packing in work.

Our careers officer was one of the masters called Mr Hartson, a man of around 50 I guess who had the annoying habit of strumming the nearest available hard surface with his forefingers. He had big, bushy eyebrows which resembled two caterpillars wriggling on his face every time he frowned. On reflection it seemed the only careers he'd really considered outside of his duties as one of the school's science masters were town and country planning, a career in customs and excise or a steady job in a bank.

Anything that might have crossed your mind outside the boundaries of his own ideas was invariably met with 'Ah yes, but the thing you've got to consider is whether it's an avenue that will provide you with employment for the rest of your life?'

And so I thought better of mentioning the Wacky Races option. The fact that my command of mathematics probably amounted to something nearing numerical dyslexia still didn't stop Mr Hartson suggesting I might like to consider a career in banking.

'You'll never be out of work if you get a job in a bank,' he insisted, a prophecy which I'd now like to put to him, though I suspect he's almost certainly dead or if not considering his life options, dribbling Complan down his face in some old people's home somewhere.

'But I'm no good at maths sir.'

'A basic working knowledge of mental arithmetic and maths 'O' level would see you through that.'

'But I'm not going to get maths 'O' level sir.'

'You'd have to be a complete idiot not to get your maths 'O' Dunn.'

'Well that being the case sir, I think we'd better move on to careers for complete idiots then . . .'

To work in a bank - to even think about working in a bank - was my idea of hell even at 13. Thirty years on I applaud myself for astuteness beyond my years. What sort of a person works in one? You're stuck behind a glass screen and the only people you are really dealing with is either those who've got money, usually a complete load of tossers; or those who haven't who get angry with you because you're not willing to give them any. And the whole working principle of the system is totally to shit. If you've got money they bend over backwards to give you more. Do you want a loan for this or that? No problem. They'll move heaven and earth to give money to people who don't need or want it. The

113

poor bastards who are having a hard time of things get fuck all but penalty payments. They've got no chance of a loan unless the bank works out that they can just about afford to pay it back at a phenomenal interest rate. When you're struggling hand to mouth and you write a cheque that bounces by just a few quid, they then charge you some extortionate fee for the privilege. Banking is an institute where they give you a brolly in the summer and then whip it away from you when it's raining. As long as they don't shoot anybody, I have a lot of time for bank robbers - and the hours are good - but I resisted the temptation to offer that as a suggestion on the grounds that it would serve banks right as they've been robbing people for years. I could just imagine Mr Hartson's face!

'Wouldn't mind being a bank robber, sir. Good hours, exciting and providing you really did your homework you'd only need to work a couple of days a year.'

Mr Hartson reverted to his tried-and-tested town and country planning and the civil service. Fuck me, get a life. Even then I'd rather have just sold double glazing or got a job at WH Smiths or something. I feel sorry for people who get into that sort of stuff and because of pensions, prospects or whatever find themselves stuck in it and have to see it out for life. It's a long time, life.

'Have you given any thought to customs and excise then?' he said wearily, as if I didn't see that one coming.

'Not really sir.'

'Have you thought about anything Dunn?'

'Well, not really sir.'

'Don't you think it's about time you did start thinking then boy?'

Looking back I'd have been well in order to tell him to fuck off; that I was only 13, and was more concerned with who was top of the hit parade than what I wanted to do in X years' time. I wanted a job that paid me good money for as little effort as possible. I was no different to anyone else of my age. I'd got important things on my mind and no hairs on my body.

And somehow he thought it was easy for me?

He gave me a leaflet on the work of the customs and excise and I couldn't help thinking that you could have some great parties if you were a customs and excise officer - all those fags and the booze that you snatch off holidaymakers

Even now it makes me smile when you see the police and customs men on TV making a big show of setting light to a mountain of fags or hardcore porn and ceremoniously glugging thousands of litres of contraband booze down the drain. Yeah, OK lads we believe you. Are you honestly telling me they don't dip in there and have a bit of a share out? Of course they fucking do. Some poor bastard works 48 weeks of the year in a factory, scrimps enough money together to take the wife and kids to Majorca and then has the end of his holiday spoiled by some twat in a bad mood because the missus has got the hump with him and takes it out on Joe Average by confiscating a few fags. The more I thought about it, the more resentful about being one of them I became. They're just agents for a government that takes the piss out of smokers with crippling taxes. And then to compound that you get more than the odd MP spouting off that doctors want to refuse treating people with smoking-related illnesses. Fuck me, if it wasn't for the taxes the smokers pay there'd be no health service

The injustice of it set me thinking . . . We could save the government a fortune by employing fewer customs men and letting all the beagles out of those testing labs. It would be extremely popular legislation. Let the beagles out and take them to the airports and docks to replace two thirds of the customs officers. Jesus, if they hadn't a fag for a few hours, there's no one who would get past those buggers and they'd cost next to nothing to employ. A few tins of chum and 20 Bensons and they'd be happy.

Politician? Mmmm . . . now there's a thought. How many 'O' levels do you need for that?

21

ALL THAT GLITTERS . . .

'Your mom's going to take you shopping this afternoon to get you a skirt,' dad mumbled waiting for my answer. I thought he'd just been mad at me for being sick drunk, but that was only part of it.

'I'm not with you?' I replied, knowing I was on a loser whatever gem I'd been able to muster over the breakfast table.

'Bloody right you're not with me. And before you even ask, you're grounded for a month.'

'What for?'

'What for? I'll give you what for. Where do you want me to start?'

'I'm sorry about being sick . . . something upset me.'

'Yeah well something's bloody well upset me as well. One, you were drunk when you came in last night.'

'I ermm . . .'

'Two' dad jabbed his finger towards my off-white face. 'You were late.'

'Only . . .'

'And three, you're a pansy,' dad jabbed again.

'I was err . . .'

'That's nancy boy just in case you didn't get my meaning. It's a bad do when you bring a lad up to 13 years of age and find out he's a big poofter.'

'Dad! It's not like that.'

'Well, come on then Shirley bloody Temple you tell me what it's about then. I'm all bloody ears. And when I've finished with you, you can take that upstairs . . .' dad pointed to the Hoover and

116

a dustpan and brush, conveniently, but I suspect not accidentally, just a few feet from the yellow formica table which had become my trial dock.

'I'll do that love,' said mom eager to ease the tension.

'No you won't, SHE'LL do it. SHE got it there; SHE wants to act like a girl so SHE can go and clean up and do some housework cos' that's what girls do isn't it Shirley?'

'S'pose so,' I said meekly, deciding any form of defiance might have resulted in sterner sanctions. Being grounded for a month made a bit of housework seem inconsequential. If I thought the knock on the back door was going to rescue me, I could hardly have got it more wrong. Mom opened the door and kind of mumbled that no I wasn't coming out and I recognised it was Pele's voice though I'd guessed as much from the over the top rat -a-tat-tat on the door which annoyed the fuck out of my dad at the best of times. This *wasn't* the best of times, but before Pele had been given the chance to make a hasty retreat he found himself on the sharp end of another of my prosecuting counsel's questions.

'Ah, Pele just the man. Come in a minute.'

'Lo Mr Dunn.'

'Pele my son, you look a bit brighter than this one this morning. Didn't you go to the disco last night or did you just drink coke like you were supposed to?'

'My dad wouldn't let me go Mr Dunn,' replied Pele and though I'd thought it damned unreasonable not 12 hours ago, I was wishing my dad had stopped me now. I wouldn't be on the wrong end of this fucking inquisition that's for sure.

'So you didn't fall over drunk last night then Pele?'

'No Mr Dunn.'

'Sensible lad. And Pele, while you're here. You didn't get one of these last night did you?' asked dad pointing at the side of my neck.

'No Mr Dunn.'

'Good lad. You've obviously got more sense haven't you Pele?'

'I don't know Mr Dunn."

'Do you know what that is Pele?'

'Looks like a bruise Mr Dunn.'

'It's not a bruise Pele, it's what is known as a lovebite.'

'Oh' mumbled Pele trying not to sound impressed.

'And do you know what this is Pele?' Dad continued pointing at my head.

'What, Mr Dunn?'

'That there' dad fingered my hair. 'And there . . . and there . . . and all in your bloody bedding as well.'

'Not sure, Mr Dunn,' my friend said, being as supportive as he could under testing circumstances.

'I'll tell you what that is son. It's glitter, Pele. It's that stuff that all those poncy pop stars put in their hair. That Mark Boland and The Sweeties.'

'Oh right. Who threw that at you?' Pele said helpfully, glancing in my direction. Fucking brilliant - what a star.

'One of the big lads did it Pel,'

'Oh right.'

'Listen, you are in deep enough water without trying to take me for a bloody idiot as well my boy. You think you're that Mark Boland don't you?

'No, it was . . .'

'I suppose a big lad came up and sucked your neck as well did he? It wouldn't surprise me. Looking like that he probably fancied you. Mind you, the state you were in you wouldn't have been able to stop him anyway. You could hardly walk.'

Dad signalled to Pele that he would be best making a quick about-turn, a suggestion which was seized upon gratefully.

'So what were you drinking?'

'I just had a few swigs of cider. It doesn't agree with me.'

'It's not the only thing that doesn't agree with you right now. Few swigs? Yeah okay. So, who did that then? Glitter or lovebite take your pick.'

'One of the girls just did it for a laugh, you know?'

'No I don't bloody know actually.' That didn't surprise me

but this was hardly the time for such an observation.

'The glitter stuff, was just messing about. A few of the lads were throwing it on each other, you know?'

'Don't keep asking me if I know! I don't know and whatsmore I don't want to know. There won't be a repeat of this, my lad, believe you me. Now go upstairs.' He pointed skywards.

'And get all that crap out of your bed. Thank god you weren't sick in it. You can die you know. Choke on your own vomit. It's easily done.'

Drowning in regurgitated cider and carrots seemed quite an appealing option right now as I whisked up the Hoover and headed for the stairs.

'Can't be bloody trusted,' I just about heard him say over the thudding of my feet on the stairs. There was glitter all in the bed and on the floor by the side of it.

'I'll kill Muldoon,' I muttered to myself.

It had been Muldoon's idea to get two big bottles of Woodpecker and hide it over by the pavilion and it was Muldoon who had urged us all to sprinkle some glitter in our hair as he attempted a ridiculous Gary Glitter impression while chanting 'I'm the Leader!'

The disco had been at the Gym, loosely a gymnasium but more of a box-shaped hangar where we played football and attended youth club. We'd gone into the disco for an hour before venturing out onto the seats of the pavilion a couple of hundred yards away. We persuaded Sue and Tanya to come along too and though Rob's presence made it a disproportionate male-female ratio, it didn't matter. The lovebite I had been so proud of the night before refused to be hidden by some of my mom's Aqua Manda talc, though it did tone it down a bit. I toyed with putting a bit of foundation on it, but that really would have given my dad needless material. Sue had given it to me in a very matter-of-fact way. Dad had built up this picture of a red-hot sex romp which it certainly wasn't but I wasn't complaining - until now.

Sue had swigged from the bottle after me and, I can't

remember how, had sort of . . . wow! We kissed and then, out of the blue, she'd slipped her tongue into my mouth.

'What yer doing?' I asked.

'Frenching.'

'What's that'

'French kissing. Don't tell me you don't know what Frenching is?'

'Course I do, I just didn't know it was called that.'

'It's proper snogging, French kissing is,' she smiled, inviting me to try it on her.

I did and it felt really funny and then she went down onto my neck and administered the wound which next morning so nearly threatened to be fatal. Rob and Tanya had gone around the other side towards the swings but I hadn't had time to get the lowdown on that liaison, while Muldoon larked about by the paddling pool pretending not to be bothered. I was dying to meet up with them but while I doubted I'd be grounded for a month, I could see it being a week at the very least. Muldoon had been a bit pissed but it wasn't so bad for him because since his parents had split, he was at home with just his dad. He'd probably get a bit of a bollocking, but with no lovebite, his catalogue of offences didn't look half as bad. Mind you with the spots on Muldoon's neck he could consider himself fortunate if a famished vampire had dared have a nibble let alone any self-respecting teenage girl. Rob hadn't really got drunk because by the time he'd come back from the other side of the pavilion our fun and games had been severely interrupted by Jimmy Hunt and a couple of his mates who had got wind that we had got some cider and had unceremoniously swiped it and told the girls they were wasting their time with three wets like us in the first place. God I loathed him but he was a fucking hard case and not a pleasant one at that, and we had to sit there and watch him empty the bottle down his throat and make out that we'd have given him some anyway if we'd only have thought to ask . . .

That apart, everything had gone really well. I'd scuffed my shirt too, which I hadn't dared show my mom yet. She wouldn't tell dad, I was sure of that, but she wasn't best pleased with me right now, so caution was the key word. As we'd giggled the evening away, the group of us had made a half-arrangement to go to the fair which was coming to town in a couple of weeks. I wasn't as optimistic about making that date now as I had been last night. I could have sworn they said it was another two weeks. I was hoping I'd be back in circulation by then, but I'd not seen my dad as mad as that before and all I could do was try and keep my nose clean, do everything that was asked of me, and see how it went.

One thing was for sure . . . this was not a good time to tell dad I'd been thinking of having a perm!

22

THE PAIN NOW STANDING ON...
PLATFORM SHOES

I'd been walking, albeit with some difficulty, a bit of a tightrope
with dad even before the glitter episode. My growth spurts
shouldn't have been such a surprise to him seeing as he was very
tall himself but it was when I shot up two inches in the space of
five minutes that he seemed genuinely perplexed. I thought my
platform shoes were the absolute business, but dad had a
completely different take on it, which was both understandable
and entirely predictable.

'Oh my God, what's he been bloody well buying now?'

'What?'

'WHAT? Like what the hell have you got on your feet? You've
forgotten to take your shoes out of the bloody boxes'

'They're the shoes - what do you think I'm likely to have on my
feet?' I answered back a little too cockily.

'Is that what you call them?'

'Everyone's got 'em dad.'

'I haven't but I don't suppose that counts. Well forgive me for
asking then. I just hope you realise you look bloody ridiculous.'

I felt like saying thanks but thought better of it. Anything that
invoked ridicule in my father was almost certainly cool. And
let's have it straight, here and now, my green and black platforms
were most certainly cool.

'Like you really need something to make you stick out in a
crowd don't you? You know you're almost six foot and you want
to stick a couple of feet on top just in case anyone thinks you're
not tall enough.

Well, I never . . . I give up.'

A couple of feet was, as usual, something of an exaggeration to simply emphasise the point. The only two feet in the argument here were the ones firmly entrenched in my magnificent platforms.

'Well, I'll tell you one thing. You'll end up crippled and don't expect me to push you around in a wheelchair when you can't get around because I won't.'

Dad had this thing about pushing me around in a wheelchair, like it was something that he'd readily do for me as long as I'd been struck down by some dreadful disease, but not if I'd been knocked down by a car because that would have been my own stupid fault. Dad was more than happy to push Complan or rusks into his teenage son's face if I'd been struck down by Motor Neurone Disease or something which he felt was acceptable, but he just couldn't stand the thought of having to explain to concerned onlookers outside the local shop that the reason his once athletic son was now being pushed around with a tartan blanket to keep his legs warm was because he'd fallen off a pair of platforms. God, I could just imagine the conversation.

Some interfering old bag, asking dad what mystery ailment I'd been struck down by.

Could just see dad replying: 'No, he was fine until he was 14 and then he fell off a couple of platforms.'

'Ooh and did he fall onto the track?' says the concerned old dear.

'No, not at a railway station love, he was wearing them at the time.'

Anything that constituted bringing about my own downfall would have seen dad steadfastly refusing to show a father's concern and devotion by pushing me around in a wheelchair. Whenever I went out in the depths of winter, I'd get the warning about the perils of going on frozen ponds and I didn't take a blind bit of notice.

'And don't get going anywhere near any ponds. Never mind drowning, it's so cold you can soon go into a coma and . . .'

Yeah don't tell me dad. 'Don't expect me to push you around in a wheelchair 'cos I won't.' Big surprise.

Anything remotely resembling danger, dad's stock answer was that I'd face the ultimate penalty of being made to sit in the house, staring morosely out of the window because no one would be there to push me around in my wheelchair. It scared me to death. My mom wouldn't do it; dad wouldn't do it, my friends wouldn't want to play with me because they wouldn't want to push me around either. They'd soon get fed-up with it. Be warned. Fuck me, a life of abject misery was no more than one dodgy drain cover or a badly judged kerbside away.

And I'm sure this is one of the reasons that the teenagers of the early 70's had such scant disregard for the unfortunate souls who had genuine afflictions. I might just be saying that to cover my shame and embarrassment at just how much we used to take the piss out of mongols, spastics and the like, but we all did it and while that doesn't make it right, maybe I've now stumbled on the reason. Kids are cruel - and we were very cruel. The very mention of a Blue Peter appeal to help children with spina-bifida, was tantamount to giving us an overdose of laughing gas.

While Lesley Judd and Peter Purves congratulated our generation on our kindness and thanked us wholeheartedly for our response to their record-breaking appeal, we actually couldn't have given a toss. 'Spineys' or 'Biffos' as they became known were jolly good material and the sight of any single one of your mates with his arms stuffed down his blazer with just his hand sticking out of the sleeves like stumps was guaranteed to have us all pissing ourselves. 'Spaz' and 'Mong' almost became terms of endearment and though I'm deeply ashamed of it now and it ranks almost on a par with trying to slaughter the newt population of this world, you can't escape it.

Long before Sir Bob, we had Blue Peter appeals for the starving people of Biafra and to the man, or boy, we thought it was fucking hilarious. Dreadful but true. Any kid at school who was slim in stature was, inevitably, 'Biafran'. Fuck me, what did John Noakes really expect? We didn't know where Biafra was and, in truth, we didn't give a flying fuck either. Was I really such a horrible child? Well yes, probably, but surely not awful enough NOT to be pushed around in a wheelchair?

And what happened to Biafrans? Did they all die off or did they all get better and decide to call their country something else? Don't hear of it now do you? Mongs became Down's Syndrome and Spastics became, well whatever they became, which I can't help thinking must have really pissed off the Spastics Society because it must have cost a bloody fortune just to change all those collection boxes, particularly those lifesize ones with calipers which stood outside shop doorways. They obviously went the way of sausage dogs.

Dad hadn't finished. His gaze was now piercing me up around the leg region and you could just sense there was more to come.

'And what in God's name do you call them then?' he exclaimed shaking his head from side to side as he took a long, slow, look at my trousers. My trousers were fantastic; baggy with patch pockets and enough buttons up the waistband to keep Ronco in business for years. They were dark green to match my shoes. I just knew I looked cool. Dad wasn't so sure.

'Enough material in them to make two pairs of my trousers.'

'Exactly.'

'Don't cheek me.'

'Wasn't'

'You look stupid.'

'Well everyone must look stupid then dad. All the lads are wearing these.'

'Oh and that makes it right does it?'

'It's not supposed to be right. It's just . . . it's just the way it is.'

'Well I'm just glad these things have passed me by that's all I can say. You must have more money than sense. Bugger off.'

23

FAIR INDICATIONS

If you want to know exactly how your girlfriend, daughter, sister, or favourite aunty rates in the shagability stakes, just take her on the waltzers. Save yourself the needless time and expense of discreet approaches to modelling agencies and make a visit to the nearest fairground. Just leave it all in the hands of a greasy, illiterate tattooed youth with the personal hygiene of a hedgehog and judge the outcome for yourself. It's a harsh fact of life but ugly birds rarely get spun on the waltzer cars. If they are afforded the luxury of a quick 360 degrees it's more likely to be an act of pity than a brief moment of compassion from the man who can't spell his own name but pirouettes on a piece of fast spinning machinery with the dexterity of an Olympic ice dancer. A more likely conclusion is the fact that she either has a huge pair of tits or a skirt showing so much leg that despite her resemblance to a moose, she looks distinctly up for it. Girls stepping uneasily from waltzer cars so dizzy they can hardly stand all have one thing in common - they are either real lookers or they were unfortunate enough to be strapped in with a friend who is.

Thirty years on, only now do I fully understand that those magical first trips to the funfair should teach you so much. There's a case for schools organising trips to the fairground simply to teach you of the pitfalls lurking around every single corner of life from there on in. But like most teenagers either on, or in search of that first romantic liaison, the flashing lights, the sweet smell of donuts and candy floss somehow mingling perfectly with the engine oil, I was oblivious to the wider implications. Weeks short of your 14th birthday, just how are you to know that you would leave the place penniless, having been shamefully or quite cunningly cheated, facing an hour's walk home, with a chalk poodle , a small portion of chips and batter bits your only comfort? If ever you needed to be shown a microcosm of the perils of adult life then a trip into Travellersville really ought to stand you in good stead.

And hopefully from that point on, as you trod gingerly through your teens towards a career, wife, family and a mortgage, not necessarily in that order, you would be ever grateful for the lessons learnt from an adults-eye view of the inner workings of a common or garden fairground. You'd learn how education or moral upbringing wouldn't necessarily be reflected in your pay packet; that the inability to read or write was, in a number of instances, virtually a pre-requisite to becoming a millionaire and that when you realised a fool and his money are soon parted, you were half way home to cracking what really was the stuff of life. Just the briefest of observation of the scruff trying his damndest to cajole you onto his stall or stuffing your money into his pocket before whizzing you around on a waltzer or some equally grubby attraction, would allow you to see that cash in hand was so often the only way to go.

Bullshit baffles brains, my old man used to say, and with each advancing year the truth of that statement acquires a flavour and maturity of a fine Cheddar. The tricks of the fairground should teach you a painful lesson, yet they don't and the dishonesty of the whole darned thing somehow gets disguised in the magic of it all. They rob you blind, let you leave thinking what a great time you've had, knowing that you'll return again to let them empty your pockets. It's so blatant, it's brilliant. They shag your town's girls and then fuck off. You can't help but admire it.

'Everyone wins a prize' the sign boldly proclaimed, sitting as it did in front of an array of attractive rewards for sticking three darts in three separate cards. There were mirrors and posters with the faces of Donny Osmond, Michael Jackson, David Cassidy, Gary Glitter and even Gilbert O'Fucking Sullivan on them. How did Gilbert become a sex symbol? For the more advanced there were various prizes emblazoned with Slade or just plain common or garden teddy bears. And the darts were blunt and different weights so they travelled the four feet or so to the board virtually sideways on and after you'd had about three goes and just got lucky to complete the task, the harsh truth of advertising was rammed home to you as if the guy with the tattoos and the Bill Sikes grin really wanted to make a point much sharper than any of the darts on offer.

'I'll take one of those,' I said pointing somewhat sheepishly at the Donny Osmond mirror, Sue Thompson, the immediate object of my misplaced desire, was urging me towards.

'Not got enough mate,' said Sikes.

I didn't much care for being asked to repeat the fact that the reward I was seeking for my near legendary marksmanship was a small Donny Osmond mirror, but nonetheless I persevered.

'One of those . . .'

'Nah, they're four wins pal.'

'But the sign . . . the sign'

By now Sikes was in the final throes of producing a box of prizes for twats like me who even dared to assume that one successful go out of four attempts with sabotaged arrows could possibly entitle me to a Donny Osmond mirror. Not even a Gilbert O'Fucking Sullivan poster. No.

'One win pal. You can have a Donny key ring, yo-yos, you can have a goldfish if you like,' Sikes suggested generously.

Suddenly my vain attempt to impress Sue had become tarnished. I'd won, against all the odds and ended up spending a whole lot more than I needed to in order to win her heart with a Donny key ring. And if only I could have realised that was only the start . . .

I spied my chance to get the bastards back. A different stall, a different denim and black T-shirt clad guy - more a Son of Sikes - but what the hell, my chance to get even. I was a crack shot with an air rifle as countless creatures who had the misfortune to cross my path were no longer able to testify. What I couldn't do with my BSA .22 wasn't worth doing. For the past 18 months, if it moved I could find a reason to shoot it. It troubles me now, but all lads are much the same and I try not to dwell on my role in the current perilous state of some species. It's a miracle of nature that I don't wake up in the middle of the night, a terrified victim of a recurring dream in which I am dragged off to some European Court of Justice for newts for my crimes some 30 years earlier. In Newtsville, I'm a modern day Milosevic or Saddam Hussein, a mass murderer suddenly hauled before an international panel to answer charges of ethnic cleansing. There I'd be, sitting in the dock, refusing to answer questions as a panel of about a dozen learned newts sat on an imposing bench before me with judicial robes on, considering the evidence. And as they weighed up my part in making the Great Crested Newt an endangered species, I would have to sit there silently trying to blot out the memory of mass slaughter of newts over by the First Pool.

'And it is further alleged that in the year Nineteen hundred and sixty nine and seventy, you Paul John Dunn, on unspecified dates did systematically . . .'

Jesus, I'm in a cold sweat thinking about it now. Where was I? Oh yeah, so if any good were to come out of my ability to splatter a newt at 15 yards or thump a pellet into a starling as it gratefully gorged on the crumbs I'd lured it onto the garden path with, then this was the time. This was my chance to take out my marksmanship on Son of Sikes, impress the girls and my mates I'd gone to the fair with. Impressing my mates was the last thing on my mind - they knew I was the neighbourhood's very own Jesse James. Just hearing Muldoon, Pele and Rob urging me on to give it my best shot, as it were, was almost enough. Sue and Sandra had been joined by their friend Catherine and they too were looking to me to respond to the promptings.

'Go on Dunny,' pleaded Rob, who I grudgingly had to accept was now easily regarded as the best looking one out of all of us.

'Dunny's brilliant,' observed Pele.

'Go on if you're good,' said Sue with a hint of faith, almost pride if I was reading the situation right, which quickly had me diving into my pocket for 25p.

'Show 'em Dunny,' said Muldoon.

Cometh the moment, cometh the man and I just hoped Sikes Junior realised what he was in for as he gave me three tiny feathered darts to load into the airgun barrel at my leisure.

'It says there is a prize every time,' I said, desperate to show not only that I was a quick learner but that I was quite prepared to stand up for my rights before sending three carefully guided missiles into the centre circle of the target to claim my top prize.

'Yeah, that's right mate. You good eh?'

It was a question unworthy of an answer, so I tucked the butt into my shoulder, lined up the sights and sent the first dart just inside the qualifying area.

'Fuck me,' I exclaimed.

'What's up Dunny?' asked Muldoon.

'These sights are fucked.'

'Nothing wrong with them sights mate. It's okay anyway so what you worried about? Two more needed.'

Keeping my head and working on the theory that if the sights were shooting a good half inch to the right, I corrected my aim and lined up to a point half an inch left of the bullseye - and missed.

'Jesus,' I groaned, hardly daring to believe that I'd been systematically duped again within the space of five minutes.

'Hard luck mate,' said Sikes Jnr.

'Hard luck, you're kidding me.'

'Avvin' another go?'

'You are kidding,' I replied boldly.

'Nothing wrong with them sights mate. Your sight maybe . . .' the greaser smiled, leaving me to shuffle off dejectedly.

And so Sandra thought I was just a bad shot; I detected a clear inference from Sue that I was just a bad loser while Pele somehow managed to call upon the services of every brain cell he possessed that I couldn't be a bad loser because I did it all the time. Fuck me, even Pele was getting laughs at my expense. The fact that he didn't manage to knock the cans off the shelves with the bean bags was of little consolation, nor that he wouldn't even attempt to get a football through one of the holes, much to the surprise of the girls.

'Thought you'd be good with a name like Pele. Pele's a football player ain't he? Why do they call you that?' asked Sue.

'Cos he's shit at football,' laughed Rob.

'Don't get it,' declared Sue.

They don't, do they?

We rustled some cash together to get a bag of donuts as Slade belted out Take Me Bak Ome, which on reflection might have been a fitting anthem. Sue, who had let me kiss her last week, seemed suitably unimpressed with my fairground prowess - and there was much worse to come. The night was still young, my confidence had taken a severe denting and I really should have taken Noddy Holder's advice because the humiliation of humiliations was no more than an hour away . . .

24

IN A SPIN

Telling the girls their bottoms looked fat outside the Hall of Mirrors was a seriously bad move. That wasn't the reason I was excluded from joining them on the waltzers. With the lads already secured into another car, my attempts to get in with the girls was meeting with resistance anyway when the youth running the ride, kind of shunted me to one side as he strapped the girls in and looked at me in a way which had 'fuck off' written all over it. There was a lesson to be learned there anyway. I didn't really like the waltzers, full stop, but the thought of being scrunched up against Sandra or Sue was too powerful an attraction to make me see the good sense in just standing on the sidelines watching them screaming hysterically.

'You look a bit like Rod Stewart,' Sandra giggled handing the money over to the lad with the spiked up birds' nest who was set to give them two minutes of orgasmic pleasure. Twat.

'Yeah, everyone says that. I get a bit fed up of it to be honest,' he said modestly.

Fed up with it? What a tosser. How can a guy with a dopey grin, big fucking hooter and hair deliberately styled like that claim he gets pissed off with people thinking he looks like Rod Stewart? I ask you. I didn't need persuading he was a total prat.

The fact that Maggie May came over the sound system as if by magic merely enhanced my suspicions. The two girls who looked to be around 16 in the car in front of Sandra's came in for maximum attention, getting spun around so much that they seemed in grave danger of wetting their pants. No doubt that was Rod the Sod's intention, though when he wasn't concentrating on them, he rode the wooden sea with supreme dexterity to make sure 'our' girls' car wasn't going short on the spin front. Pele, Muldoon and Pete were not exactly in Spin City for some reason which escapes me; neither were the two rather hefty girls a couple of cars behind them. One quite rightly expressed her disappointment as she disembarked, re-adjusting her hair.

'Thanks girls, come back,' said Rod.

'You'll need to spin us a bit more than that,' said one.

'Special spins for you next time girls,' grinned the rocker, who hardly needed to explain that the reason he had only wasted one spin on them was because they were unworthy of his attention. He might just as well have said that he hadn't spun them much because he thought they were Gorgons and that it would take someone with much greater strength then him to even get their weighty car to hurtle round 360 degrees, greased wheels or not. And you know what? They were fucking back 15 minutes later, reminding him that he'd promised them some special spins. Serves him fucking right, I thought to myself, as Rod pocketed another five bob with stunning ease.

'God, he spun us loads,' gasped Sue, her jiggly little breasts doing their best to heave under her skin tight white top.

'Big surprise,' I countered disconsolately.

'Didn't half look like Rod Stewart,' panted Sandra.

'More like Andy fucking Stewart,' Pele said dismissively.

'Just jealous.'

'Not.'

'Bet he gets some girls,' said Sandra.

Rockin' Robin boomed around the fairground, as it dawned on me that she was doubtless right. I bet Rod shagged not only for Britain, but all fucking well around it. I mean he just couldn't go wrong in a job like that. Instant access to an endless supply of girls out for a good time.

He didn't have to worry about making too much conversation with them because they invariably spoke to him first and though to my mind he had the social graces of a badger, he didn't have to even worry about getting straight to the point. He probably had a caravan round the back, or at least access to one where he could lure girls on the promise of a few free rides. No need for wine and roses here or a night out at the pictures; Rod could just say 'Fancy a shag' as an opening liner, secure in the knowledge that if anyone did take exception to his boldness he had a fairground full of travelling thugs to persuade the aggrieved party he was only joking when he said it. Marvellous! He'd probably quit school when he was eight, if he'd ever been, could eat fish and chips and toffee apples until they came out of his ears, smoke and have sex with all or most of the local bikes in every village he waltzed in and out of. Why was life so cruel? Rod didn't even have exams to worry about.

Betcha By Golly Wow was followed by Sweet's Little Willie, which prompted the inevitable remarks from the Rod-struck girls. Although this wasn't a date, even we knew four into three didn't go. Things just didn't seem to be going to plan.

Even the songs seemed to conspire against us. 'I'm your Screwing Machine' guffawed Sandra to no one in particular as Hawkwind ripped through the air. And so it went on: All the Young Dudes; Hold Your Head Up; Rock and Roll Part II; Seaside Shuffle, Locomotion, Walkin' in the Rain with the One I Love etc etc.

School's Out was the one anthem I could really identify with and as it thumped through the corridors between stalls, it felt good knowing that I didn't have to think about going into the fourth year at Grammar School - for now. Alice Cooper reminding me that school was in fact out only served to put the thought back in my head. In fairness it wasn't that bad, but lost in the neon warmth of the fair, I'd almost forgotten about it.

That was only temporary as my ears cocked in recognition of someone calling my name with a certain urgency.

'Dunny. Dunny . . .'

I half-recognised the voice but it just wasn't one I would have associated with a fairground.

'Dunny!!'

As I glanced around to my right, towards the queue for the Mad Mouse, my arm was tugged by a young girl and as I turned around quickly I realised it was Rob's little sister.

It wasn't her voice that was calling me though, and Rosie quickly alerted me to the urgency of the situation.

'Dunny,' squealed Rob's mom. 'Where's our Rob?'

Pele and Rob had gone over to the toilets on the far side of the fairground, escorting a couple of the girls in the process. Mrs Robinson breathlessly explained that she was in the very next group to go on the Mad Mouse, Rob's dad had steadfastly refused to go anywhere near it and Rosie had turned chicken on her.

Mrs Robinson begged me to rescue her by going on the ride. In this environment she just didn't look like Rob's mom, or anybody's mom for that matter. She had a turquoise tanktop on and a mid-thigh length blue leather skirt which showed off her shapely figure. These days I was more used to seeing her in a white lab coat.

By the time Rob and the rest had found us, I was crammed into the tiny car which was already being tugged up the first steep rise. Mrs Robinson begged me to take her hand, explaining she'd only agreed to go on it because Katie wanted to and she had handed over the money just before she'd pulled out. Suddenly the fairground seemed everything I wanted it to be. Mrs Robinson clutched my hand as we hurtled around the track, her screams and gasps fuelling my imagination before we finally ended up at the step-off point. As she leant across me to release the belt, I couldn't help noticing glistening fine gold hairs on the inside of her thighs. She was my best mate's mom; she was over-30 for God's sake; she was an older woman; she was respectable . . . she was totally fucking gorgeous.

While we were sharing three candy flosses between the seven of us we were drawn into the slot machine arcade by the sound of the Theme From Shaft. Pele, hardly discreet at the exact moment he needed to be, discovered that a machine he'd been pumping 5p pieces into was paying out when it shouldn't.

'Fucking hell, lads come here,' he chortled.

'That shouldn't have paid then.'

'I know - it's going fuckin' mental.'

'Jesus. Let's have a go.'

Pele plundered the machine when our frantic activities alerted a huge guy standing next to the change kiosk. Before we could calm down, a man with huge forearms and Ray Dorsey sideburns, stood behind us.

'Oi you!'

'Who?'

'You lot - you're taking the piss.'

'Sorry?'

'You bloody well will be. Piss off. Go on, scarper.'

He didn't look like a guy to argue with and it seemed a bit ironic that the one time you briefly manage to turn the tables on them you get rumbled and threatened with the death of a thousand cuts.

Somehow we managed to rustle together enough money to make our way into the queue for the big wheel and with the time at almost 9.30, we would need to make our way home shortly. I was praying Sue would encourage me to walk with her and I bristled with the hope that she might be kissing me with the enthusiasm she'd shown before.

A whole new world had opened up to me and as we stepped into the cars, I contemplated that avenue of pleasure might not be too far away now. I was encouraged by her holding my hand as we got into the cars, making sure she got in with me and Pele; the others getting into the one which followed.

She snuggled up against me as the dangling seat with the umbrella canopy slowly cranked its way up.

Horror of horrors though, as the speed built up and I looked out over the left hand side of the car to shout down to Rob and the rest a few cars back below, I could feel myself retching and knew there was no holding back. I had no alternative, try as I might, and though Sue and Pele were giggling away obliviously at first, they quickly became aware of my multi-coloured yawn which was seconds away from splattering the car beneath.

'Oh Christ, no,' Sue exclaimed.

Pele was sympathetic, clutching his stomach as he was consumed by convulsions of laughter while I was vainly trying to make the best of a very bad job, realising there was also a commotion in the car beneath. I felt dreadful - even worse when I disembarked to discover Sandra and Rob moaning because they thought someone had tipped something over them from on high.

'Fucking bastards,' groaned Rob. 'It's gone all over the bottom of my Levis.'

'And it's caught my top,' shrieked Sandra.

'Come on Pele. What's the big fucking joke?' urged Rob.

'It was me Rob,' I admitted meekly.

'Twat. What did you tip out of there then? '

'Only his stomach,' Pele screamed.

'You what!'

'Dunny chucked his ring up. Great shot though eh? '

'Dunny, you arsehole.'

'Sorry mate. Sorry Sandra. I couldn't help it. You know I wouldn't do that on purpose.'

My humble apologies were grudgingly accepted which made the situation easier, but I didn't need it spelling out to me that my hopes of a goodnight kiss had gone over the side with my half-digested hot dog.

25

CANE AND UNABLE

I had a lot of important things on my mind that chill, January morning, and none of them concerned double English with Mr Woolf in Room 16. It was Tuesday - charts day. I was blissfully unaware that I was about to stumble or, perhaps more accurately, slide, into a life-changing moment. I got the cane.

I'd never had it before; never had it since, but if anything served to remind me of whether that irritating little wanker Jimmy Osmond remained at No1 with Long Haired Lover from Liverpool, then the cane takes some beating. I hadn't too many cares up to that point in late morning where the announcement of the new charts was imminent and the only thrashing I've ever had was little under an hour away. I'd been congratulating myself on saving enough of the vouchers off the KP Crisps packets to send off for a free top five single when disaster struck. There was no way I could have known what was in store and for all those people who try to comfort you by saying sometimes that's best, believe me - it fucking isn't.

First, the important things. Because I wasn't sure of how stringently the bosses at KP would insist the record of my choice would have had to have been in the actual Top Five, I'd made the decision not to risk pissing them off by sending in a crawly note asking if I could have one that, for example, had only managed to get to No8. Therefore, what comprised the best five selling singles in Britain this particular morning was more important than usual. Jimmy Osmond was obviously out. Bowie was No2 with Jean Genie, which was a definite possibility; and just in and sure to blast it's way towards the top was a record which apart from the distinctive siren, sounded just like the start of Bowie's record - Blockbuster by Sweet. Fuckin' hell, the first time I heard that. Wow! Wig Wam Bam, Little Willy, Co Co and Funny Funny hadn't given any indication they would suddenly turn out like this and suddenly here it was BLOCKBUSTER. It was seriously good, no matter how much the sixth formers mocked it. That air raid siren was just so bloody distinctive and when I think of my dad's disbelieving face as he saw them on Top of The Pops I still chuckle. His jaw dropped at least a foot when Brian and the boys came on looking like an explosion in a make-up factory - he just hadn't got a clue what to do. God bless Sweet. More front than Brighton; boy were they outrageous?

Boland, as dad called him, was in there with Solid Gold Easy Action and The Osmonds had caught everyone totally unawares by suddenly releasing a proper record that even their biggest critics had to concede wasn't bad. Crazy Horses had one huge disadvantage - it was by The Osmonds. That apart it was a gutsy effort which would instinctively have you dragging your arm across the front of your body - provided no one was watching - when Donny (mauve scarf 'n' all) made that strange sound with his keyboard. Unfortunately the fact that it was Donny and Co instantly prohibited it from being my choice, but the fact that it was even considered for the faintest of seconds is the biggest tribute I can pay the bloody record. Roy Wood was there with Ball Park Incident - absolutely not. Well done Roy. The man who left The Move must have thought the rest of the band would disappear up their own arses without him and his silly beard. For Move read Bad Fucking Move. So Jeff Lynne and The Electric Light Orchestra become one of the very top bands of all time. Stick that up your bum with your Angel Fingers Roy and go do some panto.

Carly Simon was currently No7 with You're So Vain and while the debate raged on about who it had been written about - Mick Jagger, Cat Stevens, James Taylor, Warren Fucking Beattie - I, quite frankly couldn't have given a toss. I just liked her skin tight jeans and her gorgeous, big lips and unless she poked her head from out of a bag of KP Crisps and offered to give me a blow job, which did seem a shade unlikely, she had no chance. Judge Dread of all people was at No9 with Big Seven. He was becoming something of a cult, a description I'm sure he would have appreciated, after mischievous teenagers had flocked to buy the banned Big Five and Big Six. Gary Glitter was sure to go higher with Do You Wanna Touch Me? When he said 'Where? There? Yeah!' we were pretty sure we knew what he meant, it just wasn't until years later that we realised that at 14 we were a good six years too old for his liking.

At No10 was Shotgun Wedding by Roy C, a pile of old shite if only for the fact that it starts off with the sound of a bullet ricocheting all around the place. Now I don't want to be picky but if you've ever heard a shotgun ricochet then you're a better person than me. I'll give him the benefit of the doubt because I suppose Colt 45 Wedding or Luger Wedding doesn't have quite the same effect.

So, this particular Tuesday morning was going just fine and as I strolled into Mr Woolf's class immediately after assembly, all was pretty much well with the world. English; no problem. Mr Woolf; no problem. Free period to follow, then single Geog to take me into lunch and chart time. Brilliant. Something about the best laid plans springs to mind . . .

As I made my way around the school's inner quadrangle, the sound of the numerous segs in my brogues pierced the thin morning air with a sharp clipping sound. The sound of several pairs of horseshoe studded shoes clicking away at the same time was the norm these days and as I made my way towards the library, massive trouble was waiting to smack me in the face.

Miss Frost was an imposing figure who ruled the library and its immediate vicinity with the proverbial rod of iron. A starchy woman who I assumed to be in her mid-50s, it wasn't much of a surprise to me or anyone who had the misfortune to bump into her that she had never married. I could be kind and say she probably had her opportunities, but somehow I doubted it. I wouldn't have keeled back in surprise if someone had told me that she'd never been intimate with a man in her life, such was her disarming demeanour. Just like Belinda, Miss Frost had a name that suited her, but there the similarity ended. She always wore tweedy-type skirts and those thin, tight-stitched woollen crew-necked jumpers that were worn by, well, women like her. She had large breasts but in an attempt to disguise the fact that she was ample-bosomed, she had the slightest of forward stoops which made it look like she was suffering from some kind of back complaint. She wore those horrid supposedly flesh coloured tights and soft suede flat shoes befitting a librarian who liked stalking up behind people in total silence, taking them unawares like some sort of literary barn owl. When she sat at her desk, surveying her territory, her head seemed to move from side to side without another muscle in her entire body flickering as she took in all before her over her horn-rimmed spectacles. Miss Frost had been commandant of the library for 27 years as she often reminded people and was not a woman to be messed with.

I hadn't intended messing with her because when I poked my head around the library door to try and see if Wagger was there, I could hardly help but notice her seat was vacated and a couple of first years were chattering about something by the first set of cubicles which never would have happened had she been within 50 yards of the place. Confirming her absence, I stepped in and decided to ignore the instruction that segged shoes or any type of footwear which might mark the wooden floor was strictly prohibited. In the past, I'd slipped them off, but with Miss Frost unusually roosting somewhere else for now, I marched across the library floor with the air of a man making the most of a temporary reprieve. I hadn't seen a prefect called Mortimer follow me in let alone take any account of what a horrible bastard he really was. That was to be my undoing and before I could get back towards the library door to slip my shoes off, I glanced up to see Mortimer pointing in my general direction with Miss Frost at the side of him. Shite. What a toerag! I mean to say what was he going to get out of this except a few brownie points from that icy cow, while I now stood to get at least a detention? To my horror as I glanced down to make my way towards her beckoning finger, I could see that I had scratched the floor with my brogues and just prayed she hadn't noticed. I'm not saying she wouldn't have, but my cause was hardly helped by Mortimer who now, informed her that the reason he'd seen fit to bring my intrusion to her attention was that he feared the library floor would get damaged. Words can't truly express my gut feeling of total disgust and contempt for a tosser like the spotty creep who was smirking in front of me.

'What on earth do you think you are doing you horrible boy?' she enquired peering menacingly at me.

'Sorry Miss.'

'You know the rules boy. Dunn isn't it?'

'Miss'

'You'll be done if I have my way you wretched creature. Follow me. Mortimer, keep your eye on things for me please. Thank you.'

Miss Frost grabbed me by the ear and led me out of the open door into the quadrangle and didn't need to tell me that the headmaster's office was the next port of call. She did anyway.

'We'll see what the headmaster has to say about this because he knows how fed-up I am of telling boys like you not to desecrate my floor.'

Desecrate it? What the fuck was she on about? This was a boys' school. If nothing else, I was a boy and the fucking thing in question she was talking about in almost revered terms was neither The Shroud of Turin not the Cistine Chapel ceiling. It was a library floor for God's sake. I trusted the head, a mousey sort of man called Mr Porter, would see things in their proper perspective and see fit to give me nothing more than a stern telling off and possibly a detention.

'It's not as if there isn't a big sign on the inside of the door, warning you,' she wittered on.

The school secretary Mrs White was given chapter and verse of what had happened and pointed me towards a chair on the other side of the room at the same time assuring Miss Frost that she would inform Mr Porter straight away. It seemed like an eternity before he called me in and in the meantime, while Mrs White was in with him, Beefy Bulmer had seen me from outside and popped his head round the door to assure me that the cane wasn't as bad as a lot of people made out.

'First one stings, you don't really feel the rest,' he grinned, wishing me luck.

'Thanks pal,' I said somewhat dismissively. I wasn't going to let anyone wind me up. I wouldn't get caned for scratching the library floor. This wasn't the dark ages after all.

It was a darker age than I'd envisaged. Mr Porter lectured me on how much the new floor in the library had cost; how if it was looked after it might last for so many more years and basically pointed out that despite Miss Frost's perfectly clear sign, I had chosen to ignore everything and be a law unto myself. Brilliant. The way he was going on seemed like double detention for sure. It was 1.15 and it crossed my mind to ask him if Jimmy Osmond had been knocked off No1 just to break the ice. Perhaps not.

'Any reasons you can think of as to why I shouldn't cane you Dunn?'

Well the fact that I didn't want him to and that it was going to hurt like shit was two for starters, but I needed something better than that.

'Well?'

'Well it seems a *bit* harsh sir.'

'I'll be the judge of that Dunn.'

'Y'sir but if I offered to clean up the scratches would that help sir?'

'Well it would, but I've already decided you'll do that anyway. I CAN not and WILL not put up with this blatant disregard of things Dunn.'

'I'm sorry sir.'

'So you will be boy,' said Mr Porter reaching for the top drawer. This was a bad dream only made worse when he asked me to loosen my trousers and bend over.

'Loosen my trousers sir?'

'Yes Dunn, I don't whack pupils very often but I don't want to rip your trousers so loosen them up and just ease them down over your pants boy.'

What the fuck was this all about? If it hadn't been so serious it would have been funny, but I certainly wasn't laughing and there was an additional reason for that. For the past three or four weeks I'd been suffering from a terrible sweat rash right at the top of my legs. It had got so bad after games, that I'd told my mom and she'd winced when she'd seen it. Solution: vaseline and a pair of my dad's pants so, as she put it, 'it'll let some air in and stop the rubbing.' They looked bloody ridiculous, but in fairness they were more comfortable under extremely pressing circumstances, and she had said just to wear them on non-games days, to try and sort the problem out. I didn't have games on this particular Tuesday so I'd put them on, not for one moment imagining I was seconds away from bending over the head's desk with them on full display. This was a fucking nightmare.

'Right Dunn, before I cane you have you got anything you want to say?'

Boldness got the better of me because I just knew I was going to cry and along with the humiliation of my Demis Roussos pants, it really couldn't get a lot worse. All the lads would know I'd blabbed so any street cred from being whacked would evaporate anyway.

'I know what I'd like to say sir.'

'Well. I always feel under these circumstances that if there's anything you want to get off your chest, then now is the time to do it Dunn.'

God, it sounded more like an execution was about to take place never mind a caning.

'Anything sir?'

'Within reason Dunn yes.'

'Right then ... Mortimer's a low-life creep and a grass, sir.'

'You're allowed to THINK that Dunn but you're certainly not allowed to say it. Got it?'

'Y'sir. Okay, *I think* he's a low-life creep and a grass sir.'

Porter smiled thankfully. 'I like your style Dunn. Between you and me I'm not much into tell-tales either but that's not the point right now.'

'Well it is the point to me sir. How many are you going to give me?'

'Let me see Dunn. It was going to be six. I'll half that to three and bearing in mind that you've not been in trouble before, we'll call it two eh?'

'Thanks sir,' I muttered. Thanks? What the fuck was I on about? I'm going to get two hefty whacks right on my baggy pants, that wouldn't fit me until I was 38, and I was thanking him. Barmy.

I took the punishment but just couldn't stop the tears which had welled in my eyes from cascading down my face and tried to compose myself as I obeyed Mr Porter's instruction to make my way to lessons. I thought it was really good of my mates to be so sympathetic that they were all crying too, but once their laughter had subsided, I made my way towards the cloakroom to wash my face and calm down.

Most of the other lads had made their way to lessons as I stood under coat peg 202 and winced at the stinging sensation on my backside. I could only have been there no more than five minutes when I could make out a commotion immediately outside the cloakroom and Mrs Robinson came charging in. She turned midstream and bellowed to someone standing outside.

'You, my lad, stay there and make sure no one comes in. And I'll speak to you later. You'll find out one day that there's nothing worse than someone who tells tales about other people. So stay there, shut up and wait for me to come back.'

'Yes, miss,' I could hear come back from someone who sounded remarkably like Mortimer. How on earth Mrs Robinson had got to hear about my caning so quickly was beyond me, but I was going to have to ask her not to tell my dad.

'And shut the door Mortimer' she bellowed, beside herself with rage

'You okay?' came the enquiry as she sat down next to me and

cupped my face with her hand.

'Yes Miss.'

'Is it right you got caned on the say so of that sour-faced old battleaxe in the library?'

'I'm not sure what she said Miss to be honest.'

'I'm not having this,' she whispered. 'You shouldn't get the cane for this. How many did he give you?'

'Two Miss.'

'The boys all think you've had six.'

'That's because I told them I'd had six.'

'Good lad. You go and wash your face and I'm going to have a word with her about this.'

'I'd rather you didn't Miss. It's done now.'

'I'm going to let her know exactly what I think about it, don't you worry about that.'

'Miss . . .'

'What?'

'I'd be really grateful if you didn't tell my dad.'

'I wouldn't do that sweetheart. Not been a good week has it?'

'Not exactly Miss, no.'

'Run along,' she said giving me a hug, assuring me no one could see. 'Course I won't tell your dad. Now go and get yourself off to whatever lesson you've got and if they ask why you're late just say you had to see the head, okay?'

'Okay Miss.'

As I shuffled towards the washbasins, I could hear Mrs Robinson tearing a strip off Mortimer and telling him in no uncertain terms that no one liked a snitch.

'Snitch?' I wasn't happy with that word because it sounded kind of cute and harmless. Tosser was a far better word and if any good had come out of this whole sorry affair then at least I'd had the satisfaction of seeing the head, somewhat reluctantly agree with the observation. And Jimmy Osmond was still number fucking one . . .

26

IMPURE MATHS

June, 1973 and the sunshine glinting on the rugby posts outside only served to make the prospect of a double science period all the more daunting.

'Load up, load up, load up, with ruuuu-bber johnnies,' John Wagstaffe mouthed quietly prompting giggles among the five of us occupying one of the two back benches in Lab 30. The laughter hadn't quite diminished enough for the liking of Mr Hartson who promptly restored order with a sharp rap of the blackboard duster and a deftly aimed piece of chalk which just missed Wagger's left ear and ricocheted off the wall immediately behind us.

'QUIET!' he screamed, mouthing instructions to Mrs Robinson who was peering around the door of the back room, situated to the right of the blackboard,

'Right you rabble. Wagstaffe!!! Cut it out. Today we will be doing an experiment exploring the principles of streamlining and aerodynamics,' declared Mr Hartson pointing towards two thin glass tubes, which must have been all of five feet high standing upright, at the front of the class.

Mr Hartson moved carefully towards the tubes explaining that they were to be filled with a mystery solution and that we should now each break the lumps of blue plasticine at each desk into pieces and make various shaped objects.

'Now we are all aware of the basics of streamlining because we see it in our everyday lives. Why is a car shaped as it is for example? How does a dolphin's shape help it through the water? And so on. So what I want you all to do is to make a number of

147

different shapes and when we drop them into the tubes we can analyse which ones move through the tube quickest and just how much difference in terms of time there is between, for example, a cube and a torpedo shape,' he explained.

'Now Mrs Robinson is just preparing some solution for the tubes so while she's doing that, if you lot would like to make some shapes, let's have a nice variety eh? And then we'll split up into two groups.'

Wagger suggested a penis shape which prompted a further bout of chuckling and a warning from Hartson that anyone not taking the experiment seriously wouldn't do it because they'd be standing outside with their hands on their heads. Wagger was now backing his enthusiasm for a dick-shaped projectile with sound scientific reasoning for it being aerodynamic but quickly rolled it up into a ball when Hartson started walking behind the desks line-by-line to see how we were all getting on. Then Wagger came out with an absolutely astonishing revelation as he jabbed away at his calculator.

'You know that Rubber Johnnies song . . .'

'Bullets'

'Yeah that one,' he continued. 'You know how 10cc came up with their name?'

'Go on' said Billy Downes sitting immediately next to Professor Wagstaffe.

'It's how much you shoot when you come.'

'Bollocks,' said Phil Edwards, staggered by the suggestion.

'No, from your bollocks you mong. S'right you know.'

'That's shite,' guffawed John Ellis.

'S'right. I read it in Melody Maker. They are all brainy bastards you know and one of 'em was reading somewhere when he was at university and he read that when you shoot your load there's roughly 10cc of it.'

'What . . . spunk?'

'Course you twat. What do you shoot from yours, Turkish Delight?'

'So they decided to call the band after that?'

'I've never heard anything so soft in my life,' I countered.

'Gospel. I read it.'

'Why didn't they call themselves Spunk then?'

''Cos you can't call a band Spunk, can you? They'd ban it.'

'Well they've banned the record anyway so what's the difference.'

'Yeah but that's different,' countered Wagger, refusing to budge on his theory.

'You couldn't call it that because the DJ's would refuse to say it and people wouldn't be able to ask for it in shops and stuff like that.'

'Be a good laugh though wouldn't it?' smiled Ian. 'Just imagine a girl going into a shop and saying she wanted Spunk or Whispering Bob Harris saying that he thought Spunk would shoot up the charts.'

'Bet she's had some in her time,' Wagger mumbled as Mrs Robinson momentarily appeared from the back room to pick up a measuring jug from Hartson's desk.

'You're fucking horrible Wagger,' I interrupted.

Mrs Robinson was indeed looking particularly fine today. She had a lovely tan and her golden brown face was lightly freckled. She had a slight quiff in her fringe and her hair seemed a little longer at the back as it nudged the collar of the pristine white lab coat.

Wagger was jabbing frantically at his calculator, tittering to himself as he jotted down calculations and was now desperately motioning us to move within earshot.

'How many boys at this school?' he whispered.

'About 600-odd'

'Well, lets call that 500 just in case there are any poofters or limpdicks. Let's just say there's 10 of the masters and there must be 10 of her neighbours who fantasise about her as well - Dunny for a start - that's 520,' Wagger continued.

'So?'

'Right, well, here's my theory. Just say there's 520 who have one off the wrist over her at least once a week.'

'What d'ya mean over her?'

'Not literally you twat, just imagining they're doing it with her. So that's 520 10cc's a week for her alone. That means that Mrs Robinson is responsible for about 5000 cc's every single week. And that's just a rough estimate.'

'You are one sicko Wagger,' John interrupted.

'Well, work it out yourself. It's an unbelievable figure. So, lets go one step further. If there's 16 waking hours in the day . . . that's 112 in a week. Multiply that by . . . sixty' Wagger jabbed frantically.

"So that's 6,720 minutes and divide that by the 520. Fuckin' hell. That's 12.923076, call it 13. Every 13 minutes of every single day someone is shooting their load over Mrs Robinson.'

'Good job it isn't actually over her then,' tittered Ian. 'Poor woman would practically be embalmed. She'd drown in it.'

'Yeah, what a thought, eh?'

'You are one sick twat Wagger,' I observed.

'Sick? Me? Fucking hell if only she knew what an incredible ratio she'd got she ought to be very, very proud.'

'Oh yeah, I'm sure she'd be delighted.'

'We'll leave you to tell her Dunny.'

'Oh marvellous yeah, will do. "Oh Mrs Robinson , thought you ought to know you are personally responsible for severe wrist injuries at school. There's about 500 lads, at least 10 masters and 10 of your neighbours who have all got permanent hard-ons thinking about you. At the last count there was a cock going off about every 13 minutes Mrs Robinson, you should be very proud.'

'That's more semen than in the Royal Navy!' Wagger exclaimed, unable to contain his amusement.

Hartson was homing in on the back bench once again.

'I've warned you once Wagstaffe. One more disruption and you're out and I'll give you a detention.'

'Sir.'

'That goes for the lot of you,' he added pointing to our group.

'I won't have it. Right, bring your shapes and form yourself into two groups at the front of the class. And mind the tubes because they won't take much knocking over."

Hartson poked his head around the door and signalled to Mrs Robinson that he was now ready for the tubes to be filled with what transpired to be a weak mixture of Polycell wallpaper paste. Mrs Robinson came in carrying a red plastic bucket and a funnel and carefully started to fill the first tube. Wagger was in major difficulty and in grave danger of bursting into an uncontrollable fit of laughter. As she finished filling the first tube, you could see her mentally mulling over how to get the funnel into the second tube without making a mess, and she ended up putting her hand over the bottom of it, while passing the still half full bucket to Hartson. Placing the funnel into the second tube, Mrs Robinson spread her hand out in front of her to reveal long strings of wallpaper paste dangling from her fingers. Wagger could contain himself no longer. The sight of Hartson coming to her aid, by producing a handkerchief from his pocket, was the signal for Wagger to erupt into violent giggles and he was frogmarched out of the room by his ear with tears streaming down his face. Mrs Robinson smiled seemingly perplexed by the commotion the spillage had caused. It was a couple of days later as I waited for Rob to find his football boots that she begged to be let in on the secret.

'What did Wagstaffe find so funny the other day?'

'Oh I don't know it was nothing really.'

'Seemed to cause quite a bit of amusement considering it was nothing.'

'Oh it was you know, just something that was said a bit earlier and we were giggling.'

'About me?'

'No not directly, no, it was nothing honestly.'

Not directly about her, no. How can you discuss Wagger's Mrs Robinson theory and say it wasn't about her directly. Then again, how do you tell the school lab assistant who is also your best mate's mom that she is the object of sexual curiosity to 500 boys at various stages of puberty, a number of her colleagues and half

151

the neighbourhood. 'So come on then. What was said?'

'Nothing, honest. You know I think he's just got a bit of a crush on you, that kind of thing . . . ' I blurted out stupidly.

'On me? You're joking. I'm old enough to be his mother.'

'Well, you know, just . . . er. You know how it is,' I babbled.

'No I don't really but I suppose I should be flattered. Struth I'm 33 for God's sake. He must be hard-up or fed-up. John Wagstaffe . . . well, I never,' Mrs Robinson smiled.

27

IN AT THE DEEP END

News of Jimmy Hunt's accident had the neighbours out in the streets - not in celebration, but more morbid curiosity. It was serious. Lucky to be alive, was the general feedback; chance he'd never come out of his coma. Even though I would never have dared say it, I just wasn't bothered. How much had he ever bothered about me? The square root of fuck-all, that's how much. It would have been bad form to do cartwheels in the street shouting 'Who's the spaz now then?' but inside that's exactly what I felt like doing. And if that sounds a trifle cruel, then so be it, the manner of his plunge onto the critical list, amused me even more. It seemed like bullying and being an obnoxious twat was his only forte - when it came to getting anything else right he struggled. No one wants to die or be in a serious accident, but there is a certain kudos in doing it gloriously if the situation arises. Elvis might have been The King, the greatest entertainer who ever lived and a sex symbol to boot, but the image of him being found on the bathroom floor halfway through having a shit, does kind of stick with you.

And so not only did I wish Jimmy to be on the wrong end of a serious mishap, the icing on the cake would have been for it to have some sort of comic element. Plunging into a swimming pool and breaking your neck along with serious head injuries because it was empty does take some beating. There is a God after all. The fact that Jimmy missed the last 12 days of his 14-day holiday in Spain was neither here nor there. The early indications were not good. The only plus to it all was that his court hearing to answer a number of offences ranging from petty theft to assault, had been postponed indefinitely. Presumably the police wanted time to wipe their eyes.

If not, and without wishing to pre-judge the case against him, he might have suffered a long and lingering death in borstal with 100 points on the driving licence he never actually had. As it happened, not by so much a stroke of luck but rather unbelievable misfortune, he beat the judicial system to it. Now he could do his time in the luxury of his own wheelchair. News of Jimmy's accident just a few weeks short of his 17th birthday - when he actually would have been eligible to apply for a driving licence - spread through the village like a bushfire. You know how your parents always say that they can remember exactly where they were when they heard the news that John F. Kennedy had been assasinated, well, it was the same with me, Muldoon, Pele and the crew when a mutual acquaintance of ours - Mr Tate the newsagent - enquired as to whether we'd heard about the untimely fate which had befallen Jimmy. Pointing to the headline 'EMPTY POOL YOUTH CRITICAL', Mr Tate grabbed our attention more than adequately enough to distract us from the magazine shelves.

'Mate of yours isn't he?' asked Mr Tate, a rotund man with a jolly, fleshy face.

'Jesus, it's Jimmy Hunt,' exclaimed Rob.

'Sounds bad,' said Pele.

'Mystery surrounds the circumstances of the accident,'Rob went on. 'Spanish police are appealing for witnesses.'

Though Jimmy hadn't a friend among us, reading of his ordeal in cold print was something of a shock.

When you are kids, unless some particularly horrific tragedy befalls your family, death isn't something that really affects you. Okay, so you might have a gran that dies or something like that, but it's hardly front page news unless she was scuba diving at the time. But here it was, on the front page of the local evening paper. Jimmy Hunt had been critically injured. Forget any notions that hardnut Jimmy had lost control of his 750 Kawasaki and slid under a milk lorry at high speed. Oh no, not Jimmy. He probably could have coped with that. Dying in a James Dean kind of way might have been considered a fitting end, but he wasn't to enjoy such a glorious fate. Jimmy hadn't even got a motorbike - he used to tazz around the place on a souped up Honda moped which looked like a mini-motorbike. They were all the craze because you could have them at 16 without having to take any test and they really used to shift. They might only have been 49.999cc so as to classify as a moped but everyone knew it was the biggest case of bending the law possible and they were like shit off a shovel. What had happened to Jimmy bordered on the comical if splitting your head open like an over-ripe water melon lends itself to such a description.

As the weeks went by Jimmy's accident acquired a stamp of immortality on it for all the wrong reasons. Long after the national papers had lost interest in the story, the Shropshire Star billboards identified him as 'EMPTY POOL YOUTH.' Apparently Jimmy's mother had phoned to complain but to no avail. And so Jimmy, Joe Fucking Cool, local hard case would forever be remembered as the empty pool youth. EMPTY POOL YOUTH LATEST was followed by various permutations like POOL YOUTH HOME or POOL YOUTH 'STABLE'. Jimmy's family must have been chuffed to little cotton balls. Certain deaths which reach the public domain do have a certain coolness. No matter which theory you subscribe to, John F Kennedy's final seconds in the Dallas motorcade have a certain mystique about them. The grassy knoll, poor Jackie cradling his head in her lap - the part of it that wasn't smeared over her dress that is - the conspiracy theory, it's compelling stuff. In a way it's a fitting and dramatic way for a charismatic president to be remembered. It's peculiarly glorious in the same morbid way Jimmy Dean's car crash guaranteed him iconic status even though he only made three piss-poor films. Even if the circumstances aren't so great, if it's fitting it works. Take

Tommy Cooper for example, getting a standing ovation as he popped his clogs behind the curtain on stage - that's cool. Sid Vicious might have died in squalor, drowning in vomit with a big, fat, fishnet stockinged tart at his side but somehow it was a fitting way to go for a punk star. What must be really hard to stomach if you knew anything about it, is dying in either unfitting or particularly distasteful circumstances. Elvis would have been devastated if he'd known just how he was going to go. Marvin Gaye's another. Top guy, Motown legend and master of the all-time great love songs, the man whose music most people have shagged to at one time or another and look what happens to him. There's not too much romance in having your head shot off by your own father now is there? Bob Marley . . . the list is endless. All time Mr Cool, Mr Ganja, Mr Dreadlocked rebel and how does he eventually go - cancer of the toe. Fuck me - very uncool Bob. The trouble is when you are in the public eye, every last detail comes out and is given a right blast by the media. How about the guy who drowned in Michael Barrymore's pool? Now if he'd have known what was in store for him that night, he'd have left that fucking nightclub a lot earlier. Bad enough that you're found floating face down in a swimming pool, albeit a celebrity's, but then the inquest comes out and reveals that your body had a sexual injury which would have probably made it difficult to walk! Brilliant - now that's really what you'd need to be made public isn't it? At least the pool wasn't empty.

It struck me that Jimmy had done a kind of Christopher Reeve. It just doesn't seem right that a man who can save the planet as Superman and fly around the earth six times in the time it takes you to eat your tea, becomes a quadriplegic after falling off the family horse. It's just incongruous. One minute he's saving the world and the next he's in a wheelchair. Don't get me wrong, I've nothing but total admiration for Christopher and his brave fight in the face of adversity, but I struggle with it and I don't feel any better for admitting that. Anyway, how would he get that fucking wheelchair in a phone box for a start off? Eddie

Kidd's another. Christ, he was cool. He had smouldering good looks and a pop star lifestyle and what happens? Just when he needs a really good fucking jump, it all goes wrong at the end and he goes over the edge of that mound. I could have told him - when you need help from a bank, you just don't get it . . .

28

ONE HUNDRED AND EIGHTEE . . .

I had such a long list of things I could brag that I'd done before losing my virginity that had it not been for the fact that I was 6ft 2in and just 16, you could have been forgiven for assuming that I was an extremely sad and unattractive 60-year-old. Getting laid just hadn't happened despite my best efforts and it had become a bit of an ache. I'd been for a pint with my dad - not bad; I'd seen Soldier Blue in all it's gory glory; reeled back in horror at The Exorcist, especially when Rob had dropped a wine gum down my back just as Linda Blair's head was doing the full 360; and seen Lynda Bellingham get her tits out in that Confessions masterpiece. A reasonably impressive list, I think you'd agree. Sure I'd been close, but that's like a frustrated striker hitting the woodwork on several occasions and trudging off bemoaning his luck. No fucking goal - end of story. I was desperate to score with a girl - almost any girl. There were a few exceptions even if the exempt list got smaller by the day. One off-limits was most definitely Linda Blair- Regan to her friends! The Exorcist just had to be the the No1 scare-the-shit out of you film of a generation. If seeing Linda transform from a pretty 10-year-old whose only crime was to piss on the carpet at an important dinner party into a raging monster who loved nothing better than projecting Batchelor's pea soup into people's faces from a good 15 yards didn't put you off slipping between the sheets with the fairer sex, then nothing would. Wow, that was some film and guess what? Yeah, right first time, they BANNED it. I was hoping that perhaps by the time I'd got towards the end of my teens the powers-that-be might have all fucked off and

158

given us a break, but no. If it's any good, ban it - and it didn't stop there. Soldier Blue, a terrific film -BANNED. Clockwork Orange - BANNED. Fortunately for Rob and me, we beat them to it and managed to get into all three of those(there should be some sort of decoration or certificate for that) at the sleaziest picture house in town. Rob could get in because he had really filled out in the past 12 months thanks to rugby practice and virtually had a beard. I was still alarmingly fresh-faced but I was bigger than the attendants who asked me my age out of a sense of duty and didn't seem that bothered anyway. The Exorcist frightened the living daylights out of us. It was that scary that we didn't need to go through the tough-guy pretext of telling your mates who couldn't get in that it wasn't that scary. It was ultra-frightening in fairness. There were rumours that young Linda was supposedly mentally damaged by it all and I don't have a problem with that because I can still remember leaving The Grand cinema that night puffing out into the night air in relief just to have got through the darned thing. This Regan was scarier than anything John Thaw was about to throw up in The Sweeney, that's for sure. I couldn't help wondering about the sanity of the poor sod who ended up marrying her. Just imagine having cleaned your teeth and going into the bedroom to where she was waiting for you and by chance she was back on to the way you were facing. Oh my God! Don't turn round love, I'll be there in a minute. I just still have visions of her exploding into festering blisters and shouting 'Fuck ME!' in that voice from the bottom of the pit of hell. Cheers Linda, nice thought, but I'll watch a bit of telly if it's all the same to you.

The opening scene of Soldier Blue is still imprinted on my psyche even after all these years. I remember the scene where the US cavalry man gets that Indian squaw's breast and just cuts it off like he was slicing into an orange, and a woman dashing out of the cinema shouting 'You fucking bastards' quickly followed by her rather embarrassed boyfriend, spilling Clarnico mint creams all over the place. I'm not sure how that spontaneous outburst compares with another cracker I witnessed when watching Carrie at the pictures. That was a bit different at the time too. There's a scene in Carrie where Cissy Spacek gets seriously pissed off with her lunatic mom and starts projecting things through the air with the power of thought. Mad mom, eventually gets pinned against the door or whatever by these flying daggers which even by Carrie's barmy standards, did seem a trifle harsh. Anyway, I'm sitting there at the cinema when THWACK, the first dagger impales mom by the arm; THWACK a second pins back her other arm. You can cut the atmosphere in The Grand with the proverbial knife, but when a third one hits mom full in the chest with a bone-crunching THWACK, a lad in the audience shouts 'ONE HUNDRED AND EIGHTEEEE!' Superb. You couldn't make it up. Clockwork Orange was serious shit too. Great film - but try reading the book. It's not the best decision I ever made. Anthony Burgess might have been brilliant but he was one strange bloody guy. And they banned it, of course, but I didn't give a toss because my coolness factor multiplied by 100 merely because I'd got in to see it. And, while we're boasting, even the Oxo mom wasn't safe from my attentions. Yeah, Lynda Bellingham, who would have thought it? let Robin Asquith get her not inconsiderable charms out in the Confessions film and set a million teenage hearts pounding. This was as hard as it got and I could never have imagined that a couple of decades later she'd be wheeling out gravy dinners to her grateful family as the bastion of middle-aged mums the length and breadth of the land.

So that leaves going for a pint with my dad; a turning point in any young man's life. This should have been bonding of the highest order, and that a good 25 years before bonding was fashionable and acceptable. In the mid-70s there were only three kind of bonds - Premium, James and Brooke. In fact, on the day that dad casually asked me if I fancied going for a pint as if it was something he did all the time, I should have guessed there might be a hidden agenda somewhere. I can recall it like it was yesterday. He'd always been pretty good on that front and I'd had the odd shandy on special occasions before. But to actually go out for a pint? To a pub no less? Brilliant. It was around midday on a Saturday afternoon and he just kind of came out with it. Something just had to be afoot.

'Fancy a pint, son?'

'What?'

'I said, d'ya fancy a beer?'

'Yeah okay,' I replied, thoroughly expecting him to go into the garage and appear with two bottles of Watney's or whatever.

'Stick something decent on then and we'll pop down The Granville or The Black for an hour.'

Fucking hell. The Granville? The Granville Arms was a pub at the bottom of our road and thus far, the outdoor was as far as I'd ventured on my occasional trips to get my mom 10 Gold Leaf and 20 Players for dad in the more liberal times when youngsters could go and get fags without the accompanying sound of screeching brakes as the Flying Squad pulled up outside and bundled you into the back of a brown Ford Granada. The Black was The Foresters Arms, but you very rarely heard people call it by it's proper name. It was a black and white pub, hence The Black. It was no more profound than that. I should have known something was brewing as I went upstairs, combed my hair, slipped out of my patched jeans and slipped some patch-pocket cords on. Checking my shirt wasn't flapping around at the back, I signalled I was ready as dad motioned me towards the front door.

'Come on then. Oi, just don't tell your mother,' said dad with a wink. He often said that these days and I was never quite sure if he knew how often she said 'Don't tell your dad.'

My chest was bursting with pride, my mind laced with suspicion. This was unusual behaviour. I knew Arthur Jeffs, the landlord, was well aware I wasn't 18, but it was a local of dad's so I knew he must have been absolutely confident I would not only be allowed in, but that I was also at liberty to order a pint. Arthur was a dapper man who always wore a tie no matter what the weather or the occasion. He'd been landlord for around five years after taking early retirement from the police force. He had silver hair and a matching, neat, moustache and stood exactly 5ft 7inches and a quarter in his stockinged feet. The reason I can be so precise on that measurement is that he'd had good reason to be grateful for that quarter-of-an inch. It had played a not insignificant part in Arthur's life when he was trying to get into the force. Although he was a local man by birth he had tried, with considerable gusto, but no success to join the West Mercia Constabulary but fell short of their minimum height limit. He told the story against himself that even after sticking padded bunion plasters to the soles of his feet, one on top of the other, he still hadn't been able to elevate himself to the heady height of 5ft 8in required to realise his ambition. Such was his desire to become a bobby that he'd moved to London to join the Met, which was suffering a recruitment crisis and had lowered its requirement by an inch, leaving the door open for Arthur to get in. The story goes that as a raw, young beat bobby he had been given a notoriously rough area in the East End docks to patrol one night when he became aware of some suspicious activity over on the far side of the canal path where he was walking his beat. Over-enthusiastic and more than a little curious to investigate, Arthur had made his way towards the commotion and with the aid of his torch picked out the silhouette of a giant of a man with a crate under each arm. This guy was about 6ft 6in and as far across, according to Arthur but, undeterred, the slightly-built and diminutive rookie decided to enquire as to what was going on. Chest puffed out and virtually walking tippy-toe, Arthur approaches the man mountain and makes enquiries.

'What you got under your arms mate?' says Arthur.

The brute looks him full in the face and snaps 'Fucking hairs! What you got under yours?'

It was a lovely tale which had matured beautifully with age and the assured delivery of a man who had told it on more occasions than he cared to recall.

'Hope you've got some money,' said dad.

'Course,' I replied.

162

'Bit of advice, son - nowt worse than a bloke who doesn't stand his round,' he smiled.

'No problem,' I replied, just praying that when he said 'round' he meant mine and his and not five or six of his drinking buddies who might be in there.

"What's this about?' I couldn't help but enquire.

'What's all what about?'

'This.'

'Bloody hell. Bad job when a grown man can't take his son for a pint isn't it?'

'Well . . .'

'Listen. You're growing up fast. I'd rather you feel you can go for a pint than skulk off doing it and thinking it's something out of the ordinary. I won't be able to stop you shortly anyway so what's the point? Might as well do it in the open.'

'Excellent. Why don't you want me to tell mom then?'

'No reason. Tell her if you want, but you know what women are like?'

Well, not in the biblical sense, but a couple of pints would certainly do for now, I mused, not realising as we walked through the door that dad was about to unleash another bombshell in my direction immediately after he walked back from the bar with two creamy pints of bitter.

'Cheers, son. Good health.'

'Yeah, cheers dad,' I replied, glass raised, head cocked slightly sideways.

We exchanged small talk; we recalled the day he'd taken me to Wolves to see George Best and Bobby Charlton play for Manchester United; the subject of my 'A' levels was merely raised in passing and then it came. I fucking knew it . . .

'Keeps a good pint here does Arthur . . .'

'Yeah, seems fine.'

'Ron, my mate at work, tells me he's been seeing a bit of you just lately. Do you know Ron?'

Thinks: Think I've met him once. Don't really know. How's he seen me? Where's he seen me? What's this leading to?'

163

'Not sure, why?'

'Oh he just mentioned it in passing the other day. Just said that he thought he'd seen you up in Chestnut Drive - up in Ketley. Said I wasn't sure . . .'

Thinks: Fucking hell. Chestnut Drive Christine Trollope's house. Me and a few other lads had been up there in recent weeks because her mom worked in the day and she and her mate Shelly regularly skipped school.

'Oh right yeah. Me and the boys know a couple of girls up there. If we've got free periods or after school we nip over there sometimes. They're mates of ours.'

'The one who lives at the back of Ron's. Christine is it? She's mates with quite a few people from what he tells me.'

'Yeah, she's a nice girl. She's got a lot of friends.'

'Ron says she's very popular.'

Oh oh! Come on dad, spit it out.

'Yeah, we just play records and stuff. You know. Pass a bit of time; have a coffee. You know how it is?'

'Yeah I know how it is son. Well if you want my advice . . .'

Actually I don't but odds-on I'm going to get it and right now by the sounds of it.

'Just be careful son. She's got a bit of a reputation by all accounts.'

Exactly! Christine Trollope has got quite a reputation and that's why me and half of the fifth year find her such beguiling company.

'That's unfair. She's okay.'

'Look, I'm not interfering. Just be careful that's all. Bit of fatherly advice doesn't hurt sometimes. I'm a man of the world you know . . .'

You are interfering. You are a man of the 'born in 1935' world when mom had to be in at 9.30 the week she got married world. Things have fucking well changed and I want part of it.

'I'm sure she's fine. Trollope, did you say? All I'm saying is, well, there's a lot of things about these days and you can't be too careful.'

'Like what dad?'

'Well, like VD for a kick-off. You can't be too careful.'

VD - marvellous. Oh God give me a dose of that or at least the chance to catch it. Fuck the shame. 'Just been down the clinic.' Yeah, sounded good to me. I didn't want it but what the fuck, just getting the all-clear and the swab down the end stuff, had its appeal. VD? Not the end of the world; not mine anyway.

'Come on, dad, this is 1975 for God's sake.'

'Exactly. Well anyway, don't get bringing any trouble to this door; that's all I've got to say.

The old 'Don't go bringing any trouble to this door' line. What door? The Granville Arms door? No, the No78 Sandpiper Road door I presume.'

'She's just a friend. I do have friends of the opposite sex you know. I'm not going to bring any trouble to the door, so don't worry.'

'It's my job to worry. You know what I'm saying. It's all too easy to get a girl in the family way and spend you're entire life regretting it. I don't want that for you Paul.'

Look dad, it's not that easy to get a girl pregnant from 50 fucking yards unless your sperm is so active it can by-pass two roads, a railway line and 15 yards of front lawn.'

'She's okay.'

'Enough said. All I'm saying is that, not to put it too bluntly, she's got a reputation for being a bit of a bike.

Fantastic. Just what I need right now. And this is coming from the bloke who thought a Raleigh Chopper wasn't a sensible thing to ride! Fuck me, dad. And what do you mean 'not to put it too bluntly?' Any blunter and my head would have shallow depressions in it. Okay, she's potentially a scrubber. Marvellous.

'Let's have a beer anyway. That wasn't the point of the exercise. I'm saying be careful, because, well, she's a bit loose by all accounts. Ron's missus was saying she lies out in the back garden and leaves nothing to the imagination.'

Oh fuck. Right. So Ron's perving away over the just 16-year-

old Trollope at every available opportunity. His wife's beside herself and I end up copping it- that's really fair. Loose? What's fucking loose? I want a girl whose innards are in danger of dropping out.

'End of subject. Anyway, I thought you were holding a torch for Denise down the road. Now, she's a nice girl.'

'Yeah, she's really nice.'

'Well then.'

Dad, you sound pathetic when you say 'well then'. Like as if that's sorted that all out then. Mom will be pleased. Denise is a very nice girl. Yes, she's well mannered. Yes, she's very clean. Yes, mom and you like her. We're not talking marriage here. I'll bring a nice girl home to marry. Rest assured on that. Sleep easy on that one. I won't bring Christine home for your approval. And what do you mean 'holding a torch.' What kind of a fuckwit parent saying is that? Let me tell you dad, I'm in desperate need of some gynaecological exploration and with Denise you'd need more than a torch. If you think I'm walking down the road with a miner's lamp strapped to my head, just to please you, forget it.

'Anyway, it's good to have a chat man to man as it were. It's only 'cos I care. Enough said. D'ya wanna pint?'

'I'll get 'em dad.'

'Cheers son. That'd be great. Proud day in a man's life when his son buys him a pint for the first time. By the way . . .'

'Go on.'

'Can I have one of your fags while we're at it.'

Fucking hell what's going on here? Now he's going to give me a lecture on fucking smoking. I don't need this.'

'Errr . . .'

'Come on son, get your fags out. You've been smoking for ages. You didn't honestly think I didn't know did you?'

'Well.'

'Hey, no point being made. Get your fags out.'

I proudly ordered two pints of best bitter and turned from the bar, fumbling in my pocket for my cash and the slightly squashed pack of 10 Embassy Regal. I tossed the pack over towards my dad, sitting at the side of the one-armed bandit.

'Cheers.   Hey, another thing . . . '

'What?'

'Don't tell your mother.'

29

SOUL SISTER

I'd only had two pints, but I ended up spending most of that Saturday afternoon dozing off in the chair with only the briefest of interruptions from Dickie Davies and the ITV World of Sport programme. With the football season well and truly over, I more likely than not had the dubious attraction of World Cup skiing, athletics or rally car driving from God-knows-where to try and capture my attention - and whatever it was, it failed miserably. I had football on my mind, however, because that night I had been invited to a meeting at the Cross Keys, a pub at the farthest end of the village to discuss the formation of a new Sunday Morning League soccer side. Rob knew the landlord's son and had been given strict instructions to be there and to bring me along. That plan had been slightly scuppered by the fact that Rob had been forced to go away on a training course from work and so he'd rung me just before I'd nipped down the Granville with dad to remind me not to miss it.

Mom had rustled up a sandwich for me before she and dad made their way off to Pat and Ken's - friends of theirs who had moved to Banbury. They were going to be staying over and as mom did one final bit of fussing just to make absolutely sure I would be all right. She reminded me there was a back door key hidden under an upturned plant pot outside, just in case, while dad slipped me a couple of quid with a wink and assured her I was more than capable of looking after myself for one night. They'd be back at lunchtime the next day and mom double-checked I'd heard her instruction that if there was any problem, Ken's number was by the side of the phone. It was turning into a bit of an unusual weekend all in all, given the unexpected lunchtime trip to the pub and everything. Rob was away; Pele had never developed an interest in football and hadn't even come into consideration for an invite to the inaugural meeting of Cross Keys United or whatever the meeting ended up deciding they would be called. After a quick bath, I slipped on my tonics, a brilliant two-tone shimmering blue and maroon and my short-sleeved Adidas top and made my way towards the door. A dab of Brut before slipping into my black loafers and I was ready to make my way towards the alley adjoining our house, across the rec and over the Manor School fields to cut my way down to the pub. Making a few last checks - key, money, fags, lighter, I clicked the front door behind me, unsure what the night held in store for me. It was 6.45, the meeting had been called for 7.30 and Pele and Muldoon had said they might pop down and meet up with me later once all that 'football team bollocks' was out of the way.

'Nice night Dunny, you off birding it I suppose?' said Mr Perry from down the road.

'Nah, I'm off to the pub,' I replied manfully.

'Pub? Lucky you. Wish I was, that's for sure. She won't rest until I've got these borders done,' he said with an exagerrated groan, flicking his head in the general direction of the house, where I presumed Mrs Perry lay in waiting.

'Ah well, can't win 'em all,' I said sympathetically.

'Yeah you go and enjoy yourself, son. You're only young once.'

'Cheers, see you Mr Perry.'

I liked the sound of the word 'cheers'. It had a certain manliness all of its own. Great word. It just sounded so profoundly right.

I popped back just to check I'd closed the windows at the rear of the house and made my way back along the side when my attention was caught by Rosie, hose pipe in hand, spraying the front lawn and borders of the Robinson's garden. I couldn't help noticing her white skimpy shorts were exceptionally tight and she had a light green bikini top on, half concealed by an unbuttoned cheesecloth top.

'Hi Dunny. Where you off to?'

'Oh I've got a football meeting.'

'Where's that?'

'Down the Keys.'

'Is that the thing our Rob was on about?'

'Yeah, he rang me this morning just to remind me.'

'Seems like everybody has got something to do 'round here except me.'

'Ahhh.'

'Oh it's all right for you. I'm stuck here on my own.'

'Oh right,' I said, recalling Mr and Mrs Robinson had gone down to the caravan in Borth for the weekend.

'How come you haven't gone with 'em?'

'Oh I couldn't be bothered. I've been that many times, it's just not the same anymore. Got better things to do.'

'What? Like watering the garden and being stuck in on your own? Sounds great.'

'Tell me about it. I didn't realise Hazel was away as well. Still, not to worry eh?'

'At least there's no one to mither you Rosie?'

'Hmm, I should be so lucky.'

'Duuunneee . . .'she said in the sort of way you just know precedes a request for something.

'What?'

'Can I borrow a couple of your LP's to listen to? I'm fed up with mine.'

'Yeah, sure. I'll pop 'em round in the morning. Which one's do you want?'

I knew Rosie was into Northern Soul and couldn't imagine that she'd want any of the stuff I'd got.

'I haven't got Wigan's Chosen Few you know? Or Kenny or The Rubettes for that matter.'

'Fuck off Dunny' she said somewhat harshly.

'Rob said you've got Sheer Heart Attack. I wouldn't mind

170

borrowin' that.'

'Okay. But look after it. I don't want it coming back scratched.'

'Course I will. You got Band on the Run, as well?'

'You know I have.'

'Wouldn't mind listening to that too.'

'Oh okay.'

'Dunneee . . .'

'Oh what Rosie?'

'Can you pop and get them for me now?'

'Jesus, Rosie I've got a meeting to get to.'

'Oh go on, please' she pleaded.

'Ok. I'll nip back and get them.'

I returned two minutes later with the the Queen and Wings albums and handed them over, imploring her to take maximum care or risk an untimely death.

'Ta, Dunny. Would you do me one more favour?'

'What now?'

'Can I nick a couple of fags off you. I'll give 'em back.'

'I didn't know you smoked Rose.'

'I've grown up a bit, you know.'

'I'm sure, but . . .'

'Oh don't start Dunny.'

'I wasn't starting. Here.' I handed over two cigarettes and she popped them into the top pocket of her shirt.

'Thanks, You're an angel.'

'I know.'

'What time does the meeting finish?'

'Dunno. Why?'

'Well, I was just wondering . . .'

'Go on.'

'Well if it wasn't too late. D'ya fancy coming 'round later and listening to your records.'

'Can't do that.'

'Why not?'

'Well what would the neighbours think for a start-off what

171

with your mom and dad being away and all?'

'So.'

'Never mind *so*. Come on Rosie. It'd look a bit funny for a start off.'

'Scaredy cat.'

'It's not that. You know how it is . . .'

'I can't believe you Dunny. We're mates aren't we?'

'It'd look a bit funny, that's all.'

'Who'd know?'

'Well . . . what would people say if they saw me coming around?'

'Is that all you're worried about?'

'It's enough innit?'

'Come round the back then. I could leave the back door open if I knew you were definitely coming round.'

'Yeah and how would you know that?'

'Jesus, Dunny. Phone me from the pub. I'm on my own for God's sake. No one else is going to answer it. Just ring me when you're leaving and I'll leave the back door open. Not difficult is it?'

'Oh, I dunno.'

'Oh forget it. It was just a thought.'

'I'll see.'

'If I give you a quid, you could bring a bottle of cider or something. That'd be great,' she said persistently.

'Rosie. It'd be nice, but, you know if anyone found out about it, we'd be for the high jump.'

'Oh yeah, I'm really gonna tell mom and dad 'Guess what I did Saturday night. Dunny came round and we were smoking and drinking cider and he didn't go home till after midnight' am I? What do you take me for?'

'I'll see . . .'

'You won't come.'

'I'll ring . . .'

'Bet you don't.'

'I said I'll see.'

172

'If it's after 10 forget it.'

'Okay.'

'Oh come on Dunny.'

'Leave it with me Rosie.'

'Okay, but like I said, if it's after 10 forget it. I'm going to go and have a bath now and I'm not hanging around all night so please yourself. I know a lot of lads who'd jump at the chance you know?'

'I'm sure there are but . . .'

'But what, you're not fussed. Thanks Dunny.'

'It's not that.'

'Think I'm going to attack you or something?'

'No.'

'I might.'

'If I thought that I might just call.'

'Well you know the number,' Rosie smiled; there was a hint of beautiful menace hanging in the air.

'It'd be about 10 if I did.'

'More like it.'

'Okay, I'll see.'

'Hope you're not teasing Dunny.'

'I thought that was your department.'

'You've got the wrong girl.'

'Back way best eh?'

'I'll make sure the bolt's off the gate.'

'Mmmmm' I said, rubbing my chin.

'I'll be waiting.'

'OK'

'I'd better go.'

'Might see you later.'

'Yeah.'

'Hope you're not going to chicken out on me Dunny. And don't forget the cider.'

'Catch you later . . . maybe.'

'Up to you.'

My mind was in a total muddle. Rosie had never been like

this before. Certainly not with me. Although she was 12 months younger virtually to the day, her physical development had more than made up the difference. I knew Pele's younger brother Phil had been having a crack at her with limited success, but this? I hadn't been mistaken about the hint of mischief in what she'd been saying. No, I was sure I hadn't. So what was going on here? I still wasn't sure as I made my way into the Keys and ordered a pint of lager. It had been a funny old day.

The meeting had gone well and by around 9.20, three pints and an over active mind had started to play havoc with my concentration. Pele and Muldoon hadn't shown, which I was grateful for. If I was going to make a call to Rosie, it would need to be soon and I was still in a quandary about the whole business. She was 15 for Christ's sake. Well, 16, in around three weeks, if you wanted to look at it that way, but I still wasn't sure if it was a good idea to go around even if it was just to play records. I ordered another pint and by twenty-to-ten there was little time left if I was going to make the call.

The phone rang almost long enough to give me time to pull out when she picked the receiver up.

'573429'

'Rosie.'

'Who d'ya think it was?'

'It's Dunny,'I spluttered.

'I know who it is.'

'About what we were on about earlier on.'

'Yeah.'

'Well er . . .'

'You coming?'

'Yeah, that'd be good. If you still want me to that is.'

'Course.'

'Great.'

'Where are you - the Keys?'

'Yeah.'

'You leaving now?'

'Well, shortly.'

174

'Ok. You got the cider? Back gate's unbolted. It's dropping dark anyway. I'll leave the back door open.'

'Fine.'

'God, don't sound so nervous Dunny!'

'Why should I be? It's not that it's just . . .'

'See you soon.'

'Thought you weren't going to answer the phone for a minute.'

'I was drying my hair.'

'Right.'

'You gonna get some cider?'

'If you like.'

'I'll give you some money.'

'Doesn't matter. Strongbow or Woodpecker?'

'Don't mind. Anything.'

'Okay. See ya.'

'Just come straight in.'

'OK,' I said, blowing out as the receiver docked onto the payphone box. I finished my lager, said my farewells and made my way down the High Street to the Indian shop on the far corner of Manor Road. In around 10 minutes I was up near the mouth of the top alley which was lit up by the street lamp. I made my way along the path which led to the first banks and cut back through a gap in the flimsy hedge towards the Robinson's back gate, double checking no one was looking out of any of the back bedroom windows. I clicked it open quietly and scurried down the path, past Mr Robinson's shed and reached the safety of the back door, turning the catch nervously, worrying it might not be open. Rosie had left the light off, but the lamp in the living room shone through the half open living room door across the dining table.

'Dunny?'

'Yeah, who the hell do you think it is?'

Rosie emerged from the living room; damp hair falling onto her shoulders. Her lime-green baggy t-shirt hung loose outside the tight faded pair of Falmers which hugged her figure.

175

Barefoot, she tip-toed over the lino floor of the kitchen and guided me in the direction of the living room which was cosily lit by a standard lamp in the far corner of the room and the glow of the fibre-optic light sitting atop the television.

'Put that Queen album on. It's brilliant isn't it? I'll get some glasses,' she said taking the big bottle of Woodpecker from me.

I settled down on the sofa and smiled as she entered the room a minute or so later with two glasses full to the brim with cider.

'Glad you could make it. Crossed my mind you wouldn't be coming . . .'

30

CIDER WITH ROSIE

Rosie's tongue probed my mouth and I took in the heady cocktail of talc, shampoo and cider. There were surprises in store. Everything was happening so fast, almost breakneck speed, and yet now with time to reflect on it and savour the magic of that night, it seems like the whole wonderful episode gets purposely played back to me in slow motion. The stunning moment when it actually dawned on me that a key turning point of my life might be just around the corner is almost like a freeze frame moment I can tune into instantly. My two LPs had lasted only slightly longer than the cider and Rosie had fed four singles onto the arm of the record player and flicked it back so the last one kept playing over and over again. It was Pete Wingfield's Eighteen With a Bullet and though it was his only hit before he disappeared off the face of the universe it has become an anthem to me. If ever I meet the guy I'll thank him personally.

'I'm 18 with a bullet; got my finger on the trigger gonna pull it; be my 'A' side; be B-side me; just put it right there little girl, little girl . . . come on let's make out.'

Wow, in a distinctly Kate Bush unbelievable kind of way. As I roamed my hands over Rosie's beautiful full breasts, our tongues swirling from one to the other, I still had no idea where this was all going to end up. That might sound silly now, but on this fabulous July night in 1975, Rob's kid sister, of all people, was to take me there. That irritating, annoying little sister of not that long ago had become a beautiful swan and I couldn't tell her she was teaching me to fly. Rosie assumed I'd done it; I'd just assumed she hadn't. Huge mistake. The conversation took on almost comical proportions as she in her urgency not to let me down, inadvertently took control and led me to the promised land. I'd slipped my hand down to the front of her jeans more in hope than expectancy and even when Rosie said the settee wasn't very comfortable and we'd be better off upstairs, I still hadn't cottoned on properly. Call me stupid, I know but even as she asked me to take the cider glasses into the kitchen and make sure the back door was locked, I still hadn't taken in the full gravity of the situation which was perhaps just as well. Door locked and double-checked, I made my way up the stairs in the dark towards the light coming from Rosie's dimly-lit room. As I made my way in she giggled girlishly. She was in bed. On the floor were her jeans and a tiny pair of white pants; a bra and her green top. Oh fuck! Unbuttoning my trousers and sliding the zip down, I sat on the edge of the bed, coolly trying to slip them off as Rosie snuggled behind me and undid my shirt. I slipped under the sheets and as I pulled her towards me I can still smell talc and shampooed hair and warm flesh . . . and sweet cider. Rosie smiled as she pressed her nipples against my chest and we grinned as we stroked each other, neither really believing how circumstance, luck and just a touch of planning had brought us to this point.

'Don't worry Dunny, it's not my first time.'

'Err, okay. What?'

'You seem surprised.'

'No. I errr . . .' *Surprised?* I was absolutely stunned. It had crossed my mind to guide her through this gently. She could stop me if she wanted and I'd seem a really great guy for holding back and now . . . this. She was going to be guiding me - and probably awarding me marks when she met up with her mates tomorrow. Call me selfish, but while I'd have paid virtually any price to get my rocks off at long last, I really could have done without it being up for public dissection. I could just imagine it. 'Yeah, fucked Dunny last night. God was he hopeless!' Oh my God.

'Have I shocked you?' Rosie enquired.

'It's not that it's just. Oh I dunno. I err . . .'

'You're not going to give me that little girl bit are you? I've grown up Dunny.'

'I can see that.'

'I've been on the pill since I was 14.'

'What?' This was getting more incredible by the minute.

'It's okay, it's not what you're thinking. The doctor put me on it because I had an irregular cycle.'

I did my best to hide my shock. An irregular cycle indeed. It trumps a Raleigh Chopper anytime.

Oh my god! Not a virgin; on the pill for well over 18 months; not 16 for another couple of weeks and, if I'm not very much mistaken(surely I can't be) gagging for it. Yes, I didn't need to check. Rob's pretty young sister was naked in my arms in bed, her bed, and seemed to be taking the fact that she was about to go all the way with me very much in her confident stride. Supremely confident infact. It might be a bit of a 'so what' experience for her, but this was huge for me. Now I've rapidly gone from the point of wondering whether I might hurt her to whether she might hurt me. God, what was going on? I couldn't help wondering whether Rosie Robinson, aged 15 and seven-eighths, had any more surprises and I certainly wasn't disappointed. She writhed on my fingers and explored me with her tongue

'So when was your first time?'

'Oh, let me think. Christmas time. Yeah, about eight months ago. Something like that, she said with a cute smile.'

I snuggled in tightly to her and nibbled her ear gently, continuing: 'Did it hurt?'

'Yeah it did a bit. It was awful actually.'

Fucking great. Marvellous. I felt like punching the air.

'But then the next time it's okay.'

This was getting too much but you can't just come out with it can you?

'So, how many?'

'Only three,' Rosie said reassuringly.

'Oh right.'

179

'You don't think that's bad do you?'

'Lord, no. This is 1975,' I assured her.

'Exactly. Louise my friend has had six different guys and she's two months younger than me.'

'Six different blokes? What a girl.'

'Yeah that's going some a bit isn't it? That's why I don't think three's so bad.'

'Oh three . . .'

'Dunny! Three guys but the first two I only did it with once. The third one I still see but it's just an occasional thing. God, Dunny you make me feel like the village bike. Lay off will you?'

'How come it's just occasional then?

'Well, we have to be a bit careful. His wife would go mad if she found out.'

'Wife!'

'It's okay, he's split from her, but she just wouldn't like it.'

'Fucking hell Rosie. Bet she wouldn't. Be careful.'

'He wouldn't exactly be chuffed if he thought you were here.'

'Huh. Fuck him.'

Rosie was mouthing 'no' repeatedly as I spread her legs and as she groaned with pleasure I couldn't help but admire her neatly clipped thick black triangle. She repeated her 'no's' while at the same time manoeuvring her legs into position until I slipped inside her and eagerly pushed in and out excitedly.

'Oh Rosie. That was fantastic.' I fell to the side of her and locked onto her smile as I adjusted my bottom arm to get comfortable and bring her in towards me. I've always thought it might be handy if your arms had a sort of press stud so that you could detach whichever one was on the bottom if you were lying on your side. Perhaps not the time to be discussing dismembering oneself, but just a thought. I took up Rosie's invitation to stay a while and dozed off fitfully amid the aroma of talc, perfume, heat and crisp cotton sheets. It was just approaching dawn when we did it again and the next time we woke at around six, Rosie suggested that it might be best if I left before prying eyes had stirred in the neighbourhood. I kissed her on the doorstep and it was kind of uncomfortable leaving, not knowing what to say, but Rosie to her eternal credit picked up on it straight away.

'Dunny, that was a lovely night. Go on. Off you go. Don't feel awkward when everyone's back. That was lovely. Remember me like that.'

'Okay. Thanks. You were fantastic'

'Dunny. Go on. Just remember. Speak to me next time you see me, yeah? Don't get all flustered.'

'Course I will pudding head.'

'Good. See ya.'

The door clicked shut. Rosie gave me one last little wave and I crept back down the path which had led me to my unlikely destiny not eight hours earlier. I cut across the field to the top path and decided to go and sit on the rec pavilion and have a smoke; lap up the intensity of what the last few hours had served up to me. I'd done it. I'd fucking done it. Twice. Yeeees! *Rosie Fucking Robinson.* What a result. She had been lovely too. God she was under age! What if anyone found out? What if her dad found out? What about Rob? Oh my God. Who would have thought it? God, if I'd have known it would have been that easy, I wouldn't have got quite so worked up about it. Now I was getting worked up about it. Bollocks - I was a man - a real man. Wow - very much in a Kate Bush kind of way. Wow, wow, wow,wow,wow, WOOOOW. Unbelievable! Fantastic. I sat on the long, slatted wooden benches of the pavilion and contemplated. I smoked two cigarettes, one straight after the other, and decided it was time to make my way back across the top grass and down the road home. I picked up a discarded Cresta pop can and stood it on its end, lining it up for an attempted conversion between two of the fence posts which supported the hawthorn hedge surrounding the bowling green. Stepping back carefully, I toe-ended it with my right loafer and turned to acknowledge the crowd as it sailed over the two posts I'd picked out - dead centre.

'And yes, Dunn has clinched it with a magnificent effort,' I shouted.

'Dunn has done it. He's done it and the crowd are going wild!'

There was no crowd; there was no one - or so I thought. John the caretaker emerged from around the side of the hedge with Spot his terrier and smiled at me sympathetically.

'Oh. Mornin' John. Didn't see you there,' I replied sheepishly.

'I gathered that. What brings you out so early then? Looks like you've been out on the tiles.'

I had been out all night. I had made the big conversion. Okay, so there weren't 60,000 fans screaming their appreciation, but it fucking well felt like it. Straight down the middle; straight over the posts; straight as a fucking die. And Dunn has done it! Just a few weeks short of his 17th birthday and Dunn has fucking done it! Was this how Brian Kidd felt when he scored in the European Cup final for Manchester United on his 19th birthday? Perhaps, but maybe even better, I was forced to concede. *But this was good; this was very good indeed.*

31

GIANT STEPS

There aren't many original lines - particularly supposedly off the cuff ones. 'This is one small step for man, one giant leap for mankind.' Brilliant. Armstrong's first words on the moon, needed to be good . . . and fitting . . . and well delivered, not so much in deference to the venue but the occasion. History was unfolding in front of Planet Earth's very eyes and the words needed to be crisp and meaningful. But come on - our Neil must have rehearsed them in the shower a few hundred times before stepping out on the lunar surface. We'd already had 'The Eagle has landed' line - such a great outing for really coming up with them. I'd like to think my chance remark just one-and-a-half hours into 1976 was the kind of one-liner delivered with the accuracy and power of the most precise Muhammad Ali right cross. You can not underestimate the power of the verbal jab - and what's more it wasn't from a book. If there was any drawback, it is that years and countless experience and more exotic locations later, I have never bettered it - straight sixes. There are people who can have their words immortalised forever even though it should be clear to a fucking idiot that the script was written and rehearsed long before the lines that go down in history were actually delivered. Armstrong needed a damned good line, didn't he? Nothing less than brilliant would do really. Just imagine, Armstrong carefully steps onto the moon's surface and suddenly dries up. It was never going to happen. I'll bet it was practiced in the back bedroom of 135 Spaceship Close, Houston, or wherever he fucking lives, months before we all congratulated him on such a fitting thing to say. It's obvious. I mean to say, his missus must have asked him over breakfast if he'd got anything special prepared.

'Neil, love, what ya gonna say when you get on the moon?'

'Oh I dunno love. I'll just say 'It's really nice out here or something.'

'Come off it. The nation will demand something a bit better than that.'

'Well OK what about 'Hey guys, it's not made of cheese!''

'Better, but you really need to give this some thought sweetheart.'

'Fair point. Oh I don't know, I'll think of something.'

Meanwhile, Buzz Aldrin follows, a bit like the losing finalist at a Cup final. He's gallantly playing the role of the most successful straight man in history. Come on, he was fucked after that. I'll bet he was up at the top of that bacofoil ladder just knowing no matter what he did he would ONLY be the second man to step on the moon. Imagine doing something as meteoric as that, knowing someone has beaten you by about 10 seconds. How shit is that? As for Michael Collins up in the taxi that was whizzing around waiting for them - well, you can't help but feel sorry for the guy. Even as Eagle flopped onto the surface, Collins acknowledged from the command module that he was little more than an extra. Michael Collins? Is that the Irish fella? For all the rest of us cared it might just as well have been Joan Collins. This was the Armstrong and Aldrin show.

Mission Control acknowledged the feat by telling the two in the landing module 'There are lots of smiling faces here and all around the world' and Armstrong, who else?, replied 'There are two up here as well.'

Great stuff . . . at which point Joan pipes up 'Hey, guys don't forget the third one up here.' Exactly Joan, err Michael - my point exactly. Joan has just dropped two men on the moon and already is taking on the mantle of an inter-galactic cab. From that point on there was only one way he was ever going to end up more famous than the other two - fuck off and leave them there. Joan could have been the first serial killer in space with

Mission Control acting as hostage negotiators, trying to beg him not to make things worse for himself! Imagine it . . .what a fantastic bit of upstaging.

'Mission Control, this is Columbia - if you're so fucking fond of those two, you come and pick 'em up because I'm off.'

'Columbia this is Houston - don't be silly. You're going to become the most infamous man on the planet. You wouldn't want that, would you?

'I'm not on the fucking planet in case you haven't noticed - which you never do! Houston YOU have a problem.'

Meanwhile, Armstrong chips in 'Mission Control, where's the taxi?'

'Taxi? This is Columbia. If you're such a smartarse, you call your own fucking taxi. Hey and tell Buzz Gagarin or whatever he's called, he's gonna have to walk as well. Over'

See, it goes back to my childhood problems with Thunderbird Five. They can't be trusted. Make a man spend that much time on his own up there, getting no fucking credit and you are just inviting him to flip. I always felt John Tracy was a timebomb waiting to go off.

And so you see, circumstance can dictate the success or otherwise of your ad-lib. Your flashing repartee could be on your lips ready to home in on its target like a finely-honed Exocet missile, when you could be interrupted by the biggest prat on earth but once it's done the moment has gone. No second chances. It's not so much a case of you've fucked up but the other guy has bolloxed it all up for you.

The Mayor of Hiroshima wouldn't need reminding of the thin line we all walk when it comes to making a truly stunning observation only to see it go tits up in front of your very eyes.

'And so people of Imperial Japan, we will not rest until the might of our armed forces have . . . what the fuck was that?'

You can't say 'Guess what, I was just going to say there . . .' It's gone, knackered and that's why when I delivered the line that was going to make the summer of '76 the hottest of the century, it is with more than a little pride that I say it was in the kitchen of a working class, semi-detached home - a distinctly unremarkable venue. I was perched somewhat precariously between a stainless steel sink and a worktop creaking under the strain of Party Seven cans and discarded glasses and paper plates. This wasn't the fucking moon and if it had been it could hardly have had the same effect. This one changed my life and didn't have an audience of billions, but it felt good and if I say it myself, it *was* bloody good.

Armstrong didn't have to worry about being interrupted. Buzz Aldrin wouldn't have dared and Mission Control were waiting, poised and silent for his address. Bet a lot of them knew what was coming anyway. There must have been guys in that control centre whispering 'Here it comes, one small step . . . brilliant' and we were oblivious. What a stage. Was there ever a better one? Miles and miles and light years of nothingness and the only man who can cock it all up is either Buzz, who is on strict instructions, and yourself. What if he'd fallen off that bottom step? Wouldn't that have just been marvellous eh? Come the moment, come the man. Mission Control waits with baited breath for the pay off and Armstrong gets ready to deliver.

'This is one small step for man . . .' cameras whizz around like a scene from those awful collections of home movies that went wrong.

'Oh bollocks. Fuck me.'

'Mission Control here. Are you okay Neil?'

How about if Armstrong had deliberately decided to tear up the script and stamp his own mark on one of the landmark moments in history?

'This is one small step for man . . . one almighty kick in the bollocks for the Russians.' Yeah, now we're talking Neil. Or what about . . .

'Houston we have a problem - I'm dying for a shit.' You're the man Neil. Improvisation, now that's the thing.

So July 21, 1969 might have had greater universal implications but the early hours of New Year's Day, 1976 was the precise moment when I made one giant leap towards manhood.

The party at The Robinson's had been fantastic - fancy dress, not particularly fancy food and, for an awful lot of the revellers, fancy having so much to drink. Big Ben chimed via the radio in the year that was to see me celebrate my 18th birthday in not inconsiderable style. But that was eight months away and more pertinently, Mrs Robinson turned 36 in the few minutes it took to sing Auld Lang Syne and go around kissing and shaking hands.

She looked sensational and the lads at school would have given their right arm, a not inconsiderable sacrifice at that age, to see the outfit she had chosen. Rob hinted his dad was pissed off about it but I thought it was magnificent and I wasn't in an exclusive club. Mrs Robinson had knocked up, perhaps I should re-phrase that, a St Trinians outfit, stockings, suspenders, hockey stick, exagerrated freckles the lot. Her hair had been put up in deliberately untidy bunches and she had a Wellington Grammar School tie with a massive knot in it, barely hanging over a white blouse. Enhanced by the effects of god knows how many Sweet Martini and Lemonades and frequent visits to the big silver bowl which contained high-octane punch, Mrs Robinson was in full flow. She was doing The Bump and The Hustle with gusto and her swivelling interpretation of Let's Twist Again met with widespread approval, Rob's dad apart, who clearly felt she was making a bit of an exhibition of herself.

'I think he thinks I'm being a naughty little girl' she giggled in my ear, first removing the glistening red lollipop from her mouth.

'You don't think I'm being naughty do you Dunny?' she asked
'No Mrs Robinson. Not at all.'

She leaned over towards me and beckoned me to lower my ear towards her. 'I'm not sure I can let you call me Mrs Robinson much longer. Look at the size of you. You're making me feel old. I think it should be Penny from now on eh Dunny?'

'If you like'

'I do - you'll make me feel old before my time and it's my birthday,' she tittered urging me to join her in the middle of the living room dance floor as the distinctive start of Sweet's Wig Wam Bam came through the speakers. I was Hiawatha - she was my Mini Ha Ha. I wanted to be Running Bear so she could be my Little White Dove.

The last guests had not long gone when from somewhere deep within an alcohol-fuelled haze, I came up with a reply which under most other circumstances might well have put me in grave danger of a slap.

Mr Robinson, Rob and Rosie had all crashed out upstairs when Penny took my hand gently and invited me out onto the patio for a last cigarette before calling it a day. As we carefully picked our way around the debris in the kitchen, she smiled warmly and, looking up at me, said: 'I'm sure you are getting bigger Dunny?'

I pressed the launch button instantly. The Exocet was fired and homed in. There was no stopping the fucker.

'I think it's that outfit.'

Her eyes locked on mine for a split second longer than might have normally been appropriate as she considered not only the remark - but her own response.

'Dunny!! I can't believe you just said that' she tittered, trying to make light of it.'

'God. Sorry.'

'Don't be. You are sweet.'

Sweet? Jesus the last thing I wanted to be was sweet. This was serious stuff. I'd just told my mate's mother, the school lab assistant, the neighbour from across the road, that she gave me hard-ons and I was *sweet*. Obviously my inexperience had told and what I considered was a clever play had stupidly backfired. How would I ever look her in the face again?

Sweet? I didn't want to be sweet. Brian Connolly was Sweet? Sweet were the poncey fuckers who wore make-up and said 'We just haven't got a clue what to do.' Maybe I hadn't but I longed for Penny to take me to the silver stream. There she could whisper words like I'd never heard and make me all shudder inside.

32

STOCKINGED FEAT

As we all know, 'fancy dress optional' means that in any party of 100 people you'll be lucky if 20 make the effort. Rob and myself had been ordered to comply . . . I'd chosen to go as a tramp, which, although not ranking in the top 100 original outfits, was fairly easy to do. Rob was a monk and as we entered the hall, I was quickly to discover the costume that Mrs Robinson had been keeping secret and which had understandably met with some reservations by Rob's dad. The music was blaring which didn't matter because all the immediate neighbours were either there or on their way when we walked in at around 9pm. Mrs Robinson greeted us, gave us both a warm peck on the cheek and took the six cans of Long Life and bottle of cider which I had brought along.

'Oh you shouldn't have bothered, we've got plenty of stuff,' she said, but I wasn't aware that not bringing anything was also optional. You learn that it's just one of those things people say when they are welcoming you to a party. Come with nothing or a particularly nasty bottle of Pink Lady, large size or not, and you can guarantee it won't be forgotten. People might accept your excuse and say it doesn't matter and to think nothing of it, but we all know it does. It will be discussed at some length later on, if the poor sod is really unfortunate while the party is in full swing and they are in the kitchen helping themselves to the food the hosts have so kindly provided.

Penny looked like every schoolboy's fantasy - bloody magnificent. The glimpse of stocking top under a short navy blue skirt attracted admiring remarks. Unfortunately, Mr Robinson was just behind her in the hallway decked out in a Hawaiian shirt and Bermuda shorts, not giving us any real clues into exactly what he was supposed to be. I presumed he was just, well, an Hawaiian. Didn't they have garlands round their neck or something? Oh what the fuck, he was something like that. He'd made some effort. Muldoon and Pele were already there with beer glasses raised triumphantly in their hands, to signal our arrival. They seemed to be indicating that we were real lightweights to arrive when they had already been there ages. Laurence was on his way and as Pele kindly offered to pour me a lager, I clocked Belinda by the doorway between the kitchen and diner looking fantastic in a pair of tight white flares and a sequinned boob tube. She'd certainly made the effort, not in fancy dress mind, but who cared? She put down the glass of what appeared to be white wine and moved out of sight to dance in the living room, but with who I couldn't see as I unsuccessfully tried to negotiate the dozen or so people already congregating in the kitchen. Muldoon clearly had the top vantage point as he motioned to Rob and me to come and take a look, but we couldn't get through. Muldoon indicated he was going out of the back door to the patio and we joined him as soon as we could squeeze through having picked up our drinks and a couple of sausage rolls en route. Although it was quite cold outside, most of the smokers had congregated there and at least you had some room to move around. As we got to the backdoor David Essex's Hold Me Close was coming to a finish and as we grouped together by the half-open patio doors, Belinda treated us to 5,000 Volts worth of I'm on Fire as she gyrated provocatively in front of a tall, swarthy guy, who we were unfamiliar with. She clearly wasn't or, at least, didn't intend being.

'Who's that twat?' asked Pele.

'Dunno'

Looks a bit of a tosser if you ask me,' said Rob.

The problem was he was only a tosser to us. In our eyes he had tosser tattooed on his forehead but as he left Belinda to it as the record ended to take his position up back behind an impressive looking double record deck, the good looking DJ had clearly made an extremely quick impression on her. On fire? She looked almost combustible as she shook her head in his direction clearly affirming she approved of the disc title he'd just mouthed to her and was about to put on.

'Smooth fucker' Rob said softly as Mud's Show Me You're a Woman started to play, prompting him to try and establish the identity of the mystery DJ as his mom came out to see if we were okay.

'Oh it's Rick. Dad works with him. He kindly offered to do it for me,' she said.

'He's very good. He does it in clubs and stuff. This is only half of the gear he's got. He must make a few quid because he's got a beautiful Escort Mexico and he's only 21.'

'He would have,' Rob groaned barely audibly having established that the bright yellow car on the drive belonged to Mr Dreamboat.

'Oi' Mrs Robinson said in a reprimanding tone.

'No need to be jealous. Nice to see a young fella trying to get on and dad reckons the girls at work go potty over him.'

'Can't see why,' Rob countered.

'Well I can. He's quite dishy. Wish I was 15 years younger I can tell you, she smiled.

'You'll be a year older in a couple of hours,' teased Rob.

'Alright don't rub it in.' It was her 36th birthday on New Year's Day, though looking fleetingly at her now, as I was forced to on account of the fact that her husband was now no more than a few yards away, she could easily have passed for someone much younger.

Rob's dad seemed a little off the beat with it all and by now was holding court in the kitchen as I tried to make my way to the fridge. I guessed it might have been a mistake daring to wander too near the small group of mainly men he was talking to but had no means of escape when he blurted out 'Here you are Dunny, son - now you go to grammar school, so see what you make of this!'

Mr Robinson clearly wanted the stamp of authority from someone he considered reasonably intelligent which was nice, but I sensed it might be some time before I would be back into the dining room to give Pele and Laurence their cans.

'Right' said Mr Robinson. 'Now listen carefully.'

'Oh don't bother them with that bloody thing,' Penny intervened in a mildly agitated manner.

'Oh get off. It's brilliant this. Brilliant. But listen now, you have to listen really carefully. Got it.'

'Right, I'll start. So anyway, there's these three students right. They haven't got much money between them and they're setting up a flat together. Anyway, keeping it as brief as I can, they decide to go down to an old second hand shop to see if they can get a television for the flat at a good price.'

'So' Mr Robinson continued: 'They see a television which seems fine and the chap who owns the shop says they can have it for thirty quid. Still with me. Good. So they all get a tenner out apiece to pay for the telly, hand it to the bloke and walk out of the shop with it.

'Anyway, just after they've left the shop, the bloke who owns it says to his son that he feels a bit sorry for the students because he knows they can't have much cash and tells the boy, who is just a kid, to follow them up the road and give them a fiver back. With me so far?'

Nods and grunts give adequate confirmation prompting Mr Robinson to continue, though by now he was in full flow and it would have taken a herd of stampeding rhinos to stop him.

'The students seem genuinely surprised and pleased - obviously. But they explain to the little boy that because there's

192

three of them, they can't split the five pounds between them. So what they decide to do is have a pound back each and give the little lad the two quid that's over to buy himself some sweets. Still with me? Right.'

'So' he went on. 'So, the students have all paid nine pounds each, yes? And the little boy has got two pounds in his pocket, yes? Three nines are 27 and the little lad's two makes 29. So the question is where has the other pound gone?'

I had to admit that for once Mr Robinson had actually held me spellbound and now sadly I was more interested in discovering the whereabouts of the missing pound, than acting as drinks waiter to Pele and Laurence, admiring the robust gyrations of Belinda on the dancefloor or nabbing the occasional glimpse of Penny's thighs. Where had the fucking pound gone? There had to be a trick.

'Work that out then, Dunny,' Mr Robinson said triumphantly.

'No there must be a trick to that. Say it again.'

'God, no please. Spare us Dunny,' pleaded Penny. 'He always comes out with this one. It's his party piece. Sad, if you ask me.'

'Only because you can't get it,' Mr Robinson dismissed her observation with a self-congratulatory swig of his pint.

'I don't get it either,' I was forced to concede.

'Well' said Mr Robinson. 'Are we in any doubt that they all paid ten quid, right?'

'Right.'

'And they all got one pound back, yes?'

'Yeah.'

'And the boy's got two pound?'

'Right.'

'No trick. Where's the other pound?'

'I should go before you all die,' Penny said mockingly. As the intrigued group mulled over a truly fascinating deception, I decided to take the drinks back into the other room, though I admit to this day the bloody story haunts me. And I've told it many times to bamboozle people and wonder if I've become just as fucking sad as Mr Robinson.

Rob got on pretty well with his mom though you could sense he was a bit embarrassed at everyone seeing her in a schoolgirl's uniform, sussies 'n' all; while his dad guessed correctly that she was attracting almost as many saucy remarks as admiring glances as she flitted from guest to guest asking if they needed their glasses filling. I couldn't help wondering how much I could have got from the lads at school - and the masters for that matter -for ringside seats to see our lab assistant dressed in such a daring outfit. I was genuinely beginning to wonder if something was wrong with me as I contemplated my admiration of her, particularly in the light of the fact that I'd lost my virginity to her then 15-year-old daughter and, upstairs here, as if to really take the piss. Now I was having lustful thoughts about her. Was this normal? Was I really harbouring some deep-seated hatred for Rob's dad? I mean to say, while he wasn't exactly my favourite person, you didn't need to be Einstein to work out that the thought of me having had sex with his beloved little girl while grappling with thoughts of grappling with his wife, might quite justifiably have him reaching for an extremely sharp knife. Perhaps it was the sight of her dancing with Rosie to Hot Chocolate's You Sexy Thing which had done it - I just didn't know anymore.

Rosie and I were getting on just fine now. Despite what we'd said, things had been a little bit awkward for a while in the weeks after that monumental night and she accepted my invitation to a smoochie one to Rod Stewart's This Old Heart of Mine, pulling a face as her dad remarked on how it wasn't a patch on the Isley Brothers' original. It was the sort of thing you half-expected dads to say. Rick was still giving it loads in the direction of Belinda, who was now standing beside him sorting through the boxloads of discs, acting as his kind of Anita Harris. He seemed to be disagreeing with her choice for the next record and little wonder as the distinctive intro to the current No1 record in the universe tinkled in. Bohemian Rhapsody had become a defining moment in pop history - you were aware of that even in its own time. Having said that it was still more of a conversation point than a dance record and the living room floor cleared seconds before Freddie had the chance to confess that he'd just killed a man. Killed a dance floor more like but no one seemed to mind because, well, it was just that sort of song. Phenomenal. The first time you'd heard it was just like 'What the fuck is that?' It was just so different in a time when you arrogantly or foolishly thought nothing new remained. Most people can remember where they were when they first heard that song. I can't actually remember whether it was Simon Bates or DLT who gave prior warning that he was shortly going to be playing Queen's new single and that although there was a BBC directive that no song over three minutes would get on air, he was going to totally ignore that. He was going to play the full version, all seven minutes however many seconds long it was, and be damned with it. You wondered what the fuss was about and then instantly realised something different had gone off as this incredible song began to stun the nation. The fact that everyone is sick to fucking death of it now is immaterial. At the time it was revolutionary, a record the like of which had never been heard before.

Pele threw up in one of the flower borders at the back and was escorted home by Rob's uncle while Muldoon's 1am deadline had seen him slope off unsteadily into the night. As 2am arrived most of the guests had wandered away and Belinda was helping Dreamboat to start packing away his stuff assisted by Mr Robinson. My mom and dad were away celebrating with friends in Wolverhampton so it had been arranged for me to either go over home later on or crash out on an available chair.

To this day I'm not sure whether Rick and Belinda ended up in the same bed that particular night but for what it's worth they left together. Rosie had gone up and Rob's dad retired to bed well-pissed saying he was out on his feet, grateful that Rob and me agreed to get all the paper plates and empty cans cleared up. Mrs Robinson said she wanted to at least put some of the dishes in to soak so things might not look quite so daunting in the morning. Rob brought a sleeping bag and pillows down for me and then called it a day. I collected together one final bag of rubbish and placed it down by the side of the wire-mesh bin. It was almost a quarter to three and the air outside was fiercely sharp. Mrs Robinson peeled off her rubber gloves and said it might be an idea to have one last cigarette on the back step before calling it a day.

'Hey thanks Dunny, that's a good job done. It'll be so much easier in the morning now. That's the only trouble with parties. - the mess afterwards.'

'No problem. It was a great night.'

As we traversed the remaining debris, untouched cans and the like, Penny brushed the palm of her hand across her forehead and blew out indicating just how warm it was indoors despite the back door being half-open. And then it came:

'I'm sure you get bigger every time I see you Dunny,' she said gazing up at me.

'I think it's that outfit!'

'Dunny! I can't believe you just said that!'

'God, sorry.'

'Don't be! You are sweet,' she said nibbling her bottom lip.

'Happy Birthday . . .'

'Gissa kiss then,' she said puckering her lips together and scrunching her nose up in exaggerated fashion which enhanced the big brown freckles she'd painted on her face.

I rested my right hand on her left shoulder as she leant against the sink and edged my lips towards her cheek.

As my mouth brushed her soft skin she turned slightly towards me and guided me towards her mouth. The second my lips touched hers she opened them and slid her tongue into my mouth, teasing me in an assured, beautifully rigorous way. I pulled her towards me, my confidence growing as she declined to stop me. She was groaning and mouthing softly for me to stop, but inexperienced as I was, I was consumed by the feeling that was the last thing she wanted.

I became bolder, sliding my hand over her blouse, mouthing her frantically and hardly daring to believe what was happening, while at the same time praying she wouldn't stop my enthusiastic advances. I gripped her hair gently and kissed her more intensely, manoeuvring my tongue, taking in the sweet smell of her. Then it happened. Shit. I couldn't believe it. What an idiot. I moved my hips slightly to the side and pressed my hardness between her legs, signalling her to move away sharply and call proceedings to a halt. I was holding a small bunch of blonde hair in each hand. Penny laughed hysterically. The tears rolled down her cheeks and she turned back around and smiled gently as she observed me, still holding the two bunches of blonde hair which until a minute ago had been cutely attached to her head.

'They're clip-ons, you idiot.'

'I just errr . . .'

'I think on that note it's time for some shut-eye don't you?' she said taking the bunches and slapping the back of my hands playfully.

'Come on Dunny, there's a sleeping bag on the sofa for you, OK?'

'OK.'

'There's some pillows there too. I'll see you in the morning,' she touched my shoulder for the briefest of seconds which I took to mean that everything was all right, but I still wasn't sure.

She made her way to the door which separated the kitchen from the hall, put one of the bunches into her right hand and half opened the door with the left. As I turned to make my way into the small dining room, she whispered.

'Sweet dreams.'

'And you.'

'Bet on it'

'Night.'

'Night Dunny,' and off she sloped, leaving me in a state of wonderment, excitement, bewilderment and still not totally sure that I hadn't totally messed-up our relationship for ever.

33

IS IT A KIND OF DREAM?

I can recall an episode of Thunderbirds where . . . now before you ask where the fuck does International Rescue come into this particular part of the story, trust me, it's spot-on relevant. As I was saying, and hopefully not in a sad, anorak, kind of way, there's an episode of Thunderbirds which runs a direct parallel with exactly this point in the story. Would I lie? Well, yes, I might, but this particular offering of Supermarionation belongs right here.

Anyway, there's this kid and his dad is trapped down a mine or some other equally dire situation has befallen him and International Rescue come to his aid. Scott and the boys fly in and do what they do best and the kid then secretly decides to hitch a ride back to Tracy Island by hiding away aboard one of the Thunderbirds. Eventually he's rumbled having a right old time exploring the magical place and Geoff and the boys get wind of it and decide they've got to get him home while at the same time getting around the problem that the kid has become a breach of security. The fact that he was eternally grateful to them and only about ten anyway, makes me think perhaps Scott and Co were being a bit over-dramatic but you can't be too careful I suppose. How the hell would he know where it was? Anyway . . .

To the point . . . they fly him home; dad is mightily relieved and agrees to go along with the plan which is that when the kid wakes up, he has to convince him he's been dreaming it all. Job done. Kid wakes up, dad tells him he's got an overactive imagination and the kid falls back to sleep hardly believing that what he's dreamt about didn't really happen. Lad goes back to sleep and wakes up now convinced that it was all a dream. Brilliant. Bet he didn't doze off and get straight back into the same dream again because that just never happens does it? The number of times I've just been getting someone's top off and then I've fucking woken up, I can't count.

Right, so, one of the most life-altering, mind-blowing conversations I've ever had - and am ever likely to - crops up and a load of puppets spring immediately to mind which is the point I was making earlier - we really are a sad bunch of individuals.

* * *

God, I'm so confused and not in the least a little worried about the events in the kitchen of little over an hour ago. The consequences of my over-zealousness might well come back to haunt me. Penny hadn't given the impression that she would never speak to me again, but how would she feel in the cold light of day? Would she tell anyone? I doubted it, but this was new territory to me and while the danger of it all had a certain appeal, the repercussions were scary. What if she was forever cool with me now? I thought it was okay, I told myself time and time again, and no matter how hard I tried to convince myself that everything would be fine in the morning and she'd make me a cup of tea and everything would be just as it was before, somehow I doubted it. All in all it collectively added up to the fact that sleep was out of the question. My eyes were half closed when I stirred from the total silence to the muffled sound of what I thought was a noise in the hallway. The red numerals on the digital clock showed 3.12.am as I rolled onto my side to face out across the living room floor.

'You asleep?'

'Na' I replied somewhat sheepishly.

'Fancy a cuppa?'

'Lovely.'

'God I couldn't sleep,' Penny muttered as she made her way

past the gap where the dining table would normally have been and into the kitchen. The sound of the switch clicking on clipped through the quiet and she returned to the living room standing barefoot a yard or so from me in a pair of black karate-suit style silky pyjamas with a red dragon insignia on the front.

'Budge up a bit,' she said softly, motioning for me to make some room on the sofa before sitting on the edge of the centre cushion.

'Do we need to talk?'

The fact that we clearly were talking was a massive relief in the first instance it was just the manner of her statement had the ring of a trip to Lecture City about it. If that was as bad as it got I could probably cope with it. She got up just as the sound of the kettle boiling prompted her to make her way back into the kitchen. Penny placed the two mugs down - one on a coaster nearby and the second on top of one of an old edition of Railway Enthusiast magazine.

'Hope it doesn't get marked, or he'll moan like mad, but what the hell' she smiled, drawing on the cigarette.

'I can't believe he was boring everyone with that bloody puzzle he tells everyone who has the misfortune to listen,' she grumbled.

'It was very hard,' I said.

'Not the only thing that was Dunny?'

Oh Christ, I feared the worst - the ultimate humiliation until, in almost the same breath, she placed her hand on the back of mine and stroked it thoughtfully.

'Sorry.'

'What was all that about then Dunny? Bit too much to drink? Got carried away did we?'

'Guess so, I'm really, really sorry about that,' I said softly.

'I should think so too,' she chuckled.

'Can't remember the last time I've had that effect on someone.'

'Look, I'm err . . . I had a bit to drink.'

'Oh thanks, Dunny. You've really done my ego the world of

good.'

'I didn't mean it like that.'

'No perhaps not. Listen, I'm flattered. Honest. Just don't get pointing that thing at frustrated married women and not expect any consequences.'

'Like what?'

'You want to thank your lucky stars , we weren't on our own.'

Lucky? That was Jimmy Hunt fucking lucky.

'Oh really lucky eh?'

'For you.'

'Great.'

'Well I can't believe for one minute you'd want to get me in bed. I'm old enough to be your mother for God's sake.'

What was I supposed to say to that? This was surreal and I was loving every minute of it. Penny's hand was sweeping gently across my brow; the hush was intense.

She lowered her face towards mine and kissed me gently on the lips; pulled away allowing just enough time to smile and then brushed her tongue against my lips. As our mouths locked, I groaned and she pulled away, imploring me to be quiet.

'Sshhh . . . Not a word.'

'Sorry.'

'It's okay. Just sshhh . . .' she touched my lips with her forefinger and I nibbled the end, carefully slipping my hand inside the pyjama top to feel her breasts.

'Oh Dunny. No. no . . . no,'

'Don't stop me please, ' I implored her.

'God, this is crazy. Absolutely crazy. This is not making much sense .'

'Don't worry.'

'I do; that's the problem. God, Dunny you make me feel so horny.'

'Brilliant.'

'I can't believe I'm doing this' she added, shaking her head and gently sliding down the sleeping bag zip which had somehow worked its way round to the front of me.

'Sshhh . . .' she insisted as she slipped her hand inside, swirling it around my stomach and beyond.

'Oooh Dunny. What's that? Wow, you could make an old woman very happy with that you know.'

'I want to.'

'Hey. listen you've had a lot to drink.'

'It's not that.'

'God. And there was me thinking it was all bravado,' she sighed.

'Ooh I want it.'

'It's yours,' I tried to sit up, but was eased back down.

'Not here Dunny. Not now. Too dangerous. '

'Shit.'

'No chance. Not here. Oh God that feels so good. I can't leave you like this.'

'I don't get it.'

'Look, don't make a mess in that sleeping bag. It's Geoff's and . . . well, just don't'

I gulped as I felt Mrs Robinson tongue my naval.

'I'm sure I shouldn't be doing this . . .'

* * *

'Thanks,' seemed such a stupidly inappropriate thing to say, but I couldn't think of anything else suitable.

She adjusted her pyjama top and buttoned it back up before placing the gentlest of kisses on my cheek.

'I'd better go back up. Try and get some sleep Dunny. Feel better?'

'Not half.'

'Good. And, hey, that never happened ok?'

'OK.'

'You dreamed it!' Penny pecked me on the cheek and made her way out of the door. I glanced across at the clock which read 4.57. Nineteen seventy six wasn't even five hours old. This had all the makings of a very good year.

Talk about feeling like a tramp . . .

34

THE PENNY DROPS

'You want to put a shirt on, you stupid apeth,' Dad bellowed out of the front bedroom window. What exactly was an apeth? Fuck knows, dad was always saying *stupid apeth* this and *stupid apeth* that. It was almost midday on this first Monday morning of July, 1976, and the heat was bordering on unbearable. God, it was so hot and I wasn't even a quarter of the way through painting the first section of picket fencing at the bottom of our front garden. When Miss Orrick had given me the Tom Sawyer book, she was obviously trying to tell me there were ways and means of getting out of such drudgery, but as the sun beat down on me, it seemed like only personal intervention by Huckleberry Finn or, indeed, Mark Twain himself would give me any chance of escaping this particular chore.

Dad had given me the old 'It's not as if I ask you to do much' routine a few days earlier when he'd requested, well instructed, me to give a coat of gloss to the two sections of fencing which ran along the bottom of the front garden. The first stretched from where our garden met the adjoining house to our driveway and was a good fifteen feet in length. The second section was about 20 feet long and ran from the other side of the driveway, curving around to the post which marked the beginning of the alleyway. I was whacked and I'd only been going for about an hour; heat, fatigue and distinct lack of enthusiasm convincing me this could well take all day.

Dad made his way down the drive with a glass of green squash, that proper Tree Top pop, and repeated his earlier plea.

'Paul, go and stick a shirt on son or you're going to be sorry.

That sun is strong and you're going to end up in a frazzle if you're not careful.'

'Dad, I don't want a shirt on. Everyone moans about the weather and then we get the hottest summer in years, everyone's telling you to cover yourself up. It's barmy.'

'You're bloody barmy. Please yourself, but don't say you weren't warned.'

'I won't,' I insisted.

'Hi Penny. Warm enough for you?' dad spoke over my crouched figure.

'I never thought I'd say it, but it's too bloody hot isn't it?' came the reply.

I got up, happy to be able to take a legitimate break and turned to see Mrs Robinson, crossing the road as she made her way towards the bottom of our drive.

I hadn't seen too much of her in the last few months because Rob had been busy at work and I'd just finished at school. Reasons to get in her company had been significantly reduced and I'd hoped she hadn't been distancing herself from me. She looked absolutely stunning. Her mid-thigh length bright yellow, strappy, summer dress, only served to enhance her tanned legs and arms.

'Keeping him busy I see.'

'You're not kidding,' I groaned.

'You're looking well,' said dad.

'Thanks, feel great - it's just so damn warm.'

'You've been away haven't you?'

'Yeah. We had a couple of weeks in Spain. Came back last week and it's just been relentless ever since. No sign of a break in it is there?'

'No, the garden's suffering a bit, but what can you do? Anyway, what can I do for you?'

'Well actually John, it's your lad I could do with really. Any chance of borrowing him for an hour?'

'Sure. I don't think he'll take too much persuading to get out of painting that fence. What's the problem?'

'No problem, it's just that mom and dad have gone down to Devon for the week and I've got the job of feeding their cat and watering the hanging baskets and stuff. I'm okay in the greenhouse with the tomatoes and suchlike but I can't reach the hanging baskets properly.'

'I'll come up if you want,' said Dad.

'Oh no I wouldn't want to put you to any bother, John. You don't mind giving me a hand do you Dunny?'

'No. No problem.'

'I don't like asking but Geoff and Rob are both at work and with this sun as it is, I don't want everything to dry out. Dad'd bloody well kill me if he came back and they were all shrivelled up. He's been on the phone already and they only went yesterday, so I'm under strict orders and I'm in a bit of a fix.'

'Take him.'

'I'll drop him back off in an hour or so if that's okay.'

'Believe me, he doesn't need an excuse to get out of painting that fence. I was just thinking I might as well do it myself, the time it's taking him. By the time he's back, I'll have bloody well done it.'

'Sorry to be a pain,' she said, cutely scrunching up her nose.

'Don't mind Dunny do you?'

'No, not at all. When do you want to go?'

'Their house is only five minutes away in the car. Well, you know where it is up Lee Avenue. I'll just pop and get the car and see you in five minutes eh?'

'Fine.'

'Go on bugger off,' said dad, snatching the brush from my hand.

'You'll have to give me a few minutes,' I declared, carefully rubbing my arms down with a rag which dad had soaked in white spirit.

'Okay, don't worry,' she said, craning her neck around the slight curve of our garden towards the cul-de-sac where a barely recognisable figure was waddling towards her.

'Bet this heat is murdering you,' Penny said, talking to the balloon like figure I once knew as the beautiful Belinda. Jesus wept, what the hell was going on here? To say she was pregnant might just have been the understatement of the year; she looked like she was minutes away from giving birth to the entire James Last Orchestra, their instruments and the band's tour wagon. She was huge. You could balance a tray of drinks on her belly without spilling a drop and her face, which was also considerably chubbier than when I'd last seen her, looked like it had been stuck on someone else's body. It was horrendous and I dare say the look of shock on my face didn't go unnoticed. Her legs were all bloated and swollen and she looked grotesquely uncomfortable in the tent of a royal blue dress which she was encamped beneath.

'Yeah, I really picked the right time to go and do this didn't I? This heat is absolutely killing me. Talk about bad timing.'

'Not long now,' Penny said reassuringly. 'It'll be all over before you can say Jack Robinson.'

'Eight weeks. I'm dreading it.'

'It's nothing to worry about. That's only natural. Look I had two of 'em so if it was that bad we wouldn't go and do it again would we?'

'S'ppose. I'm just so bloody big that's all.'

'It's just water that is, love. Nothing to worry about.'

Just water! Fucking hell, I felt like informing Belinda that the Hoover Dam was just holding back water but I wouldn't want to be standing within 50 miles of it if it ever decided to burst open. Perhaps that wasn't a good idea, but hold on a minute, what had been going on here? I'd thought something was going off because on a couple of occasions when I'd entered the room, my mom and whoever she was talking to had suddenly gone quiet. Her brother hadn't said anything. Penny told her she was blooming - I felt like telling her she was blooming exploding more like. I kept my thoughts to myself and watched her shuffle down the road, a huge shadow of the gorgeous girl I had once admired so much.

'Rather her than me!' she said making sure she was out of

earshot.

'And me!' said dad.

'Such a shame. Poor girl. It's caused some heartache in that family I bet. Well I know, but they're trying to put a brave face on it. It's going to change her life that's for sure. It's always the women who suffer for one moment's madness,'

'Takes two,' said dad defensively.

'Yeah, but it's always us left holding the baby'

'I didn't know about it,' I said somewhat forlornly.

'Well there you go,' said dad, adding the inevitable 'let that be a lesson to you.'

Time to go. Mrs Robinson said she'd just get the car and in no time at all her red Mini was waiting by the kerb.

'I take it you didn't know about Belinda being in the family way then?' Penny enquired, as I wound myself into the passenger seat and slid open the window all in virtually one movement.

'No. Nobody mentioned it.'

'I don't think it's really been up for discussion. Anyway, thanks for coming to give me a hand. At least it got you out of painting the fence.'

I couldn't contain my puzzlement at the Belinda not-so-Smart revelation. The DJ guy from the party had long since disappeared from the scene, so I wasn't surprised that the news of her pregnancy had been perhaps even more of a moot point than it normally would have been.

'Maths has never been your strong point Dunny,' she laughed.

'I'm not with you.'

'She's seven months gone. We've only had six completed months this year, so by my reckoning she must have got caught early December at the latest.'

Caught? It's a strange expression isn't it? I mean it conjures up pictures of the beautiful Belinda legs akimbo with some lucky fella padded-up gleefully shouting 'Howzat!'

Caught? It's a kind of respectful female kind of saying, which you can understand and go along with but when it comes up for general discussion among the lads, you can guarantee they won't be saying 'Did you know Belinda Smart's been caught? Caught what? Shoplifting? Mugging old age pensioners? She was up the duff, in the club, up the stick, babbyed, knocked up. Whatever 'up' you wanted to put with any given expression of your choice she hadn't been caught up. She had been caught out and now the seed of The Devil was threatening to burst out of her belly like something out of The Exorcist.

It didn't bear thinking about. This was already too much for me when, as I should have known, there was worse to come.

'So if it's not Mr Cool DJ then, who's is it?' I asked.

'Well I don't know, but if it's who I think it might be, we've not heard the last of it in the street.'

'In the street?'

'Mmm. I might be talking out of turn but if it's who I think it might be there's going to be ructions.'

'Well don't say anything Dunny for God's sake, but with me only working part-time I've seen her coming in and out of No 36 at odd times. That's all I'm saying.'

'Thirty-six? Muldoon's.'

'Got it in one.'

'Not a chance. You're joking. Muldoon? No way. You honestly think Muldoon has got something to do with this? Believe you me if Muldoon had . . . I'd know about it.'

'Not Muldoon you nana.'

'You said No36.'

'Yeah.'

'Well that's Muldoon's.'

'Yeah.'

'I don't get it.'

'Obviously not, but I wouldn't be surprised if Mike hasn't.'

"Muldoon's dad!'

'You've got it.'

'Nah.'

'It wouldn't surprise me. I'm telling you, I've seen her coming from there at some unusual times. I can't think of any business she'd have being there. Can you?'

210

'I can't believe that.'

'Why?'

'That's disgusting.'

'I'd tread carefully here Dunny if I was you.'

'But he's . . .'

'He's what? 40?'

'I didn't mean that,' I spluttered.

'He's my age. Is that what you mean?'

'He's older than you.'

'Two years - big deal.'

'Yeah, but it's not the same.'

'Why not?'

'S'just not.'

'Hypocrite.'

'You know what I mean.'

'No, actually, I don't,' she interjected sharply.

'Mr Martin . . . I just can't believe it. The baaa-stard.'

'Just 'cos you'd like to!'

'Not now I wouldn't.'

'You're a hypocrite Dunny. You're just like all the rest. Typical bloke.'

'Oh come on.'

'You ARE.'

'So you're happy with the thought of Mr Martin screwing Belinda are you?'

'I didn't say I was happy with it Dunny. I just think you've got some bloody picture of her skipping through a field of forget-me-nots in white ankle socks and swinging her satchel around. She's 20 for God's sake. I don't think for one minute Mike Martin has been dragged off into a bed against his will.'

'It's not that.'

She was clearly getting more than a little agitated and guessing that my observations on the startling revelation that Belinda might be carrying Muldoon's dad's baby could have a severely detrimental effect on the advancement of my sex life, I quickly tried to get off the subject.

Penny Robinson looked fantastic. The vivid sunshine yellow, cotton dress showed off the healthy glow of her gorgeous tan and her hair seemed lighter than ever.

As I glanced carefully across at the sunlight razoring its way through the side window, I couldn't see a single fine golden hair on her legs that I'd noticed before.

As we made our way into Lee Avenue and along towards the end where her parents' small detached bungalow was, I couldn't help wondering if the hanging baskets were just an excuse.

35

SUMMER - THE FIRST TIME

Suddenly, the imminent prospect of finally reaching the Holy Grail started to fill me with some trepidation. Whether it was the sight of Belinda successfully holding at bay the entire contents of Lake Windermere or the thought that a mature woman like Penny Robinson had given birth on two occasions, the first a good 17 years ago, started to make me seriously consider whether I could cope. Put it down to total inexperience but the delights of women who had given birth was something completely new to me. I wondered just what I might find. Christ, what if it was massive? Had I maybe been a touch unprepared not to bring some crampons and harnessing equipment, just in case I fell in there or something? The prospect of what might be about to happen suddenly hit me. This was new territory. It flitted through my mind that there must be a high percentage of guys who only ever get to sleep with one woman who has had a baby and that's the one they marry, so this was hugely different. There must be a lot of blokes who never actually experience it and that didn't exactly serve to fill me with any confidence at all. I distinctly recall someone telling me, female of course, that if I wanted to imagine what having a baby was like, I should imagine trying to wee an aniseed ball.

That was far too graphic for my liking. God it must be tortuous and I recall vividly thinking even then that it was at times like that, I was grateful I hadn't been born female.

Penny was stunning and such a lovely person that I was sure the size of my equipment couldn't be an issue after what had happened. But what if it was a small issue? God, I couldn't bear the thought of her smiling and saying something comforting like 'It's okay, they are all like that to start with.' But it couldn't be, I assured myself. It wasn't that long ago that I had enjoyed that unbelievable experience on the sofa and surely if there was any question of me being a dreadful disappointment, it would have surfaced there. Perhaps she was just desperate and decided I would do. Surely not? Penny wouldn't be that cruel. Would she? As we entered the back door, she turned and smiled and went about locating the small watering can in a very matter-of-fact manner.

'Right Dunny. If you could take that out and fill it in dad's water butt, I'll get the cat fed. You'll need to reach up because they're quite high. God knows what dad was thinking of when he put the brackets on.'

'Right.'

'The butt is round the back of the shed. This hosepipe ban is a real pain. Just give them a good soaking love. They must be dry as a bone.'

Talking about bones . . . I thought to myself, making my way down the path towards the shed.

It seemed like an age before she came back out and ushered me towards the tiny greenhouse, where the neat rows of tomato plants thirstily awaited my assistance.

'Just give them a real soaking sweetheart then take a seat on the bench or wherever and I'll get us a drink.'

She returned with two large tumblers of lemon barley and sat down on the rustic garden bench which faced out onto the long, neat garden which was mainly laid to lawn. I carried on watering before she called over to me.

'That's probably enough now Dunny. Come and cool down.'

I sat down beside her and gulped the lemon gratefully. The thermometer on the outside of the greenhouse indicated it was 82F and the sweat was trickling down my chest as the full intensity of yet another glorious summer day, made its mark.

'Phew, it's hot isn't it?' she said.

'Boiling.'

'Look at you, you're sweating.'

'I know. Isn't it great?'

'Fantastic. You know, I think we'd be better off inside. That sun is far too powerful for my liking. Coming in?'

'Okay.'

'I'm just going to have a quick look around and check the house over. You can't be too careful.'

Penny disappeared for a few minutes before returning to the kitchen and calling to ask if I'd finished with my glass.

'Well bring it in then. I'll wash these up and put them on the drainer and then we can go if you like?'

I didn't want to go - truth be known I didn't know what I wanted. I wasn't sure exactly what I was supposed to do next. If anything was to happen, I needed a prompt and I wasn't to be disappointed.

'S'pose that's us done. We can get off, if you want to. Don't want to keep you from your fence painting.'

'Oh right,' I said the hint of disappointment, badly disguised.

'Well unless you've got other plans,' she said.

'I don't mind, honestly.'

'Well I suppose we ought to get out of here,' she smirked suggestively. 'I know what happens to you when you get near a sink.'

I moved towards her, praying she'd pull me in and as she placed each hand on the outside of my arms, instinctively knew the moment had arrived. Up until Christmas time, Mrs Robinson had been distinctly untouchable. She was the woman with the Soda Stream and the Buttoneer - my mate's mom in the Marigold gloves who stuck the occasional plaster on a grazed knee or had bought me a lucky bag off the back of the mobile van which used to come up our street. Suddenly it had all become so different and her urgency collided into mine with frightening force. I carefully placed my hand on the back of her neck and guided her face towards mine and in an instant we were kissing passionately.

She eased away and smiled. 'Thought I'd scared you off for a

215

minute there,' she said.

'Not a chance.'

'I'm nervous, Dunny'

'You're nervous?'

'Course. What do you think I feel like?' she said trying to reassure me.

I didn't know, but I knew I wanted to find out. Penny gasped, nibbling my neck and kissing my moist, salty face as my hands roamed all over her, down her back and over her hips where I could feel the outline of a knotted string under her figure-clinging dress. I pulled her in tightly and as my hand slipped under the hem, I gently started to ride it up to the top of her thighs where I eventually found the string. One small tug met with no resistance and she slipped her tongue back into my mouth as she parted her legs slightly allowing the white bikini bottom to fall to the floor beneath her feet. She gasped as my fingers explored her. I gained comfort from her warmth and tightness as I explored the thick, black bush between her legs, before she eased me away once more and beckoned me towards the hallway.

'Come on. I know somewhere better than this.'

She took my hand and guided me towards a door down at the bottom of the hall, bit her lip and cupped my jaw in her hand as she gently eased it open leading me into a room with a single bed in it.

Lace curtains protected our privacy and as she lowered me down towards the edge of the bed and stood right in front of me she eased my head into her midriff.

I pulled her towards me, placing my hands on the outside of her knees and raising the dress until it exposed her gorgeous thick bush to my eager tongue.

'Oooh Jesus,' she groaned, sighing deeply as she pulled the dress over her head and tossed it against the door.

She was completely naked, her beautiful chocolate-brown nipples standing out on her large breasts. She clawed at my jeans and pulled me alongside her, mouthing sweet obscenities as we

216

explored each other with frantic urgency.

Penny smiled warmly and took me in her arms, nuzzling against my neck and just kept repeating 'Thank you.'

'No, thank you,' I insisted. 'That was great.'

'Really?'

'Really!'

'You wouldn't just say that?'

'No. That was brilliant.'

'I have my moments you know. Just not that often these days!'

'It's a scandal.'

'This'd be a bloody scandal if anyone found out about it Dunny.'

'They won't.'

'And what was that you were saying about Mick Martin and Belinda. Still disgusted by it are you?'

'Course not.'

'Good, Just disappointed it wasn't you eh?'

'No . . .'

'Liar,' she grinned.

'No, honestly. That's what I wanted. I wouldn't have swapped that for anything in the world.'

'Oh Dunny,'

'Honest. That was brilliant.'

'We can do it again tomorrow if you want?'

'Great.'

'You sure now?'

'Course.'

'Same time, same place?'

'Great.'

'We'd better make tracks Dunny. Your dad will be wondering where we've got to!'

'OK,' I whispered, wiping my hand across my forehead and easing myself up from the bed.

'Jesus, Dunny.'

'What?'

217

'Your back.'

'What about it?'

'Christ it's all scratched. You're going to have to get a shirt on love.'

'But I haven't got one here.'

'We'll go up to my house and I'll find you one or something. You can't go home like that, they'll know.'

'Mine might still be on our lawn, if you pull up when we get there.'

'Put it on in the car for God's sake Dunny. I'm really sorry. I told you I get carried away.'

I could see dad crouched by the far side of the fence as we reached the brow of the hill and we pulled up alongside the kerb.

Dad stood up, balanced the paintbrush on the upturned lid of the can and exclaimed: 'Just like you to turn up when the job's done. Don't know how you manage it.'

'Sorry dad.'

'No bother.'

'Dad, do me a favour.'

'What now?'

'Just toss me that t-shirt will you?'

'Bloody hell, you wouldn't be told would you?'

I managed to wriggle into the shirt and out of the car in one far from elegant movement and stepped out onto the pavement.

'Anyway, thanks ever so Dunny.'

'Glad he's been of use because he's no bloody use to me,' sighed Dad.

'I told you you'd burn your bloody shoulders but you wouldn't listen would you? Let's have a look.'

'Nah it's okay dad. Just a touch sore that's all, Nothing to worry about.'

'You deserve to bloody well suffer.'

'Cheers dad,' I grinned. 'Hey, by the way, you've made a lovely job of that fence.

'Bugger off,' he said, raising his fist playfully.

'Think you've missed a bit there though,' I taunted him.

'You know something? If you want a job doing round here, you might as well do it yourself.'

The painted fence; dad's sweaty brow and creaking back, my satisfaction of fulfiling a thousand lads' teenage fantasy . . . so that was what Miss Orrick meant about Tom Sawyer and the whitewash. Wow.

* * *

As arranged, I was on hanging basket duties the next day, and the next and for five whole days in total, me and Penny had, as Billy Paul said, a thing going on. We both got more uninhibited and more adventurous and by the time her parents had returned, I was wonderfully knackered. We were like two mayflys, knowing our time was limited and determined to cram in as much as we could. And we did - Penny even confiding in me that it was the five days which had completely changed her outlook on life.

The heat showed no sign of relenting and the hosepipe ban looked like it would be on for the rest of the summer. The lawns were struggling on the occasional bowl of washing up water thrown on them and I had to keep my shirt on for days - which pleased dad. I felt like telling him my new sensible approach was nothing to do with him, but the fact that Penny Robinson had clawed at it like a tiger, but perhaps not.

I was making my way up the road to meet Pele on the Rec when Mr Robinson pulled up alongside me in his car, a few houses down from where he was going to pull up on his drive.

'Hey I need to see you. What's this I've been hearing about you and my missus?'

'Sorry?'

'Don't deny it. You've been spotted having a secret rendezvous with my wife. I need to have a word with you,' he said.

Mr Robinson pulled off and by the time he'd swung the car left, I had walked up and was already by the small gate at the side of the driveway.

'Hey Dunny, I know what you've been doing . . . and I want to tell you it's appreciated.'

Was it really?

'Ah think nothing of it.'

'Nah come on, you must have better things to do than watering bloody hanging baskets. Take this.' Mr Robinson offered me a fiver.

'I don't want that.'

'Why not? Take it you silly sod.'

'It's okay Mr Robinson. It was nothing,' I insisted.

'You won't get far these days, doing jobs for nowt. Here, take it.'

I tried to refuse again, but in the end it wasn't worth the bother because he was insisting I take the note as some token repayment for helping him. I felt like a gigolo. Please take a fiver off me - and, by the way, thanks for shagging my wife. Really good of you. Is a fiver enough?

'Ok if you insist. Thanks Mr Robinson,' I said.

'Hey and another thing. I think you'd better start calling me Geoff from now on. Your 18th soon isn't it and, anyway, you've been bigger than me for an age so I think it's high time you called me Geoff.'

'Ok . . . Geoff,' I said

'Thanks again anyway. You're a good lad Dunny.'

Fucking hell. Eighteen - key to the door and all that. I could do all sorts of grown-up things now! Tom's fence sprang to mind yet again. Jesus, he'd only got a load of old tat really. I'd got out of painting the fence, ended up having a five day sex romp with a gorgeous older woman and now this - her husband was paying me for being so good as to help her out. Was this really a good time to tell him I'd slept with darling Rosie as well? Maybe some other time.

36

EIGHTEEN WITH A MULLET

And while I woke up on Saturday, August 7, 1976, happily contemplating notching up 18 years, disgraced MP John Stonehouse was in his cell mulling over whether the judge summing up his corruption trial might give him 18. Formula One ace Niki Lauda was fighting for his life after his horrific crash in the German Grand Prix and sick jokes about him were being put out quicker than he was. The Montreal Olympics was being wrapped up and the long, hot summer showed no sign of letting up. Mom and dad had gone on their normal Saturday morning shop after offering me hearty congratulations and I sensed something might be going off later, by their rather furtive movements over the past few days. I put the top back on the Aramis after shave and briefly contemplated what to do with the money I'd been given, when the phone rang.

'Hello.'

'Dunny?'

'Is that you Penny?'

'Yeah. Happy birthday sweetheart.'

'Hey thanks. That's really nice of you.'

'Had loads of nice stuff?'

'Brilliant. Thanks.'

'Look can't talk for long, Geoff's upstairs having a shave. I've got a pressie for you and I'd really like to give it you personally only it's a bit difficult - can we meet at lunchtime?'

'Errm.'

'Look if it's difficult, just say. I just . . .'

'No, no. That should be okay. Here?'

'No stupid. I've got you something, but you know, I don't think other people should know. It's only something small.'

'You shouldn't have.'

'Look Dunny, going to have to shoot. How about the beer garden of The Wickets at, say, 12.30?'

'The Wickets?'

'Yeah, is that a problem? I'll explain later.'

'OK. I'll be there.'

'Great.You're old enough to buy me a drink now!'

'OK. 12.30. You do mean the one in Wellington, up by school, yeah?'

'Yeah.' The phone went dead. This was extremely strange. I knew The Wickets from the outside because it was a stone's throw from the grammar, but it was hardly the nearest place to home for a quick drink. I assumed Penny had an appointment or prior engagement in Wellington town centre and The Wickets just fitted her arrangements. I contemplated getting the bus, but scrutinising the £60 splayed out on the cushion, I decided I would ring for a taxi and sod the expense. After all, it's not every day you are 18 and the walk from the Cock Hotel bus stop to The Wickets at the other end was a good 10-15 minutes anyway. It seemed like an age since my precious week with her. Sublime intimacy for five whole days and then it had to be turned off like a tap, which though I understood and obviously went along with, didn't make it any easier. It would be nice to see her again and have a drink and maybe a laugh about the illicit, secret bond which tied us. I clicked the kettle on. It was only twenty-to-ten, but I needed to think about getting ready. This was my big day. I would shave with the new Ronson electric razor mom and dad had bought me followed by a quick soak before embarking on my big day. Mrs Robinson's call had changed things. I was guessing that Pele, Rob and some of the lads would be calling around at some point and we'd be off for a drink, but that would have to be put on hold for now. I'd catch them later.

The taxi had dropped me off outside The Wickets at around 12.10 and I was contentedly alone in the beer garden until another couple sat a few tables away around ten minutes later. Mrs Robinson arrived at just after 12.30 casually dressed in a pair of tight crushed velvet trousers and a black cotton, short sleeved top with an ace insignia in sequins. She asked for a long gin and tonic with loads of ice and sat down at the wrought iron table while I went inside.

'Cheers Dunny. Happy birthday!' she smiled, pecking me affectionately on the cheek.

'Cheers! Legal at last.' I raised my pint.

'It never feels quite the same as when you shouldn't really be doing it,' Penny said, touching her glass to mine. 'Like a lot of things . . .'

'Well, you're not a boy any more Dunny,' she giggled.

'Yeah.'

'There's nothing you can't do now. Mind, that doesn't leave much,' she said playfully, placing her hand flat on mine.

'Glad I could catch up with you. I've just got you a bit of something, that's all,'

'You shouldn't have,' I said, taking the tiny box off her.

'What is it?'

'Open it.'

'You needn't have.'

'Look, I just wanted to. It's not much but I think it's probably best if you just tell people that you bought it for yourself. It's easier that way.'

'Seems a shame.'

'I couldn't put up with the shit Dunny. Geoff stuck that fiver in your card, which was nice, but this is best just between us I think.'

'You're right.'

'Oh, it's fantastic. Thanks,' I whispered, clutching the silver ring with a round black onyx face between my thumb and forefinger.

'Really you shouldn't have. It's lovely. It must have cost a fortune. But I'm really grateful. It's lovely,' I said leaning over to kiss the side of her face once again.

'It's just a token of my appreciation. I wanted to do it and anyway, it's me who should be grateful Dunny.'

'I don't think so.'

'Oh I do. Don't worry, but, well, our friendship has given me something back you know. I don't expect you do know but I was in a rut and didn't realise just how life was passing me by. I really appreciate everything that's happened between us and it's meant a lot. More than you'll ever know.'

'That works both ways.'

'Thanks. You've no idea just what all this has done for me. Suddenly I felt like it was me who was 18 never mind you, and maybe one day in years to come, you'll know how good that felt.'

'It's meant a lot to me too.'

'Oh Dunny, you've no idea. You're so young. Don't get me wrong I love Rob and Rosie you know that and, yeah, in a way I owe Geoff a lot. But it's just not there anymore Dunny. That's not your fault. But those few days at mom's, well, oh I don't know. It was just like I was a new person. Vibrant, attractive, without a care in the world. It was just a lovely escape and it was strange being shown that by you, if you know what I mean.'

'Thanks!'

'No, I mean it. Sometimes it takes the eyes of someone younger to open yours. I don't want commitment or anything from you Dunny and you know that. But it's been fantastic and I owe you so much.'

'Listen,'I said brushing her fingers. 'You owe me nothing. I always fancied you so much.'

'Oh anyway. Enough of that. Here's to the future,' she said holding up her glass and clinking it against mine.

'I'll drink to that. Anyway, why here?'

'Ah now that'd be telling Dunny wouldn't it? No real reason, well, not really. Just thought you might fancy one last visit to school.'

'Eh?'

'It was just a thought. I'd lined up a bit of a surprise for you, but if you haven't got time or anything then it's okay. It's my sort of signing off.'

'I've got all the time in the world.'

'Great. Come on then?'

'I think you ARE 18 sometimes Penny. What's this about then?'

'Well, that depends.'

'Interesting,' I ducked under the small arched trellis which led the way back to the bar.

'Oh it could be,' she assured me.

We touched glasses once again sensing this would be, perhaps had to be, the last time we would have any proper time together. It felt like the celebration it should have been.

'So, where do you go from here then?' I asked.

'Oh nowhere just yet.'

'Eventually.'

'Rob's on his own two feet now. He's not going to be around for ever and Katie, well she's growing up by the day. She's 17 and wants to go to college. I just can't see me staying around.'

'I see.'

'Well, you probably don't, but that's the point I was making. I'm 37 and while that might sound old, there's just got to be more to it all than this. I fancy going to Australia. My brother's out there.'

'It's your life.'

'Well, exactly. Geoff won't be bothered. He's not been bothered for years if the truth be known. But anyway, enough of that. It's your big day Dunny. Last thing you want is me going all wonky on you.'

'It's okay - honest.'

'You're sweet. I know you hate that - but you are. Very sweet.'

'I'll take it.'

'Anyway Dunny, come on. We gonna go back to school or what?'

'OK.'

'Hey, there's a lot of those boys there who'd give their right arm for a secret rendezvous with me according to you.'

'Bet on it.'

'I just wanted to give you an 18th you'd never forget.'

'And when did you plan all this then.'

'Oh you make me sound such a schemer Dunny.'

'I meant . . .'

'It's just something I thought of a few days ago. I kept putting it off and I wanted to get you a little something too and then . . . oh well, I just figured if I didn't ring this morning it'd be too late.'

'Let's go then.'

'I guess it's just my way of saying goodbye,' she said jangling the huge bunch of keys.

37

SCHOOL'S OUT

The journey from The Wickets car park into the school gates was no more than a couple of minutes. The entrance to Golf Links Lane was less than a minute away and Penny negotiated the right turn before heading past the tennis courts immediately on the left and into the main entrance. It was strange going back there and the fact the place was deserted only enhanced the surreal atmosphere. She drove up to the far side of the large playground and parked just to the side of the five or six concrete steps which led up to the main building, jangling the keys which wouldn't have looked out of place on the set of Porridge.

'All coming back?' she asked.

'Not half,' I replied as I scrutinised her leading the way with keys in one hand and a black leather bag in the other with her white lab coat carefully draped through the handles.

Ushering me in through the first door which led into the inner quadrangle, she carefully locked it behind us and we continued to make our way past the old tuck shop and into the main part of the building, turning left to go past the music room which hadn't played a significant part in my secondary education.

'Where are we going?'

'Just wait and see,' she smiled mischievously.

'I need the loo,' I explained.

'Well you know where it is,' she laughed.

As I made my way straight on into the corridor which led to the main block of boys' toilets and even given the intimacy of our relationship, it still seemed rather disconcerting that Penny was still alongside me.

'I'm going to have a cigarette while I'm waiting,' she said, sensing my puzzlement.

'Oh right.'

'God Dunny, you're not going all shy on me are you?'

'No it's just . . .'

'Don't worry. I wasn't going to peep!' she slapped me on the shoulder.

'Should think not.'

'I'll be here,' she said reaching into her pocket for the cigarettes. 'Want one?'

'Yeah, I'll be back in two ticks,'

'I'll light you one.'

'Thanks.'

There were ten cubicles side by side running immediately down the left of the block. It's just one of those things you know from smoking, keeping guard and generally messing around in there for the best part of five years. It's a supposedly safe haven from the prying eyes of teachers, but you live in the knowledge that they aren't blind to most of the things that went on there. How many kids must have had their heads flushed in the cubicles of the mysterious little world of the building universally known as The Bogs? I'd seen a few scraps in there in my time too. The Bogs could tell a tale or two; bloodied noses, fagging sessions which had led to the cane, water fights, you name it. The Bogs were where it all happened. The cubicles were known by trap numbers, just like in greyhound racing, not inappropriate considering the speed kids were sometimes forced to burst out of them if the warning rang out that there was a teacher or jugger on the prowl. Trap 10 at the very far end, for geographical reasons as much as anything, always enjoyed the status of being the favourite haunt of the big lads. No one dared go near Trap 10 until you'd made at least the fifth form for fear of reprisals. Trap 10 was numero uno; once you'd progressed to that stage, you really had arrived. As I came back from around the corner, Mrs Robinson was standing in the doorway, smoke curling from two lit cigarettes.

She took a long, deliberate draw on one and handed it to me. Who could have pictured this? My 18th birthday and I was standing calmly in the school toilets smoking with the lab assistant. God, I'd have paid any price just to see Wagger's face now. It was beautifully bizarre. You couldn't make it up.

'So this is where all the boys hang out is it?' she grinned.

'Yeah this is it?'

'Not like I imagined, really,' she said.

'This place is a frequent topic of conversation in the staff room you know.'

'I bet.'

'Hardly a day passed when one of the masters wasn't moaning about something or other that had gone off in here.'

'Yeah,' I sighed nostalgically. 'I've seen some things in here, I can tell you,' I said hardly daring to believe that a block of loos could bring back such evocative memories.

'Had a few ciggies in here in your time, eh Dunny?' she said, resting her hand on one of the washbasins.

'Not half.'

'God Dunny, what is it with you? Every time I seem to be near you these days, I'm up against a sink!' she giggled, touching my arm firmly.

I moved towards her to kiss her and she softly blew a ring of smoke towards my face.

'So where's all the graffiti I used to hear so much about?' she said placing the flat of her hand against my cheek.

'God, you don't want to see that.'

'Might.'

'Believe me you wouldn't.'

'Why not? This is the only chance I'll ever get. Not a place I'm allowed to hang out you know'

229

'You're probably the subject of half of it,' I assured her.

'Ooh really. Let's have a look!'

'You really wouldn't want to, believe me.'

'Wouldn't YOU want to know what people were writing about you?' she insisted.

'Depends what they're writing. Some of the things . . . well, it's hardly Shakespeare.'

'Oh come on Dunny, don't be a spoilsport,' she urged, gently nudging me out of the way and shoving open the thick wooden door of the first cubicle.

'I wouldn't,' I warned.

Undeterred, she peered around and started to scrutinise inside. 'Well I never . . .'

'Oh God. What?'

Penny tittered as she flung the door open to reveal the crudest drawing you could imagine of a penis which was around two feet long and accompanied by the message. 'For hire - ring 247345.'

'Well, well.'

Now she emerged from what was known to me as Trap 1 and proceeded towards the next.

'I wouldn't. You'll end up finding something you wish you hadn't.'

'Oh don't be such a prude Dunny. I've always wondered what went through teenage boys' minds.'

'Absolute filth mainly,' I assured her.

It became clear her attention had been caught by some literary masterpiece on the back of the door of Trap 9 and she called me over in a fit of giggles.

'Come and look at this Dunny. Well, I never . . .'

I squeezed into the cubicle alongside her as she analysed the all-embracing list who had signed their names underneath the compass scratched instruction at the top of the door.

'Well, now I know! Who would have thought it?'

Just to the side of a felt-penned *Mr Hartson is a bummer* was an invitation to add your name to a long list. If you'd like to give Mrs Robinson a good shagging - sign here.

Didn't realise I was THAT popular Dunny' she chuckled, scrutinising a fairly impressive catalogue of willing parties. John Wagstaffe, Emlyn Jones, the entire fourth form rugby team, the headmaster's name had been signed too, the Chelsea squad, Noddy Holder, Shep, the Blue Peter collie and about 54 less well known admirers.

'Can't believe you're doing this,' I said, slightly embarrassed.

'Here' she tittered, handing me a black felt pen, 'Your name's not on it.'

'Can't think why not,' I assured her. 'I'm sure it would have been.'

'Huh. Snubbed.'

'Write something,' she insisted, lowering the seat lid down and sitting on it.

'Like what?'

'Use your imagination.'

'Oh God.'

'Dunny, you're getting so boring.'

'What do you want me to put?'

She turned me sideways on and pointed to the wall to her left which was remarkably bereft of scrawlings.

'There. Write something there.'

'Like what?'

'You're useless,' she added, placing her hand on the front of my jeans and taking the zipper catch between her thumb and forefinger.

'Write . . .' she yanked it down.

'Mrs Robinson . . .'

'Yeeees . . .' I said, following her instructions as she released the button and pulled my pants forward.

'Sucked my . . . true'

'That's outrageous,' I said, laughing.

'Best way. The more outrageous something is the less likely people are to believe it. Anyone who sees that won't imagine for one minute that it's true,' she smiled.

'Come on. Something I want to show you.'

'But . . .'

'Just come on, Dunny. Be patient!!'

I followed her out into the corridor as she urged me to follow her back up the main annex and towards the chemistry lab where she spent most of her time. She gave me the bag to hold as she searched for the key with the piece of identifying blue insulating tape on it and opened the lab door.

'Do you think I'm naughty?' she smiled.

'Yeah, very.'

'Good.'

She took the small holdall and instructed me to pull down the first blind sit on the front bench and wait for a short while.

'I'm going to give you the best birthday present you've ever had,' she assured me, making her way to her room behind Hartson's desk to the extreme right.

'Wait there. I won't be a tick.'

As I waited for her to return, in my mind the silence of the classroom was still pierced by the sounds which had been so familiar. Hartson's sergeant-major boom; Wagger's fit of uncontrollable giggles as Mrs Robinson had stood there with Polycell dripping in strings from her fingers and Hartson's desperate attempts to clean her up; you could almost smell the whiff of gas from the bunsen burners.

Penny emerged from the back room in her gleaming white lab coat and beckoned me forward. As I moved in close to her, she planted a gentle kiss on my forehead and pushed me back into Hartson's chair.

'I've been naughty Dunny . . . Very naughty.'

'In what way?' I mumbled.

'Ask me what I've done.'

'What have you done?'

'I haven't done my homework sir.'

'Well, not to worry eh?'

'DUNNY! Are you going to play this or not?'

'What'

'Jesus, Dunny, I need chastising here and you sit there and say 'Well not to worry eh?' Get a grip.'

'Okay.'

'I haven't done my homework.'

'Right - a hundred lines!'

'Lines! Fucking Lines Dunny? Jesus I'm scared out of my wits. Do you want me to carry on with this or not?'

'Just bear with me. It's a bit new to me. Don't shout.'

'That's YOUR job. YOU shout. You're angry with me. Get it.'

'Oh right.'

'Right!'

'Start again! I haven't done my homework sir.'

'Well that's very naughty isn't it?'

'Yes sir.'

'And I take a very dim view of that Penny.'

'I think you should probably call me Robinson or at least Penelope in this instance, Dunny' she laughed.

'Right, Robinson. I'm very unhappy about this.'

'I'm sorry sir.'

'So, I'm going to punish you . . .'

'Oh please don't punish me, sir. I'll do anything. No sir, please, not the cane. Anything but that', she interrupted.

'Yes, the cane.' I sensed I was getting the hang of it now. This was easy peasy.

'Did you hear me girl! You're going to get a good thrashing.'

Robinson opened Hartson's drawer and produced his fuck-off two foot cane which I'd almost forgotten about. How could I?

'Oh God how many?'

How many? Let's see . . . she wants it harsh, lets get harsh, I thought.

'Six'

'Six? For that sir? You only got two for scratching the library floor.'

'Yes. And don't be insolent, or I'll give you more!' I added assertively.

'Is there anything I could do to make you change your mind, sir?'

'Like what?'

'Oh I don't know. How about this sir?' Penny slowly undid the five buttons of her lab coat until it hung open to reveal a tiny red and black lace bra, matching suspender belt supporting sheer black nylon stockings under skimpy see-through black panties.

'Oh my God,' I exclaimed spontaneously. 'Fucking hell.'

'Surely that must be worth a reduction sir,' she whispered seductively rubbing her hand down the length of my thigh.

'Yes, perhaps I can make it a few less.'

'Ooh good sir. You're such a hard man.'

Too right! What sort of a birthday treat was this?

'Do you want me to bend over sir?'

'Yes.'

'How many are you going to give me?

Good question. 'Four?'

'Why don't you just *give me one*, sir,' she exclaimed.

'Robinson. You're very, very naughty. Make it two then'

'Don't hurt me,' she said bending over the chair.

I gently tapped her bottom with the ruler and asked her if it had hurt.

'Not too bad sir. It's the second one I'm really worried about.'

I tapped her softly again and she remained prone, turning her head to say 'You just don't get this Dunny do you?'

'What.'

'Hit me with it.'

'What *hard*?'

'Well not fantastically hard. But, well, hard enough to hurt a bit. Use your imagination for Pete's sake.'

I tapped her a little harder.

'A bit better, Dunny.'

'I'm not really sure about this.'

'Just ONE. Not too hard, not too soft. Give me a good slap with it.'

TWHACK . . .

'You bastard!' she squealed, immediately springing to her feet, to remonstrate.

'Bastard. That hurt.'

'Sorry!'

'You will be. You're going to have to make this up to me now.'

'I'm really sorry Penny . . . I err . . .'

'It's fine. Just right that was.'

'Anything you say.'

'Right. Follow me,' she insisted.

I was in a state of slight panic, wondering just what I'd done when Penny winked at me, buttoned the lab coat back up and led me out of the door and across the pathway from the lab in the direction of the library, keys jangling in her hand.

'Hope old Frosty knickers isn't in there?' she chuckled.

'I hope so too,' I said, sound in the knowledge that we were the only two in the entire building. There was only the caretaker who might be on site, but I prayed he was on holiday too.

'Well it's tough if she is. Because what I'm about to do to you might just blow the starchy old battleaxe's brains out. Penny yanked open the library door and instructed me to keep my shoes ON.

Turning acute left at the end of Miss Frost's desk, she led me to the foot of the spiral staircase leading to the balcony and ordered me to wait there.

'Follow me.'

'Jesus. Where did you learn this?'

'I didn't. I'm making it up. Like it?'

'Not half!'

'Good,' she said getting to the top stair and taking my hand as I trailed one pace behind her, to make her way between the first two partitions of books. Placing both hands on the balcony with a view over the entire library floor beneath her she bellowed: 'QUIET!'

It echoed around the room in a way that would have had Miss Frost cringing.

'That's what you say in libraries isn't it?'

'Think so.'

'QUIET!' she bawled again.

'Christ.'

'Take me Dunny - and I don't want to be quiet. Make me scream.'

Penny was fed up of being quiet - kids in the next room; neighbours next door. She was determined to let it all out and there was no one here to stop her. It was sensational - straight sixes.

* * *

I leant down and tried to take a tissue from my pocket.

'Oh don't worry about that Dunny.'

'But . . .'

'Listen, she wouldn't know what that was if it hit her in the face and I don't think there's much chance of that ever happening' she laughed.

'Chance would be a fine thing.'

'Precisely,' she agreed, checking her watch and readjusting her clothing.

'Happy birthday Dunny! Hate to be boring but have you seen

the time?'

It was twenty-five-past four and we both knew it was more than near the time we should be getting back. Penny locked the library door and we made our way back to the chemistry lab so she could change back into her day clothes. We had one lingering long kiss by Hartson's desk and smiled appreciatively at each other before making our way towards the door. She double-checked everything was locked before ushering me into the car and making our way back out. I took one last look, guessing I might never return, realising that nothing could ever top what had just happened. Perhaps it was best to leave this way. We agreed she should drop me down by The Bush and I could make my own way back up.

'Take this,' she said offering me a small, dark green plastic bag with gold writing on it.

'Put the ring box in it so if anyone asks you've been to Wellington and bought it yourself for your birthday.'

'You think of everything.'

'I have to,' she smiled, squeezing my leg and urging me to get out. I'm a married woman you know!

'You certainly do' I grinned, clicking the door shut.

'See you later sweetheart. Bye.'

The Mini disappeared up Church Street and I made my way up the hill which led to the top of the alley and lit up a cigarette. What a day! And it was only late -afternoon. Penny was right - what had happened was so unbelievable that the story became beyond recounting - not that I could anyway. Could it ever get better than that? I glanced at my watch. It was almost four o'clock. I was only half-way through the most memorable birthday of anyone's life and it was going to be impossible to beat. I took one last drag on the Embassy at the top of the alley before making my way into the top of Sandpiper Road and home. Just as I got to the top of the drive, Rob came hurtling out.

'Dunny, where the fuck have you been?'

'Ah it's a long story.'

'Me and Pel have been looking all over the place for ya.'

'Just popped into Wellington.'

'What for? We were going to go for a beer or three.'

'Just bought myself a ring and looked at some records and stuff.'

'Fuck me Dunny, it's your 18th not your 80th. You boring bastard? You out in a bit then?'

'Yeah course.'

'Okay mate, give us a ring. I'll be waiting.'

'Cool.'

Boring? Yeah, you could say that. What was I supposed to say? So now how the hell am I supposed to even try to convince him that I've been having the wildest day of my life? I might just about have got away with confessing all that I'd had my wicked way with Rosie and that she had made all the running; but to casually throw in that I'd been caning his mother over the chemistry teacher's chair, might have just about taken the biscuit.Boring? Yeah, it had been a really boring day and now I'd got the biggest birthday of my life to embark on. Marvellous. Let's keep things dull, eh?

38

PENNY'S FROM HEAVEN

Waking up to the realisation you'd had sex with someone who was dead didn't rest easily with me. I'd better rephrase that . . .

As I prepared myself to go to the funeral, I just couldn't quite get my head around the fact that someone I'd slept with was dead. Bollocks - it still doesn't sound right. Look, let's get this crystal clear. Someone I was once intimate with was now no longer with us. Not because of; certainly not during; not immediately afterwards either; oh, and certainly not as a result of some lingering, deadly disease.

The two things - the sex and the unfortunate passing away - were distanced by a not inconsiderable period. Years, to be totally accurate. They were in no way even remotely connected.

I'm sure there were no national statistics to actually clear up how many people had died as a direct result of sex. And if there were, I suspected cause of death more likely to be from a shotgun, sharp implement, deadly virus or heart attack. But this wasn't the time or place to contemplate such delicate matters. There must be some people it had happened to but it would be an extremely unfortunate and small club of which I, thankfully, was not a member.

Just imagine eh? Actually there was a time . . . it must have been all this upset which brought it back to me but, now clear as day, was a memory of just how close sex and death can sometimes be.

Myself and some of the lads had been on holiday in Ibiza and I was with this good looking girl back in my room when she gave

239

me the fright of my life. I can't remember her name now but she was from Huddersfield, and we were in mid-flight so to speak when proceedings took an unexpected twist.

I'd found her incessant moaning and writhing a real turn on up to that point and she seemed well impressed with my technique as she breathlessly writhed away in time with me. Her yelps became almost frantic only serving to accelerate my excitement as I revelled in bringing us both to a shuddering climax.

As I took my weight off her and moved to the side, her eyes rolled and she leant across the bed and fumbled around for her handbag.

'Wow that was great,' I said.

She grunted as she half-smiled and tried to grab a breath.

'Was it good for you?' I asked.

Her head nodded back and forth as I was sure I detected her trying to acknowledge my prowess in bed and as I smiled back, I caught a glimpse of what was in her hand.

'Oh I'm so sorry,' I whispered, putting my arm on hers to check she was okay.

'I just errm . . . I just . . . '

'It's okay, take it easy. It's all right,' I assured her.

'I just needed this,' she said after two almighty blasts from the inhaler she was gratefully clasping in her right hand.

'I'm an asthmatic!'

'Fucking hell. I could have killed you. Why didn't you say?'

'I was trying to dimwit.'

'And there was me just thinking you were enjoying it.'

'Well, you're a bloke aren't you?'

* * *

It still didn't make it easy coming to terms with this. I was genuinely upset anyway. Penny Robinson had played a major part in my life and had played an integral role in my formative years. I was grateful to her, if that doesn't sound crass, on a number of fronts.

And now, as I got myself ready for the funeral, it was strange to think she was no longer with us and that in a few hours my last respects would be paid and the vibrant, passionate woman I knew, would be a thing of the past. I don't mind saying it all felt a bit weird.

I planned to set out early anyway, just so that I could catch up with Rob and Rosie well before and pass on my condolences. I would have been there a few minutes earlier had it not been for getting stopped by a lollipop lady just after leaving home. Was it part of the job description that you had to be at least 17 stone? It's just one of those things you gradually come to realise that lollipop women are usually incredibly sturdy.

Is that in case they get hit or something? Maybe they have to take on the dimensions of a small roundabout, just in case. I don't know. There was hardly anyone at the church when I got there and as I pushed the small gate open, I was summoned up to the top of the path to the left of the big yew by a figure I recognised to be Rosie.

'Dunny!!!'

'Oh hi,' I mumbled motioning that I'd make my way up to her.

'Wondered whether you'd come,' she said guiding me towards the path which made its way around the back of the church.

'Was that in any doubt?'

'You tell me Dunny,' she said somewhat sharply.

'Where are we going?'

'I thought we'd go for a drink later Dunny. Just you and me eh? How's The Wickets sound.'

'Oh right. . .' I spluttered.

Rosie chose her moment perfectly and then . . . THWACK. She slapped me. Thank God we were out of sight and there was hardly anyone there. The noise seemed to echo around the place.

'Oh right. Is that all you can say? Oh fucking right?'

'What the . . . '

'You know what that's for, Dunny. You baaa..stard,' she said in that slightly exaggerated fashion which carries just a tinge of affection with it.

'Oh Jesus.'

'How dare you say that. And here of all places. Dunny, I just can't believe you. . .'

'Do you want me to go?'

'No I don't as it happens. Mom wouldn 't have wanted that.'

'Does Rob know?'

'No. No one else knows. Thank God. And stop thinking of your own skin . . .'

'I wasn't, but . . .'

'Yes you were. No, there's only me. Look, seriously, we'll go for that drink afterwards yeah? Just you and me. The Wickets.'

'Okay.'

And then she hugged me . . . and half apologised . . . and cried . . . and it was over . . . and we went inside.

* * *

It had been a lovely service. Didn't everyone always say that? So we, Rosie and me, slipped out as arranged and sat in the Wickets lounge. We raised a glass to her mom and it seemed fitting. We both just knew that she would have appreciated it. And so I asked . . .

'How did you find out?'

'You mean when did I finally confirm my suspicions?'

'Whatever.'

'About two hours ago . . . back at the church there.'

'What?'

'Yeah.'

'I don't get it.'

Rosie continued. 'Well, I didn't know for absolute certain.'

'So why?'

'Well you wouldn't would you? Look, call it intuition, but when I mentioned this place, well, your face just gave it all away. It was the final piece of the jigsaw.'

'So it was a trap then?'

'Nothing as sinister as that Dunny. Look, after mom and dad split up we got closer and closer. We were almost like sisters and towards the end, when the cancer really took hold . . .'

'She told you.'

'No. But she had said there had been a brief fling with someone years ago and that it was an impossible situation etc .etc . . . and that it was someone much younger.'

'So.'

'Yeah well, I just needed to fit in the pieces. There were clues. You know, I came to gran's house one day that hot summer years ago and couldn't get any answer even though mom's car was on the drive and I knew you'd gone there with her. I didn't attach that sort of importance to it until much later.'

'Jesus,' I said breaking her flow.

'Well Dunny, the thing is that just a couple of days before she died we were talking quite openly about the service and the music we were going to have for her and she asked me to do one last thing.'

'Go on,' I urged Rosie.

'Well, to come here stupid. She wanted me to come here and have a last drink. Said it was a special place to her and while she wouldn't go into detail, she said she'd like me to do that.'

'Oh right.'

'Exactly.'

'What?'

'And so when I mentioned it to you at the church, you said 'oh right' and your jaw almost scraped the path. And that's when I knew for sure.'

'Oh right.'

'And there you go again,' Rosie said with an understanding smile.

'So Rob . . .'

'Get serious will you? No, I think this little secret should go to the grave, so to speak.'

I clutched her hand and she indicated we would have to be making tracks soon.

Rosie left and I stayed for ten minutes to sort of pay my own last respects. It was so quiet, yet I had a warm feeling, knowing one of Penny's last wishes was being carried out. The service had been quite upbeat really, but when the vicar started off I couldn't help speculating that she would have hated the silence. A mischievous vision of her shouting 'QUIET!!!!' from one of the balconies, flashed through my mind. I suppose it wasn't the place really, but I had to hold back a smile. And then there was the final piece of music. That got to me. Ravel.

* * *

Bolero. Everyone knows it. Ever since Torvill and Dean crashed to the floor and the judges' cards went up, you just sort of instinctively knew it was never going to get any better than that. The minute that pair pulled that masterpiece off they might just as well have chucked their skates in the nearest bin and walked off, hand in hand, into a purpley sunset.

It was like they had just performed the perfect ice dance and from that point on everything else was going to be second best - at best. And that might go part way to explaining the riddle of just what happened to competitive ice dancing after that. It's like everyone jacked it in. No point. After that it disappeared up it's own arse, if that's not too vulgar a description for such a graceful pursuit. It was almost like every young hopeful had thought what's the point?

When Michaelangelo looked up at the ceiling of the Cistine

Chapel, he might just as well have said whatever Italian is for 'sod it,' chucked his brushes over the nearest wall and gone down the boozer. It was his straight sixes moment and everyone should have one.

As I walked into the lounge of The Compasses, it might just as well have had 'Memory Lane' nailed above the door.